Tears of a
Hummingbird

Cover Designers:
Maduranga (Sri Lank),
Aneeba Shoukat (Pakistan)

Page Designer: Osamudiamenabdu (Nigeria)

Interior Hummingbird Graphic: favpng.com

Editor: KYA PUBLISHING CANADA

Publisher: ELEVATEDWAVES PUBLISHING CORP.
(Garfield Heights, Ohio)

ISBN-13 (Paperback): 978-1-7331082-8-7

ISBN-13 (Hardback): 978-1-7331082-9-4

ISBN-13 (ebook): 978-0-692-89059-2

Library of Congress Control Number: 2020949061

First Edition

Printed in the United States of America

NeeNee Marie's book may be purchased in bulk for promotional, educational, or business use. Please contact your local bookseller or ElevatedWaves Publishing at ElevatedWavesPublishing@gmail.com

For more information regarding publicly for author interviews, email NeeNee Marie at authorneeneemarie@gmail.com

For Mommy.

Table of Contents

Mental Health Message

Topics discussed in this story may be disturbing and triggering for individuals living with, exposed to, and/or affected by one or multiple mental health illnesses. *Tears of a Hummingbird* is a fictional novel that ***should not*** be deemed as an official reference for mental health issues and dealings. If you — or anyone you know — are suffering from an untreated mental health illness, please consult with your primary health care physician *immediately*. If you — or anyone that you know — are experiencing a mental health crisis, please call your national emergency line (US: 911) *immediately*. If you — or anyone you know — have thoughts of suicide, please call your national emergency line or the National Suicide Prevention Lifeline at 1-800-273-TALK (8255). You can also visit https://suicidepreventionlifeline.org/, or connect with a counselor from the Crisis Text Line at: https://www.crisistextline.org/.

Domestic Violence Message

Topics discussed in this story may be disturbing and triggering for individuals living through, exposed to and/or affected by one or multiple types of domestic abuse. *Tears of a Hummingbird* is a fictional novel that ***should not*** be deemed as an official reference for issues and dealings in regard to domestic abuse. If you — or anyone you know — are suffering from any form of domestic abuse or are experiencing a domestic abuse crisis, please consult with your primary health physician *and* call your national emergency line (US: 911) *immediately*. If you — or anyone you know — have been affected by sexual assault and/or are experiencing a sexual assault crisis, please notify your primary health physician *and* call your national emergency line *immediately*. You may also contact the National Sexual Assault Hotline at *1-800-656-HOPE (4673)*, or https://www.rainn.org/.

I am a hummingbird.
I am beautiful.
I am delicate.
I am gentle.
I am tiny, yet mighty.
I am youthful and free.

There have been many who have…
Chipped away at my wings.
Plucked my beautiful, light feathers.
Fed me poisonous foods.
Tampered with my water.
Trapped me in their evil
and manipulative ring of
false perception and hope.

Those who have cut me
with their dishonesty
and shot me
with their ill intentions.

Yet, Mommy Nature has carried me...
And Karma has always come
to clean up the mess.

And I continue to fly.

Because even with blood
dripping from my wings…
I am still a hummingbird.

PROLOGUE

The Beginning to an End

Tears streamed from the corner of my eyes, down my cheek, and landed on Jay's sweaty hands, that were still locked around my neck. My hits and punches became weaker and weaker. My cries became faint as it became more apparent that *I wasn't going to make it out this time*.

My vision became blurry. My hearing started to fade and became distorted. I watched Jay grind his teeth together with all of his might as he proceeded to cut off my air pathways...completely. My body became hot. Then, cold. I was numb. My eyesight was flooded by a bright light that overpowered me entirely. This is it. I felt my spirit end the resistance against Jay's force.

I thought about my life up until this point, and instantly wished I had smiled more, laughed more, and *just* enjoyed life more. I wished I were more courageous and stood up for myself. *I wished I had not allowed myself to suffer for so long.* I wished that I set myself free long ago, so I could peacefully enjoy the glories of life.

I thought about Angelo and his beautiful smile, and all the glee that he brought to me in such a short period of time. I thought about Courtney and her angelic face. *What would she think of me after I was gone*? I prayed that she would find healthy ways to grieve my death. I broke on the inside as I wondered if she would ever forgive me for leaving her. For giving up.

CHAPTER 1

TEARS OF A COLD AND FETAL NIGHT

"She better call the police,
before he kills us this time."

The back door swung open and the brisk cold night air raced my mother into the house. I folded my arms; my shoulders shivered, trying to protect my body from the cold. I peeked around the corner, looking slowly past the refrigerator to see what was going on. I almost instantly spotted my mother's gold-dyed hair. Relieved and naively believing that I was safe, I walked quickly into the kitchen, revealing myself.

"Mommy, what was all that noise?"

Slightly startled, she jerked her head back and looked at me without saying anything. Suddenly, my heart fell through my empty stomach and onto the floor. I was scared and could not believe my eyes.

"Mommy! Your face! What happened?" were the only words I could get out.

"I'm okay. Go to bed," she said to me in a low and breathless tone, leaning against the back door, trying her best to push it completely shut...but, she was too weak. She threw her head back out of frustration and took a deep breath before letting out a grueling scream. "AHHHHH!" The screech gave her enough strength to finally shove the door closed and lock it.

"Why he do that to you?" I whined, no longer cold, but still shivering.

She grunted and limped past me, heading to the small hallway bathroom. Ignoring my dire concern altogether, she flicked the light switch on. My mother looked into the mirror and the bright light revealed the horrific chaos that covered her beautiful face. She slowly let out a pitiful cry. I didn't understand how she could even see past the thick blood that covered her eyes, leaking from the gash on her forehead.

"I *hate* him! Why God? WHY?" she wailed out as she shoved her face into her shaky hands, smearing blood all over her light brown skin.

I hate him. Why God, why? I repeated to myself in my head before asking a different question out loud.

"What happened this time?" I gripped her arm, attempting to shake her out of her sorrow.

BOOM! There was one heavy, loud bang on the back door.

"You bitch! You asked for it. This is what you wanted, right?" His words were slurred and muffled from behind the door. I could hardly make out what he was saying but understood enough to feel offended on my mother's behalf. "You can't keep a good man because you ain't a real woman!" he yelled out for the whole neighborhood to hear.

"I'm gon' call the police on yo' ass if you don't leave this property!" she attempted to match the rage in her husband's angry voice.

There was a ten-second pause before Derrick responded. "Well, let me get my things so I can leave!"

"You ain't coming in this house, dammit! Just leave!" She could barely get the last word out before her voice started to crack.

"So, I can't get my belongings? Okay, you heartless *bitch*! If this is what you want, this is what you'll get! But I'm coming back to get my shit!" he blurted out as he stomped down the back porch stairs and off into the foggy night.

My mother quickly slammed the toilet seat shut with all of her might while biting down hard on her bottom lip. She sat on the seat and continued her high-pitched, sorrowful cries that she tried so hard to keep inside.

I stood in the doorway of the bathroom, staring at the small, dingy blue trash can that was overflowing with crushed beer cans, giving myself a reason not to look in my mother's direction. I did not know what to say to her or...what *not* to say. I wanted to hug her, but something stopped me. Perhaps it was the anger I had buried deep inside of me. I hated seeing her like that and it was not the first time her and Derrick got into a physical altercation.

I finally looked up to witness her hunched over and sobbing into her lap.

"You wanna go to the hospital?" I asked, already knowing what the answer would be. I clenched my jaw tight as I waited for her predictable and disappointing response.

"I don't need them white people all in my business. Fuck them, fuck him, *FUCK ALL OF THIS!*" She was loud and belligerent. I didn't flinch one bit, as I was used to her hot and cold temper. It didn't startle me anymore.

I heard a creak on the stairs in the hallway right behind me, not too far away from where I was standing. I quickly turned around and saw my baby brother standing on the last step, in his tighty-whitey underwear, rubbing his sleepy eyes. Michael was five years old; his thick and fuzzy single braids hovered above his tiny shoulders. After a moment of adjusting his vision and trying to make sense of all of the commotion, Michael finally looked up with squinted eyes and whispered, "What's all that noise?"

"Nothing. They just arguing. Get back in the bed, Michael. We got school tomorrow." I walked in his direction, hoping to block his view of Mommy's face.

I could hear our mother's sad whimpers from the bathroom, igniting Michael's curiosity even more. He stood on his tippy toes and glanced over my shoulder to steal a glimpse of her reflection in the mirror. I stood in front of him, analyzing his facial expression. I could tell from the way his eyes widened, he had seen the pain on her flesh. I released a heavy sigh, feeling like I had failed at protecting his innocence and guarding his heart. Michael continued to stare into the bathroom, with his bottom jaw slightly dropped. He was stuck. I racked my brain, searching for the right words to bring him comfort. My thoughts raced and my heart began to pound harder. Faster. I grew more anxious by the second. Still fixated on the bathroom mirror, I watched as the base of his eyes gradually saturated with small, weary tears. I was furious. I wanted to scream to relieve myself of the sentimental buildup inside of me...but I was afraid. Afraid to reveal my raw, unfiltered emotion. Afraid of whatever the consequence might be.

I slowly fell to my feet and sat on the bottom stair, right under Michael, who was now silently sobbing to himself. The sound of his fragile cries pierced my soul. I threw my head into my hands and cradled my face. I shut my eyes tight as I began to dig my fingernails into the skin and through the soft tissues of the flesh on each side of my face. *It hurt so good.* I carefully drove my nails deeper into my skin, squeezing my eyes tighter, and focusing on the misery I was inflicting onto myself. In a twisted way, the physical discomfort drowned out the mental suffering. Though it was only temporary, my frustration and agony faded away until it was completely invisible. I embraced every second of that moment of *freedom*. After a short while, I started to decrease the amount of pressure that I used to poke into my pores with my thin, sharp fingernails. I exhaled as I slowly opened my eyes, nearly blinded by the vicious view of reality.

CLASH! BANG! This time, it wasn't a knock on the door.

A dull, red brick flew through the kitchen window, skipping the kitchen floor completely and landing right in front of me. I could hear the shatter of glass as I watched my mom stumble out of the bathroom.

"What the hell was that?" She examined the shattered kitchen window in disbelief.

"Mommy, get away from the window!" I screamed as I pushed Michael up the stairs to get him to safety.

"I know this bastard didn't just throw a brick through my house!" my mom shouted as she tiptoed closer to the window, trying to avoid the thick pieces of glass on the floor.

Michael and I hurried up the stairs and found our way to the first landing. We backed ourselves into a nearby corner of the wall, with Michael snuggled in my lap. I held my brother's head close to me, smearing his tears deep into my chest to muffle his fears momentarily, until I could think of a solution.

"Mommy, call the police!" I yelled at the top of my lungs, hoping my small voice would reach her in time.

"Fuck the police!" My heart dropped when I heard Derrick's voice through the broken window. "I told yo' mama I was coming back for my shit!"

I didn't respond.

Michael quickly turned his face away from Derrick's voice. He wrapped his arms around me with his eyes shut, as he sniffled loose mucus through his nostrils. I could hear him swallow hard and feel the muscles in his tiny frame suddenly relax, giving in to an ongoing battle he had been fighting inside. A battle that was a little too familiar. He released a quick sigh before stating very calmly in a monotonic pitch, "She better call the police, before he kills us this time." His eyes were still closed.

I could hear my mother and Derrick arguing and screaming through the shattered window but could not make out one word that was exchanged. My ears were hot, and my heart was heavy. *This is our life; this is our destiny,* I thought to myself. I lightly rested my cheek on the top of Michael's head. I closed my eyes and pushed out the air I had been storing inside of my burning throat for so long. Acceptance felt good.

"Get the hell off of me!" my mother's loud squeaky cry snatched me out of my peaceful coma. I yanked my eyes open and jumped to my feet. I threw Michael over my shoulder as I ran up the second flight of stairs towards the second floor, bursting into my bedroom. I knew Derrick had made his way into the house and I was determined to keep my brother out of harm's way. I could feel Michael's once calm heart, now pounding heavily through his trembling body. I cradled his back tightly and close to me as I surveyed my space, desperately searching for a safe zone. *Bingo.* I opened my closet door and sat a, now quivering, Michael on top of the mountain of soiled laundry.

"It's gonna be okay. I'm gonna go calm them down," I whispered to Michael, handing him the tattered blanket off my twin-sized bed.

"Here, get some sleep. We still have school in the morning," I hissed through a half, forced smile in an attempt to normalize the situation. At least for the moment. Michael sat with his knees tucked to his chest and looked up at me as I waited for him to hopefully accept my offering of momentary peace. Michael reluctantly gave a mild grin, took the blanket, and placed it around his shoulders.

"I'll be right back. I promise," I assured him as I closed the closet door, leaving a small crack so the light from the bright moon would shine through my bedroom window and into the dark space. "And don't turn the light on until I get back," I whispered, making sure Michael heard this very important instruction.

I tiptoed out of my room, carefully closing the door behind me so Michael would not witness any more of the commotion. The sounds of my mother's moans and grunts grabbed me and drove me down the steps. I was physically prepared to help her, but mentally afraid of what I might see. When I reached the bottom stair, I jerked my head towards the kitchen. My mother's upper body had completely emerged from the window. Her legs, still inside of the home, were spread apart as she kicked and felt around the floor with her bare feet. I watched as her toes searched around the kitchen floor, seeking an object that her calves could wrap around to secure her safety and prevent her from being pulled out of the window entirely.

"Symone...HELP!" She must have blindly felt my presence from behind her as she uttered my name, pleading for my assistance. I stood in place, still in the same spot trying to make sense of what I was seeing. "He's pulling me out! HELP ME."

A burning rage swallowed my body as I ran over towards the window. "Get off of her!" I roared through the opening towards Derrick's sweaty face. He held a hand full of her hair in his destructive fist with his teeth clenched tightly together. He did not look at me; he pretended I wasn't even there at all. My loud scream seemed to not faze him one bit.

I put my ninety pounds of body weight on my mother's back, hoping it would make it more difficult for her irate husband to pull her all the way out of the house. "*AHHHHHH!*" She let out a painful screech as she turned her head to me and murmured, "I'm losing blood, Symone. Call for help."

I immediately lifted my body off of her back and kneeled to view her abdominal area closely. Huge pieces of glass punctured through the flesh in her mid-section and pierced into her stomach.

"My God," I mumbled, realizing that the pieces of broken glass were stubborn window pieces that had not torn away from the windowpane once it was shattered by Derrick just moments ago. The thick, sharp pieces of glass had gauged deep inside her and were the cause of her agonizing pain.

"Stop it, you're gonna kill her!" I bellowed. I ran as fast as I could to get the cordless house phone from the dark, cold living room on the opposite side of the house. My fingers felt numb as I dialed 9-1-4. *Wrong number.* I pressed the red button to end the call, and then dialed 9-4-4. "Ahhhhh!" I cried out in frustration, fed up with my nerve-wracked fingers. It felt like hours had already passed since I left my mom's side. I ran back towards the kitchen and could now see her bright red blood drenching the dingy floor from underneath her. Derrick continued to yank and pull away at her from outside the window. I screamed with my mouth shut, trying my best to not react to the abuse in front of me. Instead, I focused on getting my hands calm enough to dial the correct numbers for emergencies: 9-1-1. *WHEW!* I let out a breath of relief as I slapped the phone to my ear, anxiously waiting for the operator to answer.

"Symone...I can't hold on much longer..." my mom cried out to me. I held air tightly inside of my cheeks as tears ran down my face. I paced the dirty kitchen floor to ease some of the tension in my body.

"Nine-one-one, what's your emergency?" the operator's voice sounded like heaven and I couldn't help but to hand her all of the hurt I was holding inside.

"He's killing my mommy!" I sobbed heavily, closing my eyes, wishing to trap the stream of tears that were now rushing down my face.

"Who's killing who? Speak clearly, sweetie, so that we can send you some help."

I took three seconds to gather myself and clear my throat. I finally opened my eyes and watched my mom's body continue to struggle as she tried to break loose from Derrick's tight grip. She fought tirelessly to pull herself back up into the house, but she was not strong enough.

"I said, HE'S KILLING MY MOMMY!"

"Okay honey, I pulled up your address. I'm sending help now. How old are you sweetie?" the concerned woman asked on the other end.

"Twelve," I wept.

CHAPTER 2

TEARS OF A WOMAN IN THE MIRROR

"I could feel the toxins of depression and heartbreak leave my body through the fresh wound. It hurt so good."

16 Years Later

I t was 10:33 p.m.; I lay in bed with my eyes glued to my phone. My thumb swiped through social media posts almost automatically, even as I drifted in and out of a light drowsy state. The bedroom was dark and cold. I pulled the thick cover up past my shoulders to the bottom of my chin to lock in the natural heat generated from my body. I carefully shifted to a more comfortable position in the king-sized bed.

"Oooouch!" I reacted to the painful discomfort. My back was now facing the bedroom door; I reached around for a pillow and placed it under the left side of my bruised rib cage.

"Better," I sang out in a quiet sigh with my eyelids shut, prepared to finally get some rest.

Just as I began to fall asleep, the sound of keys dancing loudly in the far distance sent alarm bells off in my brain. I lifted my head slightly to examine the situation, but it was difficult to hear through the loud beating thumps coming from my heart.

"He's back already?" In a panic, I decided to *play possum* and curled up under the blanket, though I was no longer cold — within seconds I had become hot and sweaty. I could hear his key connect to the front door as he grunted and groaned into our home of seven years.

"Symone," he slurred my name loudly from downstairs, in our two-story townhome. All of the lights were out and all of the TV's were off, leaving me with no excuse for not hearing his call. Still, I remained lying in the bed. Speechless.

"Hey, woman! I know you hear me," Jay's voice echoed through the house like thunder bolts in a calm, blue sky. "Listen, I'm sorry about earlier. You hear me? I said I apologize," I could tell he was standing at the bottom of the steps projecting his voice towards the second level, hoping they would reach me behind the closed bedroom door.

And what about all the other times, asshole? I thought as I rolled my eyes under their closed lids.

"See, this is what irks me," Jay barked as he stumbled his way up the long flight of stairs. "You do these types of things to get a reaction out of me," his voice grew closer and closer to the bedroom.

BOOM!

Jay threw one punch through the door.

"Oh my God! What are you doing?" I screamed, examining the pieces of door wood scattered on the bedroom floor. He slowly walked towards the bed, breathing intensely, with his fist still closed tight. Jay's devil blue eyes stared through my soul as the mixture of alcohol and sweat drained from his pores and drizzled down his pale, white skin. His short but cocky stature was strong and intimidating.

"You know I don't like to be ignored, and you do it to me all the time," he shouted through a clenched jaw as he continued towards me.

"I was sleeping, how was I supposed to hea —"

"SHUT UP! First, you ignore me, and now you're lying to my face! Why do you do this to me?" He paused. "Let me take a guess...you're not attracted to me anymore, is that it?"

"No, that's not true."

"Well, what is it? Huh? Why don't you touch me anymore?"

I thought about stating the obvious, but I knew that would add fuel to his fire and I was already weak from previous burns. I took a deep breath and looked up into Jay's eyes for the first time since he bombarded me in our bedroom. "I have been feeling under the weather lately," I whispered slowly. My eyes started to fill with sorrow. I was disappointed in myself once again. *I am not my mother. One day I will be strong.* I stated in my head as I continued to stare at Jay, trying to convince myself to be brave.

"BULLSHIT!" His words landed right on my face. I yanked my eyes shut. I could smell the rum from the drops of saliva he planted on my flesh. I kept my eyes closed, wishing I could escape through the secret doors in my mind that led to the peaceful rooms of my imagination.

Jay quickly yanked the front of my night shirt, pulling me to the edge of the bed and bending down so his nose was just inches away from mine. "Touch me...NOW," His demand was slow and aggressive. I stared at the tip of his sweaty nose, avoiding direct eye contact. I did not know what to say or what to do. I just knew what I *didn't* want to do, and I thought that was clear. I hated when he got drunk and acted irate like this. Only I knew that when he consumed alcohol, it meant he did not take his medication...which usually resulted in a nightmare for me.

"Jay...let's both get some rest and continue this conversation in the morning, please," I begged with my wide brown eyes, searching for a hint of mercy through his. He stared at me for what felt like an eternity, before he let out a frustrated roar and eventually let go of my pink, silk shirt. I laid my hand over my night shirt and proceeded to smooth it out.

Jay began pacing the white carpet with his hands on his head. "I don't like this! You know I don't like feeling like this! Rest? Talk in the morning? *How* can I rest when I'm feeling unwanted, huh? What sense does that make, Symone?"

He stopped his repetitive stride to look at me, waiting for an answer to what I thought was a rhetorical question. I closed my eyes and sighed, searching for the right words to sooth his bruised ego. I came up with nothing. With my eyes still shut, I heard Jay begin to whimper. I opened my eyes to the sight of a grown man on his knees with his head hanging to the floor.

"Why don't anyone want me?" his voice cracked as he began sobbing hysterically. I knew it wasn't fair. *How many times must I bear the burden of his deadbeat parents?* Jay's mom and dad abandoned him when he was just eight months and it was like he expected me to pay for *their* poor choices in life. When I looked down, Jay was still hunched over on the floor crying helplessly. *He's sick,* I thought to myself. Not disgustingly sick. More like mentally ill sick.

"Jay. Listen. This is totally diff—"

"Symone, I know I'm not perfect," he interrupted. "I'm fucked up in the head beyond my control and you *know* that. I'm trying my best. I am…" Jay paused as he gathered his emotions and then cleared his throat. "Sorry," Jay blurted out in a deep, crisp tone. He continued facing down towards the thick, furry carpet that covered the large bedroom floor. There was a moment of silence before I felt pressure to respond.

"I know you've been through a lot. I truly commend you on how strong you are, Jay. You went to college. You are a successful business owner. I mean, people respect and look up to you. That's real."

He lifted his head slightly so his pupils were eye level to the white nail polish on my toes, hanging slightly off the bed. Jay began to laugh without taking his eyes off my long, skinny toes.

"Jay? What's funny?" I asked as I looked down towards his thick head, trembling with laughter.

Jay remained on all fours as he lifted his head, looked directly into my eyes, and screamed from the top of his lungs. "You think you're so smart, don't you? I am not a child. Don't you talk to me that way. Don't you dare belittle me like that, anymore."

I could feel my heart shift in my chest as my body stiffened. I was afraid to move. Jay raised his hand and slapped down on my feet with all of his might.

"Get your damn feet out of my face," he roared as he stood up from the floor. I quickly gathered both of my feet and planted them under my bottom as I adjusted my position on the bed.

"You don't want to touch me, but you allow a *stranger* to touch your feet?" It took me a few moments to process Jay's ridiculous statement. I took in a deep breath and exhaled slowly...and quietly, hoping to not agitate the angry man in front of me with the sound of frustration escaping my nostrils. I quickly collected myself and swallowed my emotions before responding. "Pedicure," was the only word I could get out without completely losing it.

"What?" Jay cocked his head sideways, confused by the one-word response I set before him.

The bottled-up anger seemed to be too much for my petite body. The ache from my ribcage reminded me of all the harm and hurt this man had put me through. I was mad, and rightfully so. The anger within me fizzled to the top of my head and began to leak out of my mouth. It took over my body. Before I knew it, I exploded and yelled out, "IT'S A FUCKING PEDICURE!"

I was relieved. I smiled on the inside to celebrate my audacity to speak up for myself. Immediately after my outburst, I felt a powerful blow to my chest. *OWWW*! I wheezed and reached out for the air that had suddenly escaped my lungs.

When I was finally able to re-open my eyes, I found myself lying face-up with my back sunken into the bed. I peered at the high ceilings, trying to remember how to breathe again. My chest felt as if it had been ripped into pieces. I reached my hand up towards my heart to make sure it still had a beat. I gradually came back to full consciousness and realized what just happened. My body froze out of fear. I slowly moved my gaze from the distant ceiling, down to where Jay was standing. He stood at the foot of the bed with beads of sweat streaming down his narrow sideburns. I glanced down and gasped when I saw what he was holding in his right hand.

"What are you doing?" My voice was shattered. Jay held my favorite hummingbird knickknack that I kept on our rosewood dresser for good luck. The miniature statue of the hummingbird was blue with two bright stripes under its long, pointy beak — one a beautiful red and the other one a clean, bold yellow. The colorful decorative figure was shiny with a thick, purple lining in both the small wings that stood straight up, adjacent to the short green tail that fanned out widely. It was my symbol of true freedom; my ultimate goal.

"You got some nerve," Jay said in a stern tone. His stature was stiff, his head was low, and his eyes glued to my face. "You love this damn thing more than you love *ME*!" he spat out with increased volume in his baritone voice.

"Jay," I whispered. "It's just an object. It has no true meaning," I downplayed the value of the hummingbird hoping to prevent the beautiful keepsake from being shattered into pieces on the bedroom floor.

Jay walked towards me and placed one knee on the bed. He stared into my eyes as he placed the second knee onto the bed. He crept up on the bed closer to me and stopped at my legs. Jay climbed on top of me and placed his bottom firmly on my ankles.

I tried to wiggle my legs free, but I was stuck. He had me locked in his angry space while holding my freedom hostage. I said nothing. I stared Jay back into his eyes, hoping to disguise the fear that lived in the pit of my stomach.

"You don't want to make love to me, huh?" he flashed an evil grin at me. "Well, let's see you make love to Mr. Hummingbird."

I was baffled. "Make love to *what*?"

He quickly reached up my night shirt and grabbed my panties with his free left hand, still holding the glossy bird in his right. With two aggressive yanks, he was able to rip through the thick, black underwear that hugged my hips. It was that moment when I wished that he had just broken the damn knickknack, rather than use it against me. I lifted my leg and pressed my foot firmly against Jay's thick, moist chest as I yelled out, "*NOOO!*"

He took my defensive gesture as an opportunity to finish undressing my lower body against my will. With my leg up, Jay was able to quickly tug and slide the remainder of the ripped underwear off of my bottom. I closed my eyes to catch the tears that started to form..."*PLEASE! STOP!*" I sobbed as I felt Jay's heavy hands forcing my foot off his chest and prying my thighs open.

"This is what you want, right? I'm just giving you what you want." The sound of his deep, breathless voice stung my ears.

"*GET OFF OF ME!*" I screamed out in one last attempt to save myself. Jay ignored my cries as he bought the knickknack closer to my private area. I quickly slapped my hands over my wet eyes to block the horrific view created by the man that promised to love and protect me just seven years earlier.

I felt the cold, hard glass object enter my body slowly, then suddenly with a hard thrust. *Ahhh!* I cringed from the unorthodox pain. My teeth grinded together underneath my moist, sweaty palms. I groaned to myself, determined to not weep out loud and reward the monster on top of me with my cries. I took a deep breath with each shove to prepare my body to catch each thrust that he forced into me. I pushed against each shove by squeezing my vaginal walls to reject the pointy knickknack from entering my body entirely. After several agonizing minutes, I could feel Jay's digs into my womanhood become slower...less powerful. I kept my hands over my eyes as I listened to his heavy breathing gradually inch away from the bed. I could feel his gaze over my shivering body. Eventually, his footsteps stomped out of our bedroom, followed by a loud slam of the door.

When I lifted my trembling hands from my face, the room was still and stiff. I was afraid to move and disturb the silence. I carefully and quietly lifted from the bed and placed one of my feet on the thick carpet that covered the floor. As I pulled my lifeless body entirely off of the bed, I felt exposed, followed by the sudden urge to run and hide from reality. I ran out of the bedroom, down the hall, and into the second-floor bathroom- locking the door behind me. The pitch-black dark allowed me to hide. I didn't bother to turn on the lights because I was ashamed to face myself in the mirror. The small space was my own sanctuary. It was the one room in the house that no one else used. Here, I could shower peacefully, or listen to music while applying makeup to my face, no matter how long it took. In this space, I could sit in my thoughts and wonders...and just *be*.

I stood in front of the bathroom sink, into the mirror, somehow peering into the reflection that I could not see, in fact, but could feel. I felt my reflection staring back at me with disappointment, sorrow, and pain. The emotions were so heavy. I grabbed my chest to help carry some of the weight that my heart was bearing.

My eyes flooded as I sat down on the toilet right next to the sink and allowed the tears to flow freely. I shoved my hand into the drawer beneath the sink and reached for the one tool that would offer me temporary healing. When I felt the tip of the small Ziplock bag, I snatched it out and proceeded to unzip the old sandwich bag. I stuffed the tip of my fingers into the bag and grabbed my special *healing tool*. Some would call the rectangular, sharp object a razor...and that's exactly what it was. A razor. I personally referred to the item as my special *healing tool*. It was my saving grace during painful times like this.

I held out my left wrist to search for a fresh space to cut. Now that my eyes were adjusted to the dark bathroom, I could pinpoint the perfect spot on my flesh. I quickly took my healing tool and sliced my flesh opened. I closed my eyes to take it all in, dropping the tool onto the marble floor. I could feel the toxins of depression and heartbreak leave my body through the fresh wound. *It hurt so good.* The sore throbs in my vagina and tenderness in my ribs were now faded and mellow.

In the midst of my healing session, I was startled by two stern knocks. I froze and decided not to answer. The two knocks landed once more, followed by an innocent, soft, yet concerned voice that called from behind the door.

"Mommy?"

CHAPTER 3

TEARS OF A BEAUTIFUL DISASTER

"You need to leave. Immediately."

"Okay baby let's go—Mommy's running late." I threw the car in park and pushed the heavy door of the 2020 Audi wide open, barely missing the white sedan parked next to me. I quickly stomped my favorite work heels on the school's concrete, around the back of my shiny, black car, and to the other side where my five-year-old daughter was buckled in, yet still sleeping.

"Court," I called out to her, panicked, as I pulled open the car door and began to unbuckle her seatbelt.

Court's skin was a rich caramel color that glowed perfectly under the early morning sun. Her thick, curly, and kinky hair sat perfectly on top of her round head, right above her wide sleepy eyes. She closed her big eyes as she raised her arms above her head for a deep body stretch that seemed to have put me more behind schedule by at least twenty extra minutes. She decided to end her stretch by sliding her body out of her seat and down to the floor of the backseat of the car.

"Let's go, Court." I quickly bent down to pick my daughter up from the backseat of the car rather than waiting for her to cooperate. With Court in one arm, I opened the passenger side of the door and grabbed her bright pink and blue bookbag with Elsa's face from the hit Disney movie *Frozen* printed on the front of it. I pushed the door closed with the bottom of my heel and ran towards the school's main entrance.

"Good morning, Mrs. Michaels. Please remember to sign the late arrival form on the front desk in the office," Principal Greer greeted me as I burst through the heavy school doors. He was a tall, dark-skinned Black man who wore a suit and tie to work every day. He took his position at F. Douglass Elementary School very seriously and always made a fuss about students arriving late.

"Good morning, Mr. Greer. Thanks," I replied, nearly out of breath and on my way up the foyer stairs towards the main office.

"Now, he knows I never forget to sign that damn form," I hissed under my breath followed by a quick roll of the eyes right before entering the office.

"Courtney! Good morning pretty lady!" Courtney quickly jumped out of my arms to greet Ms. Brown behind the school office desk.

"Good morning, Ms. Brown," I smiled as I scribbled my signature on the late arrival form. The school building was built just ten years earlier; the office was clean and spacious with a plethora of natural light shining through its large windows.

"Good morning, honey!" Ms. Brown exclaimed, still facing away from me and occupied by Court's small, tight hug with her tiny arms around the short, thick woman's neck.

"Ms. Brown, I'm running late. Do you think you ca—" Before I could finish my sentence, I was interrupted by a hard wave of the woman's chubby arm in my direction.

"Hush chile and go on to work. I'll take this little one to class. Don't you worry about it. Go on!" Ms. Brown looked back at me with her eyebrows raised to let me know she was serious. I threw my hands up in the air and walked backwards towards the exit as a sign of my surrender.

"Bye, Mommy!" Court's sweet voice called out.

"See you later, baby. Mommy loves you!" I yelled right before running out the office and down the foyer stairs, past Principal Greer who was fully engaged in a conversation with another parent.

♦

"A and B Law Firm, Symone speaking, how can I assist you this morning?" I reached over to grab the message pad, prepared to fill in the details and capture all important aspects of the call. "Ma'am, Mr. Bricks and Mr. Butler are both in a meeting at this time, may I take a message?" The woman on the other side of the phone rambled off her name, number, and reason for her call as I scribbled viciously and quickly to keep up with her words.

"Thank you, Mrs. Blair. I will be sure to pass this message onto Mr. Bricks. Yes. Have a wonderful day." I hung up the phone and walked over to Mr. Alvin Bricks' mailbox to slide in the message sheet with the woman's requests and contact information listed.

A&B Law Firm had been my work home for the past two years. Once Court started pre-school, I longed for a new reason to get up in the morning. Mr. Alvin Bricks and Mr. Benjamin Butler were like night and day, but somehow it worked and, together, they built and developed a successful, well known law firm in the city of Boston. Mr. Bricks was a short, scrawny white man in his mid-fifties. He entered the firm each morning with a wide smile across his rosy cheeks. His small, perfectly round eyes were always filled with delight and squinted narrowly just behind his large glasses. He wore a thick, white button-down shirt with an awkwardly short black tie. He always kept his oversized shirt tucked in his baggy dress pants that started right above his belly button. His pants were held up by a single, skinny black belt.

Mr. Butler was a tall Black man with broad shoulders and a deep, stern voice. He spoke slowly and sharply pronounced every syllable in every word that left his lips. His suit always hugged his frame just right. I was sure that each one of his suits were professionally tailored to his liking. His shiny bald head seemed to flow naturally with his stiff, intelligent persona.

The office walls were a dark navy blue outlined in a rich, dark wood. My desk sat right in front of the office entry to welcome the potential clients and guests that entered each morning. My office desk was wide and round. The front of the desk was made of a thick, shiny glass outlined with the same wood that sat in the creases and ends of the walls.

I sat in my tall black office chair and leaned my head back against the cushion embedded in the headrest. "What a morning," I murmured to myself as I exhaled heavily, hoping to release all of the negative energy I collected throughout the first part of my day.

◆

"Over here!" I looked up and saw my best friend sitting at an intimate table for two on the small outdoor patio, right underneath the cafe's green and white business logo.

"Lynieeeeeeee," I sang her name out loud as I skipped my heels over to the table where she was now standing with her arms stretched out, prepared to receive my warm embrace.

"Monieeeeeeeee," Lynie mocked as she held me against her double D breasts, swinging us both from side to side.

"I missed you so much," I sighed as I continued to wrap my arms around my best friend's thick waist, barely able to connect my right fingers with my left fingers at the small of her warm, cozy back.

"Okay hun, let's sit and catch up while we can. Here, have a drink." Lynie took one of the margaritas from her side of the table and sat it in front of my chair.

Lynie and I had been friends since our college days at Boston State University. She was from Detroit, I was from Cleveland, and we naturally clicked. I like to describe Lynie as the missing piece to my puzzle and she just fit in perfectly. She was and had always been the ying to my yang. She said things that I would not dare to say out loud. She was my personal voice of reasoning—and sometimes a stern voice of unreasoning.

NeeNee Marie

"Lynie," I gasped as I sat down in front of the large glass of adult beverage. "I have to go back to work. Mr. Butler would kill me."

"Ah shit, live a little! Drink your alcohol, eat your little skinny girl salad, pop a peppermint in your mouth, and take your ass back to work. Simple," Lynie demanded as she removed the straw from her glass and bought the drink up to her thick lips. She proceeded to take a large gulp of the mixed drink, peeped at me through the bottom of her half empty glass, and waved her hand at me, encouraging me to follow suit. I slightly smiled in disbelief that I was actually going to drink in the middle of the workday. I quickly shoved the straw in my mouth and took a sip before placing the wide glassware back on the table and looking around, hoping to not see any familiar faces from the firm.

"Girl, you didn't even drink shit," Lynie blurted out across the table at me. There were two seconds of silence between the two of us before we both burst into belly-wrenching laughter.

I admired Me'Lynie James since the first time we met in College English 101 at BSU. We were the only Black women in the course and often challenged the white professor on the subject of African American culture. I would use quotes from texts and articles to rebut Professor Lewinsky's absurd statements and opinions on the experiences of African Americans in our country. Lynie, of course, used her strong voice, wittiness, and

Tears of a Hummingbird 38

wealth of common sense to expose the professor's blunt bigotry.

Lynie wore her beautiful brown skin with a curvy figure. Her weight was portioned perfectly in all the right places and she loved herself out loud wherever she went. Her confidence and self-love was one of the things that drew me in to her and established our close-knit friendship.

"How's LBR?" I leaned in close, eager to hear her response.

"Well you know, LBR is my baby and I try my best to stay on top of things to keep the shop growing and flourishing. But girl, keeping a Black business afloat and successful is as difficult as it sounds." Lynie squeezed her eyebrows together, threw her head back, and closed her eyes as she exhaled in frustration.

"I know, girl," I replied to comfort her, sorry that I even asked. "I can only imagine the blood, sweat, and tears that you put into that shop every single day, but you've been doing a great job and I can honestly see the results."

LBR was the acronym that Lynie gave her beauty salon: *Lynie's Beauty Retreat*. I always described Lynie as a fashionista. That trait, along with her natural ability to lead, her talent with hair care, and her bachelor's degree in business administration made it possible for her to go into that area of work and succeed effortlessly. She started her business small, doing hair and makeup in her small apartment in the inner city of Boston. She saved up enough money over time, built her brand, and enhanced her reputation as a professional and talented businesswoman. Before I knew it, she was in her very own shop with business booming.

"I know LBR is your baby, girl," I continued to console her. "Trust me, *you just might be a Black Bill Gates in the making*." We both laughed and cheered to the recited Beyonce lyrics.

"Speaking of *babies*, how's my little Court?" Lynie asked.

"She is well, though she's not exactly a baby anymore," I smiled at the thought of my precious daughter. "I can't believe she's already in kindergarten." I sipped more of my drink as I took a moment to reminisce about my daughter's infant phase.

Lynie shifted her energy and raised one eyebrow as the smile from her face faded drastically. "And that husband of yours?"

I stared down into the grilled chicken salad that the waiter placed in front of me just moments before. "Let's not even go ther—" I started, and then quickly altered my response. "We're okay. Same ole, same ole. I mean, we have a lot of work to do," I struggled to find the words that would give Lynie just enough information but not the exact truth. The truth was that my husband of seven years just beat and sexually assaulted me the day before. The truth was that my ribs and vagina still hurt from the violent encounters. The truth was, I wanted to be saved but was afraid of change and the unknown of what could happen next. The truth could cause trouble on top of my troubles and that was the last thing I wanted. I was unsure of what the truth would bring. What would the truth bring to me and my child? A divorce? Without shelter? Food insecurity? Abandonment? Separation from my child? Resentment? Another statistic? I wasn't certain. But, at that moment, I was convinced that the truth would send Lynie into a whirlwind of drama and I was not prepared to de-escalate that emotional storm.

"Symone," Lynie leaned forward and reached her right hand across the table and placed it in front of me. I looked down at her long, sky blue, coffin shaped nails that laid just inches from my empty margarita glass.

"I need you to promise me something," she continued. "If Jonathan has not changed...if he has not shown you that he would be nothing less than perfect to you and that baby, I want you to *leave*. If that low-life lay a finger on you again, you need to leave. *Immediately*. I mean it, Symone; this is not to be taken lightly. This is serious; life or death." She was now lightly, but firmly banging the side of her right fist on the table to put emphasis on her words. "Promise me that you will not be afraid to reach out and ask for help," Lynie stared deep into my face, waiting for a two-second reply that I was unable to produce in time before she blurted out my name. "Symone, this is serious!"

"Lynie, you are so dramatic," I responded in a light whispering voice as I scanned the cafe to see if anyone was listening to our conversation. I felt backed into a corner and wanted out.

"Listen," I said matter-of-factly. "I am a grown woman, Lynie. I know how to ask for help when I am in danger. I need you to remember that, okay?" Lynie shifted her position in her chair and looked away, seeming to be slightly offended by the words that I just placed upon her ears. "Lynie, look at me," I said softly as I waited for her to glance back at my face before smiling and finishing my statement. "I'm okay. Really. I am," I lied.

Lynie pulled out the black leather purse that had been dangling from her chair. She sat the huge designer bag on the table in front of her and began to dig around for her credit card.

"Look, I didn't come here to argue. I don't want to get you upset or get myself worked up," she stated while still searching her purse. "I just wanted to catch up, eat, have a drink, and be real with you like I always do."

"Lynie, I appreciate your concern. You are my best friend and I understand why you're worried, but you have to trust me. If I was in danger, you would be the first to know," I continued to lie.

"Girl, if you are in danger do not call me first," Lynie slowly loosened her stern expression and begin to smile as she finished her thought. "Call the damn police first, okay? *Then* call me." We both laughed out loud. Shortly after, my chuckling was interrupted by a vibration from my cell phone, signaling a text notification.

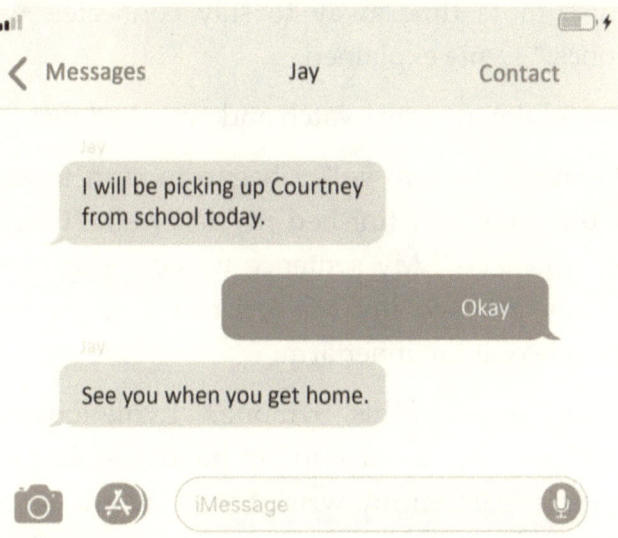

The thought of going home to Jay literally made me sick to my stomach. The more I thought about it, the more I got the urge to puke up the fresh mixture of margarita and chicken Caesar salad sitting in my belly.

"Oh wow, I have to make it back to the office. I guess time flies when you're having fun." I stood up to signal to Lynie that it was time to go. Lynie signed her receipt and left the thin, rectangular paper on the table.

"Ok love, it was nice meeting up with you," Lynie walked around the small table towards me and proceeded to wrap her warm arms around my shoulders. I leaned in to welcome her affection and exhaled heavily.

"Same here; we have to stay in touch," I demanded as I slowly pulled back from our hug.

"Definitely! You know the shop keeps me busy, but I could use more time away to stay connected with my loved ones," Lynie explained.

I looked down at my watch and panicked instantly.

"Oh shit, I have to go!" I began to rush towards the exit of the patio as I finished my farewell. "Okay girl! I will see you lat—" My sentence was cut short by Lynie who firmly grabbed my left wrist and gently turned it around to reveal my inner arm.

"What the hell is this, Symone?" Lynie looked at me while still holding my arm in her hand. I looked down at the exposed scars on my wrist. Some old and some new. They scattered perfectly across my small, fragile arm. *A beautiful disaster.* I pulled my shirt sleeve back over the scarring to cover the bruises, like it was intended to do that morning when I got dressed for the day. I had no answer for Lynie, besides the obvious. I remained silent.

"I thought you were done with this nonsense," Lynie snapped before releasing my arm and storming off away from the cafe.

CHAPTER 4

TEARS OF A SHATTERED SOUL

"If you cared about Courtney as much as you claim, you wouldn't be toying with your life."

It was 5:32 in the evening when I pulled into the driveway of our home. I turned the key in the ignition and the car went silent. I unfastened my seatbelt and reclined my driver's seat as I prepared to steal some alone time inside the car before walking into the unknown that waited for me in the townhome.

I pulled out my cell phone and clicked on the Instagram application. I slowly scrolled through memes, funny videos, and motivational messages—some posted by friends and others posted by people I never met a day in my life. I found it freeing to be able to silently move through society, without revealing my truth and without being judged. I wasn't there to troll or to cause harm. I simply wanted to watch the lives of others, or what I perceived to be the lives of others. I would often find myself lost in someone else's world, living vicariously through their social media page. I eventually came across a video of a woman on vacation at a beach in Miami with white sand, clean water, and blue skies. I re-watched the video, pretending to be the woman in the sixty second clip of paradise. Before I knew it, I was one with the video. I could feel the Miami heat on my skin. I could hear the ocean waves as I ran my toes through the sparkling sand.

I continued to scroll past a few more posts before I came across a meme that caught my attention. It read: *The key to long lasting, healthy relationships, is remembering what brought you together in the first place and nurturing that foundation of your union.* I instantly thought of my own marriage and thought back to the early days when I first fell in love with Jay. It was 2008 when I was introduced to Johnathon Michaels at Boston State University. A classmate thought we should meet to discuss our shared interest in diet and nutrition in the Black community. I was taken back when I discovered that Jay was a white man, but I did not let it cloud my judgement. Jay was smart, polite, and deeply passionate. We naturally hit it off and began to spend an enormous amount of time together. The chemistry between us was undeniable. Jay officially asked me out not even two weeks after we met one another. Before I knew it, we were in a full-blown relationship. A year later and two semesters before college graduation, we were engaged. Jay moved fast, but I didn't question it. He promised a better life and I was ready to leave the misery of my childhood behind.

That was then.

I walked up to the large, red, and tall townhome door that secured my truths and prevented my secrets from escaping and running free into the world. I inhaled and exhaled before taking out my keys to unlock the door and stroll back into reality.

When I walked in, the energy was stiff across the open floor plan of the house. The TV's were off, and the air was cool. The only light I could see from the small foyer where I stood, were dim flickering of illuminations in the dining area. I hung my keys on one of the hooks connected to the mail holder that sat mounted on the wall near the front door. I walked further into my home and placed my purse and jacket on the armrest of the royal blue plush recliner chair that sat stretched out in the living room. I walked through the living area, closer to the dining room where the candlelight fires were dancing fiercely above the red wax. I stopped in front of the staircase that separated the living room and dining room with a bright, shiny white railing and dark, stainless hardwood flooring that covered each stair. I looked up the stairs into the dark hallway.

"She's asleep," Jay's deep voice echoed from the large glass dining room table. Startled, I walked past the stairwell and fully entered the dining area to reveal myself to Jay.

He sat at the table with his head bowed, his forehead in the palm of his hand, and elbows dug into the surface of the table. On the table was a plated dinner prepared for two, along with a bottle of wine chilled in a bucket of ice. I stood near the table, scrambling for the right words to set a calm tone for the remainder of the evening. I failed.

"What's all of this?" I asked.

"You know, I left the office early, I went grocery shopping, I picked Courtney up from school, I came home to bathe her, help her with homework, and tucked her into bed. I then proceeded to prepare salmon, mashed potatoes, and asparagus for us. I watched you pull up in the driveway and sit in your car for nearly an hour," Jay looked up at me exposing the frustration in his face. "You walk in and the first thing you say is 'what's all of this'? The nerve of you!"

The nerve of me? The nerve of you to try and patch up things with some dry salmon and cheap ass wine! I thought to myself before responding.

"Jay, it has been a long day for me as well. I just needed time to recuperate before coming inside," I said calmly, hoping to ease his anger.

He took an exaggerated deep breath. "You know what, just forget it. I forgive you. Have a seat," he commanded as he began to eat his dinner. I grinded my teeth out of anger from the audacity of this man, standing for several more seconds before giving in to his order and finally taking the seat across from him. We both sat quietly as we ate the dinner that was now lukewarm and not as enjoyable as Jay hyped it up to be. I used my fork to scrape up the last of the mashed potatoes on my plate and positioned it on top of the last bite of salmon and placed it into my mouth. Jay finished with his meal five minutes before me. He sat there, shaking his foot, and picking the stale pieces of salmon out of his teeth. As soon as I swallowed the last bit of my food, he stood up immediately and walked around the table to collect the empty plate from in front of me.

I remained seated as Jay washed the few dishes that were in the sink. I wanted to scream at him and curse him out for hurting me. I wanted to hurt him back and give him a taste of his own medicine. But there was something in my soul that would not let me get to that point. Maybe it was my intuition saving me. Saving me from being beat and broken to the point of no return.

The kitchen sink water shut off and the house went back to silent. I watched Jay as he dried his hands with a paper towel and walked towards the bottom of the staircase.

"Come on," he signaled me to follow him by nodding his head towards the stairs and proceeded to jog slowly up, assuming I would follow his lead. Jay seemed to be excited about what was in store next. I rolled my eyes at his fake happiness, just as my text notification sounded off loudly.

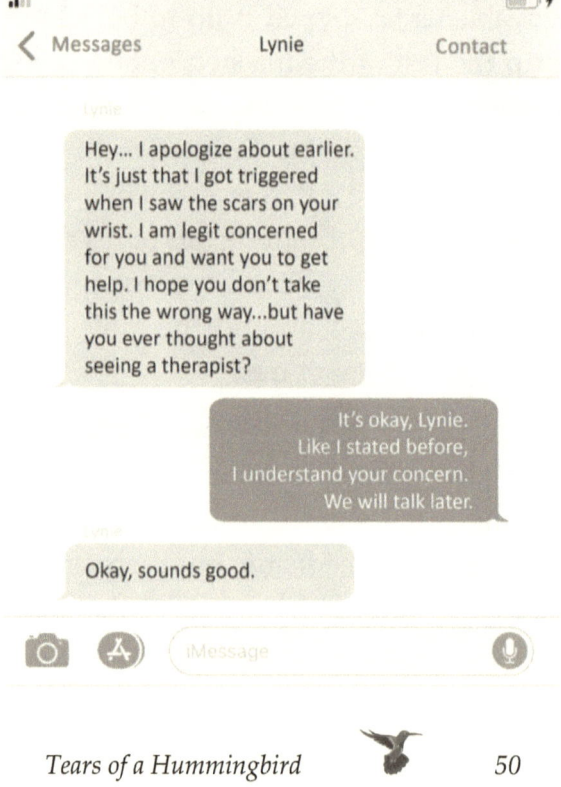

I quickly change my phone notification setting to vibrate only.

"Symone? You coming up?" I could sense that irritation had made its way back into Jay as he called down to me, pretending to give me a choice.

As I walked up the stairs, I could smell the scent of fresh roses in the air. I looked towards my daughter's room and noted that her door was closed and that she was safe. I looked down at my feet and realized there were rose petals on the ground that made a path through the master bedroom. I stopped at the doorway of our bedroom and picked up one of the red petals. I examined the piece of the flower as I wondered what Jay was up to. He was definitely a full grown "sour patch kid," only, his sweet side was never really *sweet*. It was more of a bittersweet perspective of the sourness that oozed from his pores.

I took a deep breath as I continued the path that ended in the master bathroom like I expected. When I arrived, I saw the so-called surprise Jay had orchestrated for me. The same type of red candles that accompanied us at the dinner table surrounded the white, standalone soaker tub that sat in the middle of the bathroom. Jay turned off three of the four light fixtures that occupied that area of the house. The fourth light was the furthest away from the tub and served as a dimmed light to assist the candles in setting the mood. I could hear a low jazz tune playing in the background as I slowly walked towards the tub and placed my fingers in the water to check the temperature. It was warm. I looked up and spotted Jay sitting on the bathroom stool with a thick white towel draped across his left knee.

"This is the part when you remove your clothes and get into the tub," Jay spat out sarcastically with a half grin on his face.

"What is all of th—" I stopped myself and rephrased my question to pacify Jay's obvious sensitivity to the format of that particular query. "What's the occasion?" I asked.

Jay stood up slowly and swung the towel that was on his lap over his right shoulder as he approached me. He placed his hands on each one of my shoulders and looked into my eyes.

"Symone, I know things have been rough for us these past few months. But I am hoping to rekindle that bond and love that we once shared, before the marriage, before the baby, before the money. It was just us," Jay continued to look deep into my pupils, searching for a response.

I closed my eyes to prevent him from seeing the truth. The truth was that I didn't want to rekindle our marriage. I wanted out. I wanted to leave without consequences. Without any more hurt. Without regret. I wanted to be free.

With Jay's heavy hands still resting on my small shoulders, and with my eyes still shut, I began my response. "Jay, you har—"

"Wait, wait. Before you start, let's get you in the tub before the water gets too cold," Jay requested quickly as he bent down to remove my heels from my sore feet. He then proceeded to pull my blouse over my head, and then reached behind me to unfasten my bra. Once I was completely topless, I swiftly slid off my skirt and underwear and hurried into the bathtub to hide my naked body underneath the bath bubbles that fizzled on top of the water.

Jay kneeled on the floor, beside the tub with that same ingenuine grin on his face. "You were saying?"

I hesitated. I was programmed to massage his ego and swallow the blood that marinated in my mouth from biting my tongue. But I was simply tired. Tired of being suppressed and not being able to speak my truth. I decided that I had no other choice but to use my voice to free myself, even if it was frightening.

"Jay…" I started. "You harmed me." My heart began to thump at, what seemed like, a thousand beats per minute. I looked into Jay's eyes and I could see the confused look on his face. He cocked his head to the side, still searching for comprehension in my words and perhaps surprised with my straightforward fact. He was speechless.

What the fuck is wrong with him? I thought to myself, surprised that *he* was surprised and confused about what I had just said. However, this was typical for Jay: never fully taking responsibility for his actions. He would rather sprinkle his shit with glitter and gold and expect for me to be excited when he presented it to me. This *romantic evening* was a prime example of such twisted thinking.

"Jay, a month ago you choked me against our bedroom wall because of your personal assumptions for why I came home late. It was 8:30pm. Last week you slapped me across the face for not cleaning the house spotless before your domino game night with your friends. You accused me of trying to make you look bad. Yesterday, you nearly shattered my ribs and later that night you ra—" I stopped to hold back the emotion that crept up my throat. It would be the first time that I utter the word *rape*, out loud… in front of my abuser. "Raped me," I finished the statement as tears raced down my cheeks and into the bath water.

Jay was quiet. He began to bite down hard on his bottom lip until a thin stream of blood formed from the self-inflicted wound. With the red liquid now dripping down his mouth and his jaws clenched tight, Jay began to speak.

"You know I have been struggling with taking my medication," he growled towards me.

I was more than fed up with this excuse and it was evident when I responded to him. "You don't get to hurt me because *you* can't control your anger, because *you* can't control your emotions and because *you're* not responsible enough to take your medication or at the very least, schedule an appointment to meet with Dr. Matthews to adjust your dosage. I am your *wife* for crying out loud. You promised… to love me," I remained calm, but my heart was deranged, pounding long and hard through the skin on my chest. I knew I had talked myself into a grave, but held my head high. My breaths were loud in the silence that followed my blunt statement.

Jay said nothing. I was worried. Suddenly, he jumped up from the bathroom floor and stormed out of the room and down the hallway. I could not see where he was going and had no clue as to what he was doing. Seconds later, I started to hear loud rumbling noises in the distance. My hands began to shake underneath the bath water, as I wondered what Jay was up to. I pulled my knees closely towards my bare chest and wrapped my trembling hands around my legs. The rumbling ceased. Jay's heavy footsteps grow louder as he made his way back into the master bathroom; my heartbeats mimicked his footsteps. Once Jay entered the bathroom, and before I could block my face fast enough, he threw a light object towards me. The object hit my cheek before falling into the bathwater. Once I regained focus of my vision, I saw that the object was my healing tool inside of the Ziplock bag that I kept in the bathroom down the hall.

Jay kicked the stool towards the tub and flopped down as he shoved his face into my personal space.

"If you was to ever be so stupid and decide to leave me, you'd be walking out this door by your damn self. There's NO WAY in *hell* you're taking my child with you," Jay's words were sharp and cut through my ears. The thought of living a life without my baby girl escaped my mouth in a pitiful sob as Jay continued his rant.

"Raped you? There was no gun to your head. You didn't stop me. If you *really* didn't like it, you could have left. Hell, you can leave now, what's stopping you? Courtney?" Jay pointed at the razor sitting in my hand underneath the bath water.

"If you cared about Courtney as much as you claim, you wouldn't be toying with your life and slitting your wrist," Jay leaned in closer to me. "How do you think that will hold up in divorce court during the custody battle?" His attempt to blackmail me frustrated me. I took my wet hands and wiped the hot tears off of my face, disguising them with cool water from the tub.

"Jay, how will it look that you don't take your medi—" Jay pounded his fist on the rim of the tub and stopped me in the middle of my sentence.

"At least I was a responsible parent and went to get help for my issues! You, on the other hand, are not even woman enough to deal with the death in your family in a healthy manner. Instead of seeking professional guidance and support, your ass sits in the bathroom and plays tic tac toe on your veins."

"That's not fair," I yelled through my cries. "What about your physical abuse, *huh*? How is **THAT** going to look when you try fighting me for custody?"

Jay clenched his teeth tightly and responded by moving his lips, but keeping his teeth shut together. "You know I have never harmed my daughter. And what proof do you have that I have ever physically abused you? How do I know those bruised ribs didn't come from you self-harming your damn self? The same way you do with that fucking razor," Jay took a deep breath and lowered his tone. "I know…I have been a little rough with you at times, but that doesn't equate to abuse, and definitely doesn't speak to my ability to be a father," he lost his cool, once again. "Look, I'm going out for a drink. When I return, I suggest that you be humming a different tune."

◆

After I heard the front door slammed and Jay's Range Rover screech out of the driveway, I slowly lifted myself from the bathtub. I grabbed the white fluffy towel from the floor and wrapped my body with the soft fabric. I made my way to the dark bedroom and crawled into my bed. My body felt heavy as it sank into the mattress. Just as I began to drift off into a non-peaceful, yet much needed sleep, a calendar reminder rang out from my cell phone. With my face still in the pillow, I reached my hand over towards the nightstand and felt around for my phone. I pulled my cellular device towards me to silence the alarm. When my eyes adjusted to the bright light from the screen, I was able to read the reminder: *two weeks before mom's death anniversary.* I instantly let out a sharp, pitiful wail. "Mommy...I miss you," I sobbed deep into my pillows.

CHAPTER 5

TEARS OF A GENERATIONAL CURSE

"Memories that I had locked away and buried forever...or so I thought."

I lounged on the oversized, fluffy red couch and stared right past the maple brown face that sat across from me. Gazing upon the tall walls filled with degree frames and the fancy chandelier that hung from the high ceiling, I could feel wide brown eyes piercing through me, waiting for my eyes to greet them. Instead, I skipped over the mesmerizing eyes and focused my attention on the grand bookshelf covered in an intense dark brown wood pattern. The shelves were filled with thick, hardback books. *DSM-5, Mental Health, Anxiety, Stability*. All of the foreign words jumped out at me from the shiny books that sat neatly on the shelf. I couldn't help but wonder if it was possible for one person to read every single word in every one of those books in one lifetime.

"Symone," the woman's voice was prestigious and sharp, interrupting my wandering mind. "You know, you should probably talk to me during this session."

The sarcasm irritated the back of my throat and made me gag. The crooked smile on her face mimicked Jay's face right before he dove into one of his destructive episodes. It was a smile I did not trust.

"I'm not sure what you expect me to say," I murmured as I looked down at my dancing foot.

"It's not what I expect you to say. What would you like to say?" Ms. Rita Fray wore a clean, layered, and feminine haircut with dark bangs that hovered right above her stylish eyeglasses. She carried a unique, rich gold ring on each finger with thick round wrist bracelets that dangled on her forearm. She was a beautiful, mature Black woman with a brown sugar skin complexion that glowed with the sunlight that beamed through the large crystal-clear window of her office. The window stood tall from floor to ceiling and I instantly wished I was on the other side of the glass. I did not want to talk to a stranger about *my feelings*. The whole concept seemed very cliché and not at all beneficial.

"How about we start off light, okay? Let's see..." Ms. Rita Fray placed her soft, wrinkled finger on her bottom lip, pretending to think of a conversation starter. "Ahh, I got it. Tell me about what you do for a living."

"I'm an administrative assistant at a law firm," I quickly replied.

Ms. Rita Fray smiled to herself before responding. "Can you elaborate? Just a little?"

I was reluctant. "Okay. I serve as an administrative assistant at A&B Law Firm in downtown Boston. I help schedule potential client appointments for attorneys, Mr. Bricks and Mr. Butler, depending on the case. I also manage their calendars, supervise the general operations of the office. Things like that."

"Sounds like you're the heartbeat of the firm." She gave me a warm smirk before proceeding with another question. "Tell me about yourself. Your family. Where did you grow up? What do you like to do for fun—you know, your typical get-to-know-me questions. Fire away," she prompted.

I hesitated. "Umm, well. I have a daughter, I'm married, and I grew up in Ohio." I looked up at Ms. Rita Fray to signal that I was finished with my reply and ready for the next question.

She looked at me with a hint of disappointment sprinkled across her face. She remained quiet for a moment, as if she were waiting for the rest of my response, which didn't exist. Her small dose of patience slithered away. Her faint smile faded, and I could see that she was now ready to get down to business as she shifted her position in the white office chair. My palms began to sweat.

"Symone, what brings you in today? How would you like for me to assist you? Tell me, why are you here?" Her eyes were glued to my face.

"I am here because..." I stopped to think about why I was there. I thought back to the week before when Lynie called me out about the damaged flesh on my wrist. And later that day when Jay threatened to withhold the only being on this earth that accepted and loved me unconditionally. Just as I am. "Because I love my daughter," I exhaled as I gave into my secret protest against the therapy session and decided to actively engage and participate.

"Okay, good." She stopped for a second. "What about yourself?" Ms. Rita Fray questioned. I looked up at her for the first time, slightly confused as to what she was asking me.

"I'm sorry?" I lightly chuckled to hide my discomfort with the audacity of her question.

Ms. Rita Fray challenged me with her eyes as she removed her glasses and leaned in forward before rephrasing her question. This time, with a bit of compassion behind her stern words. "Symone. Do you love yourself?"

Her words were like poison that ran through my ears and down my spine, numbing my entire body. I was paralyzed. I couldn't respond fast enough before she took the next shot.

"Have you ever had thoughts of harming yourself?"

I was frozen; cold and stiff. She continued.

"Symone, do you have a plan to harm yourself in *any way*?" Ms. Rita Fray paused as she finally gave me time to collect my heart from the floor. Only, it was too heavy for me to lift. At this point, her top shelf perfume was the loudest thing in the room. The silence ate away at me little by little. The woman shoved her glasses back onto her round face, she looked down, and flipped through the pages on the white clipboard that sat in her lap.

"Here. When asked if you have experienced any recent loss, you circled *yes*." She looked up at me. "Would you like to elaborate on this question? Or *any* of the information provided on the questionnaire?"

"I...uh..." I remained stuck. I wanted to yell for mercy, but my lips were glued shut. Ms. Rita Fray waited as I gathered the strength to speak.

"He found her," I managed to get out, in a light whisper.

"Who?" she was confused and pleaded for clarity. "Symone, who is *he* and who did *he* find?"

I released some of the tension in my face, along with a river of warm tears that rushed down my cheeks. "Michael..." I whimpered in a loud whisper. "He found our mom."

Ms. Rita Fray's big eyes began to droop as she took a moment to empathize with me. "Symone, I'm sorry." She leaned in towards me. "This seems to be very painful for you. I want to help you work through this. Yes, it's going to be difficult. But you are strong and can do hard things. Look how far you've come." Her sudden warm energy hugged my body tightly.

"Okay," I responded through my tears.

Ms. Rita Fray sighed and took a brief moment to collect herself. She sat back in her chair and proceeded to pick my brain about the sensitive topics in my life.

"Okay, let's backtrack for a second. You mentioned that Michael found *our* mom. Is Michael your brother?"

I leaned over to grab a tissue from the small glass table in front of me. "Yes, my little brother." I could feel her peering through me as I blew my nose into the thick Kleenex. "We were my mom's only kids," I continued. "My mom struggled with alcoholism, so I took care of him as much as I could; we're seven years apart." I looked down at the dampened tissue in my hand. "We were very close."

"*Were?*" She was curious.

"I haven't seen him since he traveled to Boston for my wedding. That was nearly seven years ago." My heart ached.

"Is there a reason why you are no longer close with your brother?"

I swallowed the excessive saliva that sat in my trembling jaws before responding. "I guess when I left home, I left everything and everyone that reminded me of home."

Tears of a Hummingbird   64

There was a moment of silence before Ms. Rita Fray dug in deeper. "What about your father? Do you have a relationship with your father?"

I closed my eyes and sighed. "I never met him."

She sensed my elevated anxiety and reiterated the purpose of the personal questions. "Symone, again, I am just collecting enough information so that I can know how to help you. I need to have an understanding of your history, your pain, and traumas. This will help me to identify the tools and resources needed to work through and navigate the hurt you're suffering with.

I nodded to showcase my understanding. She continued.

"Earlier you mentioned that Michael found your mom. What was this statement in reference too?"

I braced myself. "Michael found our mother…dead. In our childhood home. He had just gotten in from his high school basketball game."

"My God." Ms. Rita Fray placed her hand on her chest. "That must have been diffic—"

"I should have been there," I interjected. "He was there alone. Suffering and drowning in grief. And I was here. Hundreds of miles away living—what I perceived to be—a happy and peaceful life with my new husband." I shook my head in disgust.

"Living," she exclaimed. "You were simply living your life, which we are all entitled to do."

I reluctantly nodded in agreement.

"Symone, do you want to talk about your mom passing?" Ms. Rita Fray lowered her tone and leaned in closer to me. "How did she die?"

My body temperature increased, and I started to sweat fiercely through the pores in my armpits. The room began to spin, and I was incapable of focusing my vision on Ms. Rita Fray's soft face. I searched for the strength to speak; I was weak. I manage to shake my head horizontally followed by an, "mhm mhm." I was hoping she could translate my nervous grunt into English and understand that what I was trying to say was *no*.

"That's fair," she replied before moving on. "I understand that you have never met your father. Was your mom ever married? Did you have a father figure or a stepfather that you were close to?"

"She was married," I said quickly. My airways started to close, and I struggled to breathe.

"What was your relationship with him like?" she prowled.

I gasped for the small bits of air pockets that could fit into my now deflated lungs. "Not good," I exhaled heavily.

"Why not?" she asked. *Let up already, lady!* Is what I would have screamed if my tongue wasn't numb and my jaw wasn't heavy. I closed my eyes in an effort to regain control of my body. The inside of my eyelids presented a pitch-black display, which triggered my brain to replay disturbing memories. Memories and encounters that I had locked away forever...or so I thought.

I could see twelve-year-old me lying in the twin-sized bed that my mom surprised me with when I learned I was finally going to have my own room. I wore my favorite nightgown and snuggled up under the thick, quilted comforter that kept me warm that winter night. My walls were decorated with the hottest R&B groups and most popular hip hop artists; my small collection of stuffed animals sat neatly on my dresser just inches away from my bed. It was a dark school night. I was finally drifting off into a peaceful sleep when my bedroom door creeped open. Derrick's dark silhouette spread across the foot of my bed as he inched into my bedroom, little by little. The sour scent that he carried snatched me out of my sleep and twelve-year-old me began to panic. I could hear his raspy voice call out to me in a whisper, "Symone." I squeezed my eyes shut tighter, hoping that he would go away. But he didn't. Instead, he stood at the foot of my bed and repeated my name over and over. "Symone...Symone...Symone." Each time my name was called my heart pounded with intensity. I prayed that he would leave, but he was consistent. "Symone... Symone...Symone." I could hear his heavy footsteps move closer towards me. I prayed that I suddenly melted away as I began to sweat profusely underneath the cover that draped across my small body. "Symone...Symone," he continued right before placing his heavy hand on my back.

I yanked my eyes open and screamed out loud. "GET OFF OF ME!"

"Symone? Symone, are you okay? Do you need me to call for help?" I looked into Ms. Rita Fray's worried eyes as I remembered where I actually was. The feeling of relief that I was in a safe environment lasted only seconds before Derrick's sour smell followed me into reality and haunted me once more. I felt sick. Unable to open my mouth and speak without vomiting on the white fluffy carpet underneath my feet, I used my hands to motion for the small trash can across the room. Ms. Rita Fray shot up right away and skipped across the room to retrieve the trash can. As soon as she placed the can into my lap, the contents of my morning breakfast immediately rushed up and out of my mouth and nose all at once.

"Aw honey," Ms. Rita Fray placed her warm hand on the small of my back as I continued to purge.

Once my stomach was completely empty, I yanked my head up and quickly reached for the Kleenex on the table to dry my face. "I have to go," I blurted out.

"I understand," I could tell that Ms. Rita Fray was concerned and wanted to ask more questions, but she also wanted to keep a safe rapport with me and respect my boundaries. "Okay, but before you leave, we should schedule our next appointment. I promise, it will only take a few minu—"

"I have to go. I have to go *now*." I scrambled to retrieve my personal items from the couch, stuffed my phone and wallet inside my purse, and quickly pushed my sunglasses onto my face to cover my puffy eyes.

"Okay, well here, take my card. Please don't forget to call or email me so that we can schedule our follow-up appointment," Ms. Rita Fray pleaded as she held the shiny black card in her hand.

I took the card and shoved it in my purse as I rushed past her and headed for the door. "Thank you," I murmured right before the door slammed shut behind me.

◆

Lynie was sitting on the same furniture in the main lobby that she sat on right before I went in to visit with Ms. Rita Fray. She recommended Ms. Rita Fray and offered to accompany me to downtown Boston for my first session. I spotted her before she saw me. She wore *her version* of a comfortable outfit for a Friday afternoon, which was actually a fancy, fitted jogging pants suit that hugged all of her voluptuous curves with the popular clothing logo printed across her buttocks. She complimented her outfit with a pair of nude wedges that revealed just enough of her bright white toenail polish through the peek-a-boo style shoe.

I was emotionally drained and wanted so badly to be alone, to hide from the world and to recharge my spirit. I watched Lynie as she took a sip of her afternoon coffee and quickly peeked at the golden Rolex that snugged her wrist. She sat waiting for me. I could tell that she was growing anxious, eager to pound me with a million and one questions about my counseling appointment. I immediately regretted my decision to bring her along. I thought I would need the emotional support, but it had turned into more of an emotional burden. I didn't want to relive the painful words and memories that were discussed in that office. I contemplated walking in the opposite direction to exit the building in secrecy and to avoid Lynie's unwanted debrief session, but I knew it would only lead to a disagreement between Lynie and I, as she wouldn't understand my desperate feeling of wanting to run away.

I took a deep breath and pressed my dark sunglasses closer to my face as I prepared to rip the Band-Aid off the situation at once. I quickly walked in Lynie's direction, barely stopping to acknowledge her.

"Okay, I'm all done," I said to her, continuing to walk towards the exit.

"Symone!" Lynie called out to me as she quickly rose to her feet, swinging her leather purse over her shoulder and walking swiftly behind me. "Symone?" I could hear her confusion as I continued ahead. "What the hell, SYMONE?" Her wrath stopped me in my tracks right outside of the tall building. I slowly turned towards her, as I prepared myself for a lecture."

"What is wrong with you?" I was silent. She continued. "Umm, hello? I got up early and canceled my clients' appointments to come and support you. Why are you being so damn rude?"

I didn't have a short and easy answer for her. I was mute. Suddenly my sunglasses were being lifted up and off of my face. Before I realized what was going on, Lynie had my glasses in her hand as she glared, deep into my face, searching for the answers that I was not ready to provide. I threw my head back and exhaled heavily into the sky.

Lynie looked into my puffy, red eyes and immediately empathized with me. *"Shit,"* she cursed to herself in frustration. She hated losing her cool, especially at the expense of hurting me. "Look, I know this must be a very intense situation for you." She looked down at my eyewear in her hands, using the tip of her perfectly clean designer hoody to wipe and remove the smudge marks from my glasses before she slid them back onto my face. "I'm sorry for making this about me," she muttered.

We simultaneously sank into the bench behind us, both needing to recuperate from the brief emotional storm that had just occurred.

The cool Boston wind brushed passed my cheeks and through my coarse hair that had coiled up at its roots from the sweat that drenched my scalp.

"Lynie...I'm just tired," the statement left my lips as a sigh of relief.

"Oh hush. I know...I mean, I can only imagine." Lynie shifted her position and looked towards me. "Listen here, sis. You are strong, determined, resilient, and you are a badass. You hear me? Now, I don't know what happened in Ms. Rita Fray's office, but whatever it is, it will *not* defeat you," Lynie deposited her words into my soul.

There was silence. I glanced over the city and took in the scenery as I clung onto Lynie's encouraging words. The sun hid behind the tall skyscrapers, but its rays managed to find their way to me and gently caressed my face. It felt like a warm hug from mother nature herself. The Boston wind grew stronger and ripped through my hair, leaving it wild and free; it felt good.

"Listen," Lynie started. "I know this is supposed to be a deep moment for you right now, but we need to do something about this head of yours, *immediately.*"

We burst into uncontrollable giggles. The echoes of our laughter were carried throughout the city and dissolved into the crisp blue skies above.

♦

I parallel parked my black Audi in the first parking space labeled *special guest,* reserved specifically for family and friends. *She's so extra,* I thought to myself with a slight grin on my face. I had to admit, the unique parking space made me feel kind of important.

I turned off the ignition and looked through my car window at the medium-sized, pearl-colored brick building that stood in front of me. The walkway to the entrance was a clean concrete that led to the royal blue double doors. The windows on the building were massive and provided a way for natural light to enter the establishment; I instantly remembered how beautiful the interior of the building was. I looked up towards the top of the structure and admired the bold, gold letters that read, *Lynie's Beauty Retreat.*

After an intense and emotional session with the therapist, Lynie convinced me to follow her to the shop for a quick pampering. "You might as well Symone," she said. "Mr. Bricks and Mr. Butler gave you the entire day off and we don't know if that will ever happen again," she teased before adding, "Besides, it's free." Lynie brought up some valid points and I didn't know how to get out of her plan, so I agreed.

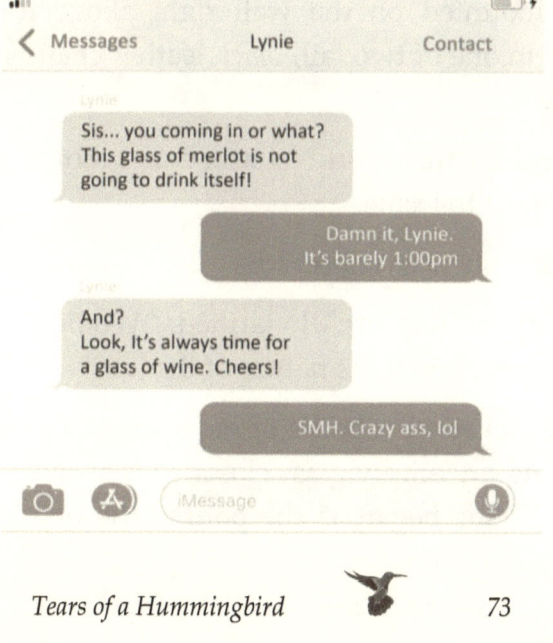

When I walked into the beauty salon, it was empty as expected, given the vacant parking lot out front.

"I gave the crew a surprise day off," Lynie's voice traveled from the back of the salon. "We got the place to ourselves," she celebrated.

I glanced around the spacious and beautiful interior. The walls were a rich blue color with a dramatic black accent wall where the hair dryers were lined up. The floors were a dark hardwood pattern that shined and captured the reflection of the lights glowing from the glass-made chandeliers that dangled from the ceiling. I walked past the stylist workstations, which were grand and laced with granite counter tops, as I made my way back to where Lynie was.

Lynie was relaxing in one of her sitting areas right in front of a modern artificial fireplace with a flatscreen TV that sat mounted on the wall right above it. She was snuggled in one of two tall, black leather chairs with wide armrests.

"How does that work?" I asked as I took my place in the chair next to Lynie.

"What?" she was confused.

"A surprise day off," I clarified. "Wouldn't they lose out on money, given the nature of the job?"

Lynie picked up a bottle of red wine and motioned for me to bring my empty glass closer so that she could fill it up. "Well," she began as she poured the rich liquid into the spotless wine glass. "To make it a *true* day off for my stylists, I attach a bonus for the day. Meaning, they each get a check from me to make up for the money they would have made."

"How much do you pay them?" I was curious.

"Well come work for me and you'll find out," she teased.

I watched Lynie swallow the wine in her glass in one huge gulp, and tried to follow suit but was unsuccessful. Lynie chuckled to herself as she handed me a napkin to wipe off the droplets of wine from the corners of my mouth and beneath my chin.

"Be careful now," she alerted me. "That's pure, organic tiger fur up under your feet. It wouldn't look as nice with wine stains on it."

"Lynie, you do know there are just as nice *vegan* area rugs that you can purchase and probably for half the price of this poor tiger that you had skinned alive just to rest your big ass feet on," I barked at her. I knew my point was going in one ear and out the other, like it always did.

Lynie finished pouring her second glass of wine right before throwing a sharp look my way. "How do you know the tiger was alive when they removed its fur?"

"Does it matter if the tiger was alive? What's really important is the fact that a fellow earthling was murdered at the expense of the decor in your salon." I threw a smirk back at Lynie because I knew she hated when I scolded her on this topic.

She threw her hand on her hip as she pushed back at my last statement. "Hey, it's all the circle of li—"

"Oh, don't you dare pull that 'circle of life' bullshit card with me," I laughed at the audacity of Lynie's cliché rebuttal.

Lynie's giggles trailed off as she regained a serious face. "And what about that poor chicken in that Caesar salad from the other day?" she mocked me.

I sighed and rolled my eyes as I tilted my empty wine glass towards Lynie to signal for a refill. "That meat on those salads at the Green Garden Cafe is so heavily processed to the point it's no longer flesh that you're digesting but more like a clump of rubber and chemicals," I stated as a matter of fact.

"I see what you did there." Lynie winked at me as she poured the rest of the wine into my glass.

"Hey, it's the truth." I shrugged.

"Hmmmm, animal flesh or heavily processed balls of rubber chemicals?" Lynie pretended to think out loud in a sarcastic demeanor. "I think I'll try my luck with the flesh," she joked.

"Disgusting." I laughed as I openly and playfully judged Lynie's choice of diet.

My muscles were relaxed, and the mild numbness triggered by the adult beverage in my hand traveled through my body. I felt light as a feather. Everything that was once so serious to me just thirty minutes ago, now seemed not as crucial. I chuckled as I replayed the moment that I puked into Ms. Rita Fray's perfectly clean and untouched trash bin just hours ago. *She probably thinks I have serious issues*, I giggled to myself.

"What's funny?" Lynie wondered as she witnessed me in my own little world.

I tried to regain my composure before responding, as I was clearly suffering from a case of *the giggles*. "So, earlier when I was meeting with the counselor, I barfed into her trash can." I burst into belly-wrenching laughter before I could even finish the sentence.

Lynie's expressed disbelief as she shifted towards me with her mouth wide open. "You did *what*?" I continued my laughter, almost unable to breathe. Lynie would not give up on receiving an explanation. "Seriously, what happened? Are you pregnant?"

I quickly caught my breath and rebuked what felt like curse words that Lynie had thrown towards me. "*GOD, NO!*" I exclaimed. I took an enormous swallow of wine to cool my sudden hot throat. Lynie looked at me with suspicion.

"So, you don't want more kids? Or...you don't want more kids with Jonathan?"

I paused for a moment. Having more children was something I definitely desired at the beginning of my marriage. I longed for a huge family that I could nurture, take care of, and create traditions with. I would imagine having children in almost every room of the house and I could visualize having a toddler following me around the home, giggling at every single face and movement I made. A third grader working on his long division math problems at the dining room table. A pre-teen son in the family room playing his favorite video games to kill time before dinner. A beautiful teenage daughter, lying across the fluffy bed in her room with her celebrity crush plastered all over her wall. I could peep through the crack of her mostly shut bedroom door and watch her with her headphones on as she sang her heart out, reciting the lyrics of the latest and most popular R&B love song, dreaming of someday falling in love and starting a family of her own. And my husband would be in the living room on his laptop, working on his next plan to save humanity. He would gently motion for me to come over and sit next to him to review his most recent idea, as he unashamedly requested my thoughts and opinions surrounding his new development.

The sound of Lynie obnoxiously clearing her throat to regain my attention brought me back to my unpreferred reality. "Both," I partially lied as I buried my face inside my wine glass, inhaling the last sip.

Lynie got up abruptly and walked over to the first chair at the shampoo station. "Let's get this head of yours together, honey!" She turned on the sink faucet and ran her fingers under the water to assess its heat level. I watched as she turned and adjusted the hot and cold knobs a few times until she finally found the perfect temperature for my hair. I lifted myself from the comfortable space and walked over to sit in the chair in front of the sink where Lynie was standing.

"It is *not* that bad," I growled at her right before leaning my head back into the warm water. I could hardly hear Lynie's sassy remark through the loud runny water that began to soak my hair. I assumed that her comment was somewhere along the lines of insisting that my hair was, indeed, *that* bad. I ignored her response, choosing to let her win this battle of the ongoing war regarding my apparent untamed hair. I closed my eyes and allowed Lynie's fingers to caress and massage my scalp. The tip of her thick, acrylic coated fingernails scraped my skull perfectly, removing the dandruff and tension all at once. Each stroke of her fingers pressing against my head implanted relief into my soul. Each scrub removed old caked up oil and pain that lingered around for far too long. I could hear and feel the shampoo lather up and apprehend all of the worries and dirt in my hair right before carrying it all down the sink drain for good.

After rinsing my hair clean of the shampoo, Lynie added a thick layer of soothing, peppermint conditioner. She rubbed the cool substance onto my hair carefully and slowly, making sure to coat and moisturize every single strand of hair. Lynie took her time, allowing the conditioner to marinate in my coils before rinsing the excess product out of my hair, leaving a fresh and shiny finish. I felt restored.

"And that's how you breathe life back into a sistah's hair, honey," Lynie tooted her own horn out loud. "Your natural curls are now hydrated and beautiful again. I'm thinking we should add some oil, additional moisture, and gel for styling a soft, bouncy wash-and-go hairstyle," Lynie thought out loud.

I lifted my head up from the sink and quickly sat up straight in the chair, eager to witness my rejuvenated curls. I looked in the mirror across from where I was sitting and instantly fell in awe. For the first time in a long time, I looked at my reflection and did not feel pain. I oddly felt sort of...*beautiful*. I sat quietly and continued to admire Lynie's work through the mirror as I watched her use hair gel and a wide tooth comb to accentuate and style my coils. She pinned the back portion up, leaving chin length bangs in the front, which created a fun and pretty hairdo.

Lynie dramatically stepped back to view her work from a distance. "Flawless," she announced.

"Thanks, girl!" I was grateful and still mesmerized by my new look.

"No problem, sis! It was done effortlessly," she bragged as she walked across the room to pull out a second bottle of wine from one of her decorative glass cabinets. She proceeded to fill two new glasses right before walking over to hand me one. "You can get out of the mirror now, *Ms. Sadity*," Lynie laughed.

"Whatever! Is there crime in appreciating my natural beauty?" I delivered the rhetorical question to Lynie as I posed in the mirror and took my first sip of my fresh glass of wine.

Lynie lifted her glass to the air and toasted to my last statement. "Definitely no crime in that!" We cheered to ourselves.

I gradually started to hear a faint tune that seemed very familiar to me, but I was unsure about where the sound was coming from. I unintentionally ignored the melody for several seconds until it stopped, and then restarted almost immediately. I jumped out of the salon chair and scurried to my purse once I realized the oddly familiar—yet annoying and repetitive melody—was my cell phone ringing. Once I reached my purse, I placed my wine on a nearby table and shoved my hand into my purse, digging around viciously until I was able to grasp the cellular device. I unlocked my screen with my six-digit code and read three missed calls from Ms. Brown, followed by a text message.

Ms. Brown

> Hi Mrs. Michaels, it's Ms. Brown. Are you coming to pick up Courtney today, or should I be expecting someone else? School ended 20 minutes ago...

Oh no! I'm stuck in traffic! I'm on my way this second— PLEASE keep her at the school until I get there, thank you.

Ms. Brown

> Principal Greer is here, and is demanding that we follow proper protocol.

Okay? So, what is the proper protocol?

Ms. Brown

> To call the second parent and/or family member listed on the emergency contact form. If there's no contact with a relative within a reasonable timeframe, I'm expected to call CPS.

Ms. Brown, no. Please, I will be there.

  iMessage

I sped up Summer Street towards Court's school, cursing at every red light along the way. I drove with the windows down, praying that the Boston air would quickly clear out my pores and sober my liver before arriving at my daughter's school. I desperately chomped on a stale piece of cool mint gum that I spotted in the cupholder to mask the smell of wine on my breath.

When I finally arrived at F. Douglass Elementary School, I was relieved to see Ms. Brown, wobbling out of the front door with a pleasant look on her face. I was more so relieved to see the absence of Principal Greer's car. Ms. Brown's short, round body began to move down the stairs just as I threw my car in park and jumped out of my vehicle to meet her at the bottom step.

"Ms. Brown thank you so much. You have no idea how helpful you have been," I pleaded to her as I simultaneously tried to catch my breath.

"No problem Ms. Michaels. You didn't have to come all the way up here just to thank me. I'm just happy I didn't have to make that phone call to CPS. I'm actually on my way out." She smiled gratefully.

Slightly discombobulated, I looked behind her and noticed that Principal Greer wasn't the only person missing from this gathering. "Where's Courtney?" I began to panic.

Ms. Brown paused for a few seconds to process my question. "Um, you didn't get my voicemail?"

I began to grow impatient. "No, where is she?" I smiled hard, trying to hide my anxiety.

"She's fine. She's with her dad, Mr. Michaels. Did your husband not call you?"

My knees weakened. "Fuck; no. He's supposed to be out of town," I thought out loud, trying to make sense of the situation.

"Mrs. Michaels? Is everything okay?" Ms. Brown's concerned eyes pierced through me as she waited for a response.

I quickly collected my emotions for the moment and assured Ms. Brown that I was okay. I placed my hands on her shoulders as I escorted her to her vehicle, steering her to the driver's side. I opened the car door and left her with an ingenuine warm smile, followed by an empty *goodnight*. Ms. Brown responded with a slightly nervous grin before sliding into her seatbelt and driving off.

I sat in my car with my forehead pressed against my steering wheel and listened to the missed voicemail that Ms. Brown left for me, moments before I arrived at the school.

"Hi Mrs. Michaels, it's Ms. Brown calling back from F. Douglass Elementary School in regard to Courtney Michaels. I know we just talked via texting, but I wanted to let you know that I was able to get in touch with your husband and Mr. Michaels has agreed to come by and pick up Courtney since he was already in the area.

Besides, this way you can take your time and drive safely in the hectic Boston traffic. I hope this helps! Talk to you later."

I squealed on the inside, imagining what evil energies Jay had brewing up back at home. The thought of running away with nothing more than the clothes on my back, my car and the $572 in my checking account came to my mind. I imagined leaving out of the school parking lot and making a right, going straight onto the freeway and never looking back. I didn't care where I would end up, just as long as it was far, far away from Jay and the demons that lived in our home. I wanted to be cleansed and reborn with a fresh start.

I immediately cursed myself for fantasizing about a peaceful life without Courtney, even if it was only for a few seconds. She was one of the few reasons, besides plain fear, why I stayed in a destructive marriage. I felt hopeless. My shoulders dropped as I exhaled heavily, watching my spirit leave my body. I started the engine and slowly made a left turn out of the school parking lot.

◆

When I entered the front door, the air was thick, and I could feel the tension crawl up my spine. The house was silent, cold, and dimmed. I removed my heels in the foyer and quietly sat them on the floor against the wall. I carefully hung my keys beneath the mailbox, squeezing them tightly to prevent them from making a lot of noise. I then proceeded to place my purse and jacket on the blue recliner in the living area.

I tiptoed towards the kitchen and noticed a distinct smell of fried fish and broccoli that I assumed Jay prepared for dinner. This, along with mac and cheese, was Courtney's favorite meal. I glanced at the kitchen clock and observed that it was barely sunset and a little too early for Courtney to be finished with her dinner and in bed, let along all done with her homework. I wondered why I couldn't hear her sweet little voice. I walked up the stairs with uncertainty.

I stopped at Courtney's bedroom door and slowly pushed it open. My heart sank into my stomach once I noticed that Courtney was not inside of her bedroom, at her miniature desk completing her homework with the colorful gel pens that she loved so much.

"She's at my sister's," Jay's voice echoed from our bedroom and created trembles through my body. I remained silent as he continued. "Don't worry, she's good. I packed her dinner, homework and night clothes."

"Night clothes?" I was suspicious. "When is she coming back home?" I asked, still standing near Courtney's door, unable to see Jay's face.

I could hear Jay chuckle at my growing fear before responding, yet completely ignoring my inquiry on our daughter's whereabouts. "I called the firm earlier and they said you were out for the day. Where were you?"

"I had an appointment, Jay. When is Court coming back home?"

"Interesting. You know, I can sense your guilty conscience from here. You think because you left our daughter at school while you were out doing God knows what, I would take her away from you? Hmmmm... maybe I should? Maybe it would be in her best interest to have a responsible parent that is capable of getting her to and from school every day." I could feel his frustration start to intensify. I remained silent. I could hear Jay lift himself from the bed, followed by his slow heavy footsteps that grew louder and closer. Soon after, his angry face appeared. His dark eyes gazed over me and stopped at my hair.

"Is *that* the reason you kept Courtney waiting at school? Because you had a lousy ass hair appointment?"

"No," I was immediately offended. "I had a—" I paused. I did not want Jay to know that I had a counseling appointment with Ms. Rita Fray. I knew that he would use context clues and conclude that I was arming myself with evidence to show that I was, in fact, a responsible mother who *is* capable of taking care of herself and her child, contrary to what Jay wanted everyone to believe. "I had something similar to a doctor's appointment and then Lynie invited me over to the shop."

"*Tsk!* So, let me get this right, your so-called friend is the reason you left my daughter on the school steps waiting in the cold?" A disgusted expression stained his face.

"What are you talking about? She was *not* in the cold," I pushed back at him with my words. "I spoke with Ms. Brown and she was safe and sound in the main office while she waited just twenty or thirty minutes for me."

"*Just* twenty or thirty minutes?" Jay moved closer to me. "You should have been there waiting to greet her the second her school day ended!" He was furious.

"Jay, I am there every day waiting for her when she gets out of school," I pleaded as he continued to move closer. "I have never been late to pick Courtney up from school. It was just this one tim—"

"That's one time too damn many!" I was interrupted by Jay's rage. He walked towards me until his nose was pressed down and against my forehead. I tried my very best to remain calm and collective, but my heart was rebellious against my wishes and began to race out of control. I could feel the heat of Jay's heavy breaths each time he exhaled.

"Are you *drunk*?" he bellowed out at me while still invading my personal space.

"No, I'm not drunk!"

"Well it sure as hell smells like it!"

"I had some *wine*, okay? I know what you're trying to do and drinking wine does not make me a bad mom and will not stand as sufficient evidence against me in divorce court, should we ever end up in such a place."

Just then, I watched all of Jay's muscular strength travel to his dominant hand as it suddenly elevated in the tensed air, hovering above me, right before it came racing down towards me. The heavy hand suddenly struck my body, connecting perfectly to the middle of my small face. The force was enormous; it pushed me through Court's bedroom door, leaving me on the floor near the foot of her princess, canopy bed.

I was frozen out of fear and pain. I pulled my hands to my nose to catch the warm, thick, and red liquid that started to fall from my nostrils.

"FUCK!" I could faintly hear Jay a few steps away from me as he reacted to his own sudden and violent action. "My intentions were to have a civilized conversation, Symone!"

I attempted to respond, but the shock factor from the painful encounter only allowed for a few groans to escape my lips.

He walked over towards my limp body and squatted down beside me. I could feel his angry eyes staring into my bloody face. "You know you really bring out the worst in me," he whispered the words through his tight jaw.

I was conscious, yet unresponsive.

"Get up and go get yourself cleaned." He rolled his eyes, seeming to be disgusted with the bloody mess on my face. "We'll finish this conversation later."

I remained curled up on my daughter's fluffy pink carpet until I could hear Jay's truck roar out of the driveway. I slowly lifted myself from the floor and dragged my spirit down the hallway and into the dark, windowless bathroom. I stood still and silent in the dark for several moments before finding the courage to flip on the light switch. The light was bright and exposed all of my emotional and physical pain. I looked deep into my reflection but could not see myself. The woman that I saw staring back at me resembled my mother. She wore the same tears, the same mistakes, and the exact same disappointments. The weight of my current reality sat heavy on my shoulders and forced me down to the bathroom floor. The feeling of sorrow invaded my chest, making it difficult to breathe. I wanted nothing more than to end the horrific cycle of unpleasantry. My trembling hand reached up towards the top drawer of the sink. I slowly pulled it open and crept my fingers inside and felt around for my *back-up healing tool*, since Jay tossed out my original one. *Not as smart as he thinks,* I thought to myself once I was able to grasp the brand-new razor, realizing Jay had overlooked it on his quest to locate evidence that would prove me to be an unfit mother.

I immediately thought of my own mother and connected with the betrayal and hopelessness she must have felt when she was being terrorized in her own home.

I expected her to do something I was unable to do myself: live through the trauma. "Mama, I know you were suffering," I wept to myself. "I forgive you mama, I forgive you." I began to unravel the thick, tightly folded napkin that swaddled my healing tool. I removed the sharp object and brought it close to my wrist. "Mama, please forgive me! I promise I tried my best," I sobbed. "Court, my beautiful baby. Mommy loves you."

I imagined the night my mother ended her own suffering. She was alone in a cold and dark place, just as I was. She reached her shivering fingers for both bottles, the alcohol and the pills. She consumed them both until she drifted off into, what I like to believe was, a peaceful sleep that never ended. I envied her everlasting paradise and longed to join her.

I dug the corner of my healing tool deep into the skin of my wrist, with the intention of dragging the blade through my flesh and to the other side of my hand. I took what I thought would be, one of the last deep breaths I would take in my lifetime, right before exhaling sharply through my dry, chapped lips. "Lord, make me numb," I whispered to myself as I prepared for my soul to slither away from my physical being. I closed my eyes in an attempt to work up the courage to go through with the plan. I began to count down. "Three...two...on—"

DING!

The message notification from my cell phone seemed louder than usual; the intense sound pierced through my body abruptly. Completely startled, I dropped the razor onto the bathroom floor right in between my thighs. I quickly reached in between my legs to retrieve the tool but was once again distracted by my cell phone.

DING!

I looked up and spotted the cellular device on the counter of the bathroom sink.

DING!

It rang out once more. Agitated by its interference, I shot up off the floor, flicked on the bathroom light and snatched the phone from the counter. There were three unread messages.

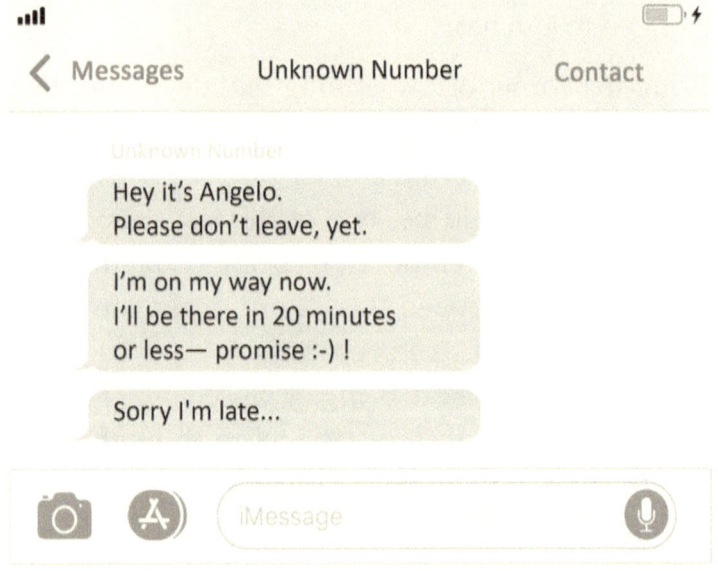

Hey it's Angelo.
Please don't leave, yet.

I'm on my way now.
I'll be there in 20 minutes
or less— promise :-) !

Sorry I'm late...

CHAPTER 6

TEARS OF A LIFE-SAVING INTERCEPTION

"If you ever contemplated suicide... I'm glad you're still here with us."

Confused, I reread the words a couple of times to make sense of the messages. The texts were from an unknown number and I was sure that the person on the other end sent the messages to me by accident. I tossed the phone back on the counter, choosing to ignore the lost person. I exhaled sharply before looking back into the mirror and staring at myself once more. Only this time, a thick layer of shame covered me. I was disappointed in myself for nearly giving in to the weak moment. "*AHHHHHHHH!*" I screamed at the top of my lungs, projecting all of my guilt, sorrow, and anger towards the pitiful woman in the mirror.

"How dare you?" I yelled at her. "How dare you contemplate leaving your daughter behind with that monster? You weak *bitch*! Maybe you don't deserve her, you poor excuse for a mother," I sobbed uncontrollably. "I'm sorry." Seconds later I found myself back on the bathroom floor. I pressed my cheek against the blue, plush rug. The soft texture soaked up my heavy tears and offered some temporary comfort. I opened my eyes and focused my blurry vision on a silver object that laid just inches away from the tip of my nose. It was my *healing* tool. The site of the razor reignited a fury inside of me. I quickly lifted my face from the floor and snatched the silver object from the rug. I stood up completely and dunked the blade into the small restroom trash can with extreme force.

I was exhausted and my muscles were tense. I turned on the shower and increased the temperature until it was steaming hot, yet comfortable enough for my skin to marinate in. The moment I stepped into the strong streams of water, the steam flooded my pores and caressed each inch of my petite figure. I closed my eyes and walked closer to the shower, allowing the water to splatter over my body. I welcomed the pressure from the streams to penetrate me entirely. The hot water cleansed my face. I watched the red liquid from my wounded nose as it intertwined with the fresh water and rushed down my neck, in between my breasts, passed the stretch marks on my belly, down my long legs, and into the shower drain. I followed up with a deep soap scrub, removing any unwanted bacteria from my flesh. I turned off the shower and grabbed the clean, white towel that hung on the wall nearby, wrapping the fabric tightly around my body. Immediately after leaving the shower, I was greeted with a beautiful, yet overwhelming feeling of restoration. I was reborn.

I slid into a light and comfortable nightgown and slithered my way underneath the fresh comforter that stretched across my bed. My body melted onto the surface of the soft mattress. In that very moment I felt a sense of peace as I slowly drifted into a cozy state of rest.

RING!

The intense sound yanked me out of my sleep. I sat up in bed, a bit disoriented and wondering what the noise was coming from.

RING!

I realized that my phone was ringing out from the bathroom counter where I had it last. I looked over at the small clock on the nightstand and saw that it was close to midnight. "Courtney," I said to myself as I jumped out of bed and ran towards the bathroom. I hoped that the ringing phone would soon notify me that my baby girl was on her way home. I snatched the cellphone off of the countertop of the bathroom sink. Once my eyes focused in on the screen of the buzzing device, a sigh of disappointment slipped out from my lips. I stared at the same unknown number that had disturbed me earlier, frustrated that the stranger was still obviously lost and confused. I ignored the call and immediately proceeded to check on Courtney's whereabouts.

I was relieved. My body slowly let go of the tension that it had quickly accumulated within the past five minutes of being awake. I reached my arms straight up above my head to welcome a full body stretch followed by a wide yawn. My feet began to guide me back to the huge fluffy pillows that sat on my bed, waiting to re-greet me.

RING!

What the hell? My teeth grinded against each other. I stomped back to the bathroom and screamed at the noisy device. "LET ME SLEEP!" The unknown number was starting to become oddly familiar.

RING!

The person on the other end just would not let up. I decided it was time for them to catch my wrath, and I accepted the call. Before the man on the other end could get a piece of his first word out, I yelled into the phone: "WRONG NUMBER!" I could hear a smooth, gentle-yet-strong, and baritone voice pleading for my attention.

"Please don't hang up! Look, I know this might sound crazy, but I've been waiting at this restaurant for two whole hours, Mariah. We had a date scheduled for this evening. I know I was a little late and I'm sorry for that. Are you coming? Or is it safe to assume that I'm being stoo—"

"Yes, sir! I think It's safe to assume that Mariah has stood you up." I was annoyed.

"Wait, who is this? Where's Mariah?" He was flustered.

"I think it's also safe to assume that this Mariah lady *also* gave you the wrong number. Which explains *why* you have been texting and calling my phone all night disturbing my peace of mind!" I could hear the lightbulb in the man's head click on as he finally realized he had been dialing the wrong number the whole time.

"Ma'am," I could hear the small amount of hope he possessed at the beginning of the phone call slowly start to melt away. "I'm sorry for interrupting your Friday night. Good evening," he ended the call before I could say anything else. Part of me empathized with the man and regretted the way I approached the situation. However, I honestly was too exhausted to dwell on the feeling of guilt for longer than a few seconds. I moseyed my drained body towards my bed and instantly fell back into a deep sleep.

◆

"Mommy... Mommy... Mommy," I could hear a light, warm voice in my right ear. "Mommy, wake up," the voice sang out to me, soft and sweet as a hummingbird's tune. My eyes were heavy, yet I managed to open them. The bright brown eyes and wide smile on the beautiful melanated face that stood just centimeters away from mine, made the struggle to wake up all worth it. Courtney's burst of joyful energy shined bright and naturally lit up the room. "Look mama, I made this picture for you at Auntie Lisa's house."

I sat up in bed to get a better look at the beautiful art that Court held so proudly in her small hands. The artwork was spread across a pale purple piece of construction paper. There were two stick figures with gorgeous curly hair. One of the figures was significantly taller than the other; beside the smaller figures was a huge vibrant red heart that took up a big chunk of the paper. On the opposite side and next to the taller figure was a sun colored in with a bright yellow. "I love it!" I smiled while still examining the artwork.

Courtney chimed in and explained her illustration. "Mommy, this one is you and this one is me." She pointed her tiny finger to the shorter stick figure. "This heart is here because you give me so much love! And I love you and you love me! And all of this love created a *big* heart!" She used her miniature arms to demonstrate the amount of love we have for each other. "And this sun is next to you because you make me feel happy like the sun," Court began to sing in a soft and jolly hum as she swayed her body side to side. "You are my sunshine, my only sunshine, you make me happy when life feels gray! Hm hm hm hmm hmmmm hm hm hm hmm hmmmm…"

My heart was full as I watched my baby girl dance and glorify my existence and unconditional love for her. The two emotions of gratitude and guilt tugged and fought for a place in my heart. It was a draw, but there was not enough room for both. The combination of the two energies overflowed in my chest and resulted in a fresh, warm batch of tears that quickly flooded my eyes.

"Mama? Why are you crying?" Court stopped her humming and prancing to attend to my silent tears.

"These are tears of joy, baby." I flashed a grin at my daughter as I wiped away the tears that concerned her. "I'm just happy that I'm here with you." I leaned over to kiss Court on her soft, precious forehead. She wrapped her arms around me and squeezed as tight as her heart would allow. "I'm never going to leave you baby girl, I promise. Okay?" I looked Courtney into her eyes as I awaited her response.

"Okay, Mama," she looked back into my eyes with a strong sense of trust. I was absolutely disgusted with myself and could not believe I almost gave up moments like this for good. It was difficult to fathom the fact that I would have literally missed out on the rich interaction with Courtney if it wasn't for—. I stopped mid thought and realized the technical truth as to why I was still alive and able to hold my daughter in my arms. "Angelo," I whispered to myself. I was now oddly grateful for the stranger's misdials and desperation to contact the date that stood him up. I was now happy that she issued him the wrong cell phone number, and reflected on the unwanted texts and calls that I was now beyond thankful for. I held Courtney close to my chest and placed a second kiss on her face.

"Mommy, who's *Angelo*?" Court looked up at me with scrunched together eyes.

"I don't know baby." I smiled down at Court right before squeezing her with a tight hug.

"Good morning, Symone," Jay's voice ripped through the room. He stood in the doorway of the bedroom with the both of his hands behind his back.

"Daddy!" Court ran across the carpet and wrapped her arms around her father's legs.

"Guess what?" Jay bent down and whispered towards Court. "There's warm muffins in the kitchen."

Court's bottom jaw dropped as she jumped up and down out of excitement. Jay smiled and nodded his head towards the hallway to signal to Court that the muffins were ready for her to devour them. Courtney accepted the invite to the kitchen where the warm treat waited for her, and anxiously ran downstairs.

"I said, good morning," Jay repeated as he slowly walked towards me, with his hands still placed behind his back.

It was a good morning before you walked in, I thought to myself. "Morning," I replied to Jay.

He continued towards me. His unseen arms created a ball of suspicion at the pit of my stomach. Yet, I was determined to hide any fear that lived within me. Jay stared deep into my eyes, seeming to seek out any uncertainty. I calmly held my breath as I watched him begin to remove his arm from hiding. He slowly brought his hands from around his back and before I knew it, there were a dozen of fresh roses in my face. "These are for you," Jay said with a slight grin on his face.

The bright red flowers he held in his huge hands resembled the bright red fluid those same hands caused to rush down my face just hours before. I reached out and collected the roses from him, bringing them to my face and drowning my aching nose in its healing scent. "Thanks," I murmured through the flowers.

I cringed on the inside as Jay sat next to me on the bed. He exhaled sharply. "Symone, do you remember when we first met? How close we were?"

I was silent.

"Last night, I was thinking back to how things were when we first met. I was a complete wreck before you came along, and you just made everything better. You were my peace." Jay stopped for a moment to swallow what sounded like an emotional lump in his throat. "And dammit, I want that back."

I looked over at Jay and watched one lonely tear slide down his face. I had no words. Jay quickly stood up and removed the roses from my lap to make room for himself. He got on his knees and shimmied his way in between my legs and looked into my eyes.

"Do you remember our vows?" he asked.

"For better or for worse," I replied softly.

"Baby, I know we have been experiencing a lot of *worse*, but I want to make it better," he implored.

I never knew the *for better* parts of our marriage would equate to the days when I was *not* in my husband's presence. That those days would mean I was safe from the physical harm and emotional suffering my husband forced on me whenever his life seemed to be anything but perfect. That, those *better days* would be the days I was fortunate enough to escape the heavy, painful loads that my husband was eager to drop on to me, just to temporarily lighten up the emotional weight on his own shoulders. Those *better days* would be the days that I was given a chance to breathe and hope for more… *better days*.

I never imagined *for worse* would lead to bruised ribs and busted noses. That those days would mean I was lucky enough to still be alive. That those days would make me feel unlucky to still be alive. When my husband looked me in my eyes seven years ago and promised to love me for better or for worse, I never knew he would become the *worse*. Had I known then…I would have ripped the ivory white gown off my body and ran back down the aisle, away from the altar, away from the vows, away from the commitment to evil and never looked back. Had I known the *worse* days would include my husband's forced manhood into my innocence, I would have not created life with it early on.

Jay laid his heavy head on my lap. "Symone, let's start over," he began to weep.

Choose your battles wisely, I thought to myself. I knew that if I agreed to a clean slate with Jay, I would be agreeing to disregard all of the pain he had caused me up until that point in our marriage. Agreeing to a clean slate would be re-committing to for better or for worse. I knew this was a battle I *had to* fight with everything I had inside of me.

Suddenly, Court's perfectly glowing, smiling face burst into the bedroom. Her eyes lit up as she glanced over at us from the doorway. I watched as the muffin crumbs on her face shifted once her smile grew even wider than before. I suspected that Court was thrilled to witness her parents having what she perceived to be an intimate and loving moment. "Mommy and Daddy," Court charged at us with her arms open, prepared to receive some of the joy she was so sure we were sharing with one another. "I love you, Mommy, and I love you, Daddy," Court squeezed us tight, projecting her enthusiasm onto the both of us.

Jay looked up at me. His eyes awaited a response to his earlier proposal. Courtney continued to cling onto our group hug; her sense of joy and protection was all that mattered to me at that very moment. *Perhaps, this is a battle that I will fight later*, I negotiated with myself. "Okay," I mumbled to Jay.

♦

"A and B Law Firm, Symone speaking, how can I assist you this morning?" The woman on the other end was frustrated and demanded to speak with Mr. Butler.

"Ma'am, I understand your concern and I apologize for any inconvenience. Unfortunately, Mr. Butler is out. But, if you'd like, I can put you on a line with Mr. Bricks?" I waited patiently as the woman complained for several seconds before ultimately agreeing to speak with Mr. Bricks. "Great, one moment please," I pressed the hold button on the large black office phone, walked across the lobby to Mr. Bricks' office, and placed two soft knocks on his door.

"Oh, come on in," I heard Mr. Bricks' high-pitched, jolly voice yell out to me.

"Good morning Mr. Bricks, sorry to disturb you. I—"

"Oh, don't be silly, Mrs. Michaels. How are you?" He stood up and walked around to the front of his desk. Mr. Bricks proceeded to plant his bottom on the edge of his desk as he folded his arms and leaned in towards me with a warm smile.

"Oh, me? I'm...I'm doing well. Um...thanks for asking," I stuttered, mirroring the smile on his face.

Mr. Bricks raised his eyebrows. "Now, that wasn't very convincing at all," he teased.

I let out a calm giggle to fill in the awkward silence. "Oh! Umm, I have Mrs. Blair on the line again. She wanted to speak with Mr. Butler. I informed her he was out and suggested she address her concerns with you. Is that okay?"

"Of course! Transfer her back," Mr. Bricks grinned as he walked back to his office chair. He quickly plopped down and reached towards his phone, prepared to take the call.

"Thanks, sir." I skipped back across the lobby towards my phone. "Hi, Mrs. Blair? Yes, thank you for waiting. Mr. Bricks is now available and ready to take your call. Is it okay if I transfer you now? Great." I pressed the transfer button as I prepared to hang up the phone immediately.

The office became quiet and still. I looked out towards the grand windows of the firm's beautiful lobby and admired the rays of sunshine that beamed into the building and through my space. *What a gorgeous sight,* I thought to myself. I continued to watch as the healthy leaves on the tall, bright green trees danced in the rich blue sky as the wind blew through the branches and offered nature a relaxing, cool breeze. The amazing view overwhelmed me. I briefly thought back to the darkness that took over me just a few days earlier. *Just think, I would have missed all of this.* I smiled as I continued to gaze out of the window. "Thank God for misdials, I guess," I chuckled to myself, half joking and half serious.

I thought about the man that found his way to me during a crucial moment in my life...just as I was about to end it. The coincidence of a stranger texting and calling the wrong number and ultimately saving a life was a thought I could not shake—it had been weighing heavy on my mind and heart. I thought of the lost voice that I was so blunt and rude to, and regretted the aggressive manner in which I approached the caller. There was a strong urge deep inside of me to make it right—I toyed with the idea of reaching out to Angelo and offering an apology. *That would be stupid and creepy,* I scoffed to myself.

"Mrs. Micheals, can you schedule Mrs. Blair with Mr. Butler? Next Tuesday at ten a.m.?" Mr. Bricks startled me as he poked his head out of his office.

"Uh...yes, sure thing Mr. Bricks." I shuffled around my desk to find a pen.

"Perfect." Mr. Bricks winked at me.

I quickly pressed down on the white letters on the black keyboard as I responded to Mr. Bricks' request.

"A and B Law Firm, Symone speaking, how can I assist you this morning?" I quickly picked up the ringing phone. "Ah yes, Mrs. Blair. I am scheduling your appointment now...and there! I have you scheduled for Tuesday at ten a.m. with Mr. Butler. Yes, ma'am. Same location. Thanks, and enjoy the rest of your day." I placed the phone on the hook and exhaled loudly. "That lady sure is consistent," I said to myself.

I anxiously looked over at the clock on the wall. It read 11:03 a.m. I mindlessly clicked around the browser with my mouse and wandered through my social media accounts, as I usually did to kill time. I enjoyed viewing the glimpse of life that my relatives and friends shared openly through the internet, and I was sure it was the only way I was able to stay somewhat in touch with any of them. My small life in Boston somehow managed to swallow all of me, including my time and energy to have a life outside of my family of three. I continued to scroll and stopped at a meme that read: *If you ever contemplated suicide...I'm glad you're still here with us.*

Chills raced through my body. I suddenly felt there were millions of eyes on me as I sat alone at my work desk. "I'm glad that I am still here, too," I silently whimpered to myself. The words of the meme cut me open and made it impossible for me to hold in my emotions.

"I'm heading out to an early lun—" Mr. Bricks stopped in his tracks. I quickly wiped the unexpected tears off my face and flashed a forced smile towards the small, worried man.

"Sounds good, I will see you once you return," my voice cracked all the way through the sentence.

Mr. Bricks continued to slowly put on his hat and jacket, but I could see the hesitation in his face as he walked towards the exit. He stopped right at the door and turned back towards me. "Mrs. Michaels," he paused for a second. "Is everything okay back at home?"

I felt exposed. It was not often that someone directly asked me about my home life. I was torn. My eyes cried out for help as they looked through Mr. Bricks, pleading for help...but my lips had other plans. "Yes, home is great. I uh, I just came across a sad news story online," I fibbed. "Got me all teary eyed," I chuckled nervously as I lied to his face.

"Okay," Mr. Bricks responded with a stale smile. "If you need anything—and I mean anything at all—don't you think twice about reaching out to me."

"Thank you, sir."

"See you in about an hour." Mr. Bricks softly closed the door behind him.

I exhaled sharply as I reached for a Kleenex to dry my face. I looked down at my phone and scrolled through my contacts. I stopped at the stranger's contact information that was saved under what I remembered his name to be: Angelo.

Well, it wouldn't be that weird, I convinced myself.

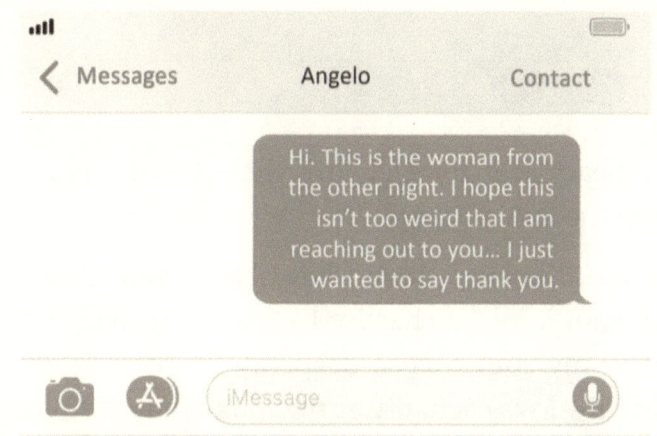

I screeched loudly right after I hit *send*. I couldn't believe that I actually typed and sent a thank you text to a complete stranger. *"Ahhhh!"* I partially regretted my choice to press send. I re-read my text several times and critiqued every single letter in every single word. *Why didn't I tell him my name? I didn't even explain why I was thanking him. Well, that would have been too much, right? Ugh, I don't know!* The thoughts raced through my head at one-hundred and twenty miles per hour.

DING!

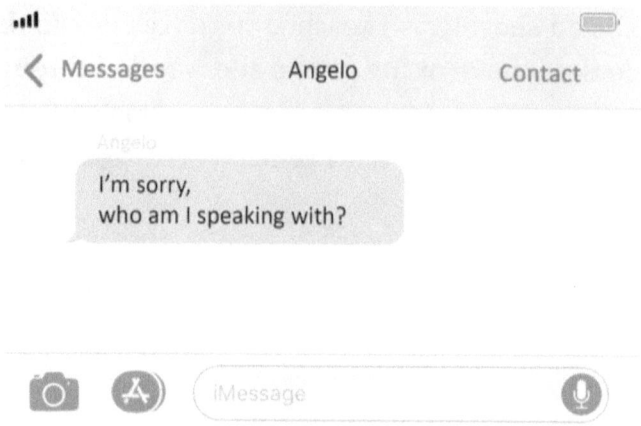

My heart beat through my chest loudly as my eyes digested the text message.

"Damn. I knew I should have been more clear, now I look like an idiot," I chastised myself out loud. I had no idea why my soul was so desperate to connect with this individual—I was actually suspicious of my own motives. I did not know why I wanted to, I just knew it was something I had to do. I replied to the text.

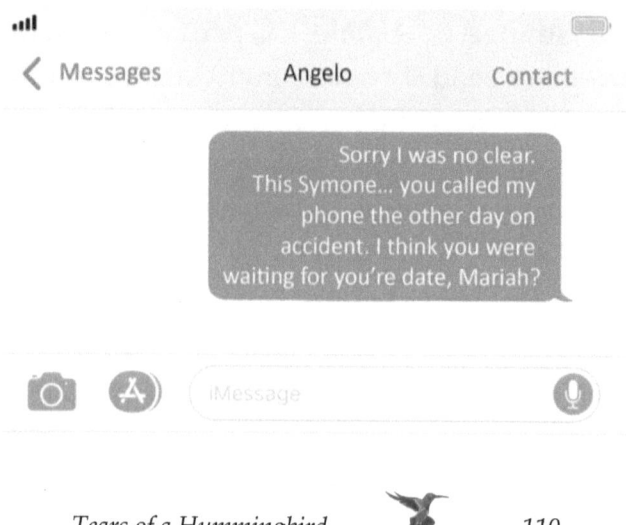

I softly nibbled on my nails as I awaited a reply. My body was stiff, and I could not think of anything else other than what the man would say next. I re-read the message that I sent and immediately bellowed out, "Oh, gosh. A typo!" I rolled my eyes at my own mistake. "Great, now he's going to think I am weird *and* illiterate." I instantly sent a follow-up text to correct my grammar.

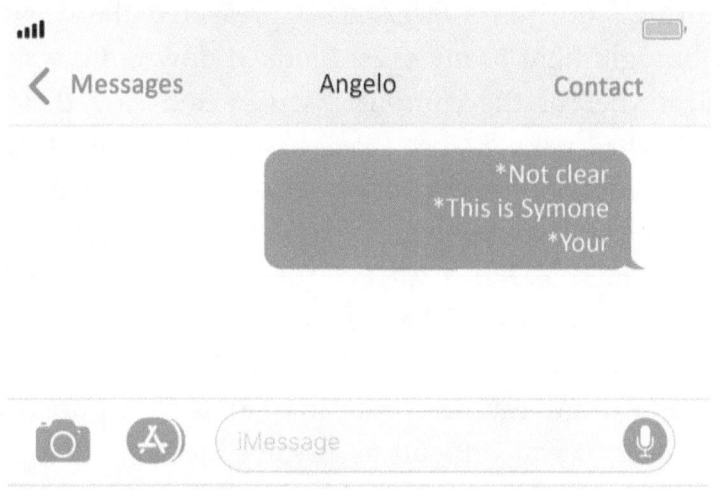

I quickly switched my ringer mode to silent and turned my phone face down, so I was not immediately notified once—and if—he decided to respond. I snatched my mouse and began to browse through online shopping sites. *Why the hell am I being so crazy about this? Sheesh,* I thought to myself as I tried my best to force my mind off of the phone for as long as I could. "Oooohhh! This would be cute on Courtney," I said out loud when I came across a beautiful yellow dress with glittery bows on the shoulders. "Ahhhhh, and these heels are something serious. Now, I can see myself dancing around in these," I laughed to myself as I tried to remember the last time I had been out dancing. *I wonder if he texted back? Nope. Symone, chill out,* I encouraged myself. *Calm down, girl. Finish doing what you're doing, and if you just so happen to pick up your phone and he just so happens to respond, then maybe you can text back.* I fooled myself.

I added the two items into my online shopping cart; picturing Courtney's face once I presented the dress to her brought light to my eyes. I looked down to the right-hand corner of the computer screen and saw that ten minutes had passed since I last messaged Angelo. *What if he texted back nine minutes ago and has been waiting for me to respond? Then he's going to think I'm playing on his phone.* I worried myself. *But, what if I flip this phone over and he hasn't texted back, yet? What if he never texts back at all? Ugh! I should have never texted him in the first place.* I closed my eyes and threw my head into my hands to suppress my frustration. It was difficult to dissolve the thirst to further communicate with this individual. When I reopened my eyes, my cell phone sat loudly in my peripheral vision. The anticipation was too heavy for me to bear any longer. I quickly reached out across the desk and pulled the phone towards me. I turned on the screen and saw that I had two unread messages from Angelo, sent ten minutes ago. My heart dropped.

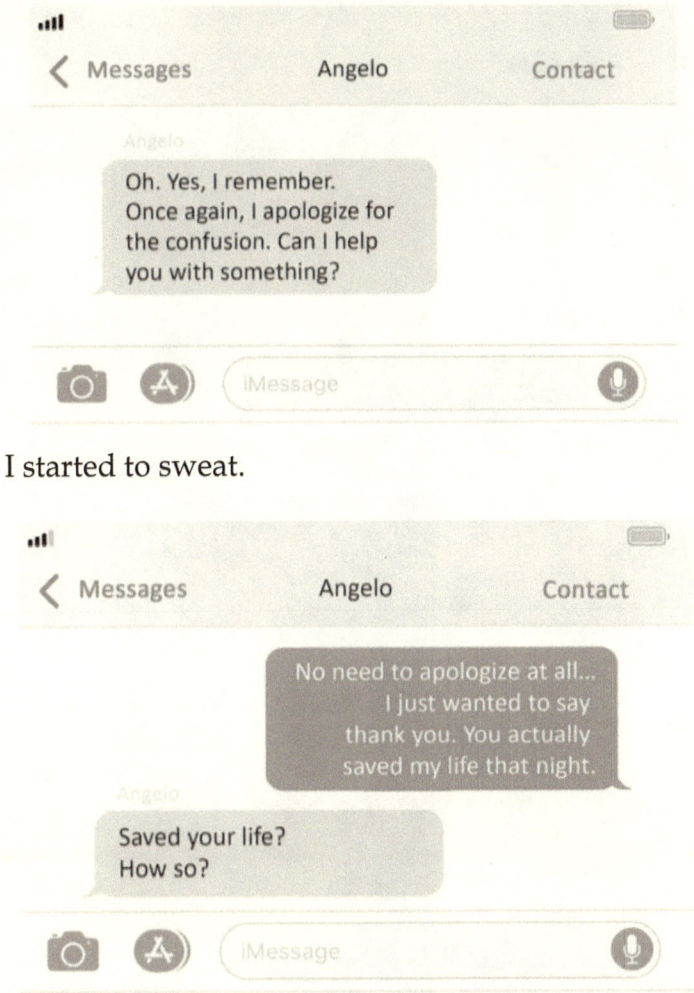

I started to sweat.

Whoa. Such an empty question could have such a loaded answer. I was not expecting the man on the other end to fully engage and had not prepared myself to fully answer his question. *I guess I could just tell him the truth. There's no harm in that, right?* I asked myself. *But he's a stranger. Yes he is, but it feels good to be honest and open for once. Even if it's with a stranger.* I enlightened myself.

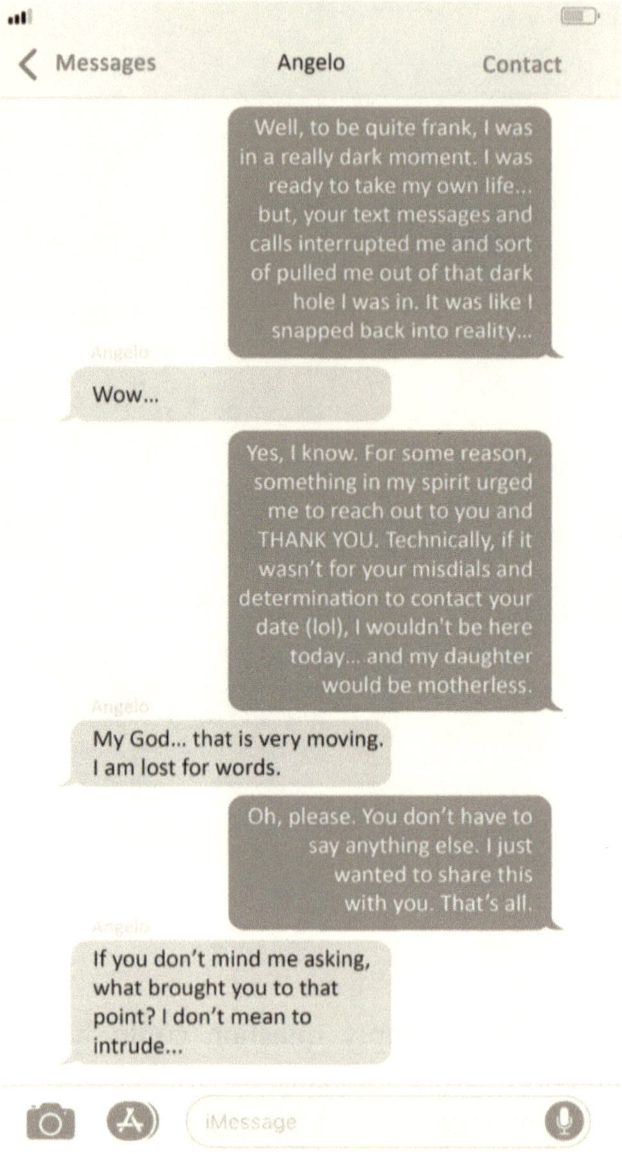

all 📶 🔋

< Messages   Angelo   Contact

> Well, to be quite frank, I was in a really dark moment. I was ready to take my own life... but, your text messages and calls interrupted me and sort of pulled me out of that dark hole I was in. It was like I snapped back into reality...

Angelo
Wow...

> Yes, I know. For some reason, something in my spirit urged me to reach out to you and THANK YOU. Technically, if it wasn't for your misdials and determination to contact your date (lol), I wouldn't be here today... and my daughter would be motherless.

Angelo
My God... that is very moving. I am lost for words.

> Oh, please. You don't have to say anything else. I just wanted to share this with you. That's all.

Angelo
If you don't mind me asking, what brought you to that point? I don't mean to intrude...

📷 Ⓐ (iMessage) 🎤

My body tensed up. What brought me to the point of suicide? This was a great question, but was not easy to answer. What do I say? My husband shoves foreign objects into my vagina and beats me up? I feel trapped? I miss my mother dearly, who by the way, was successful in her suicide attempt? I have no idea where my only sibling is, and I feel guilty that I haven't tried harder to find him? I never knew my dad? At night, I was violated by the man that consoled my mom in the daytime?

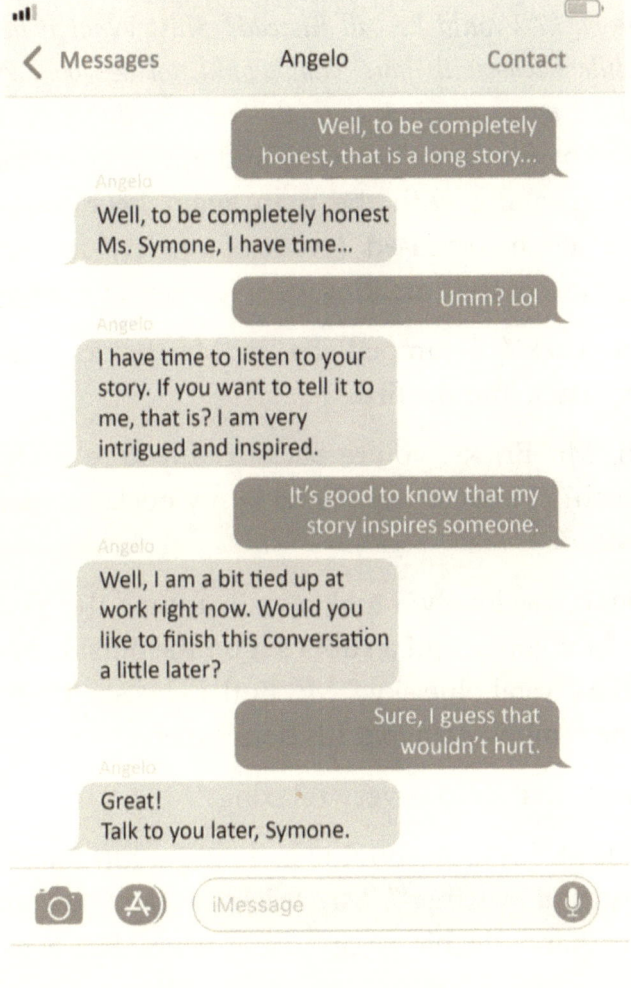

< Messages   Angelo   Contact

Well, to be completely honest, that is a long story...

Angelo

Well, to be completely honest Ms. Symone, I have time...

Umm? Lol

Angelo

I have time to listen to your story. If you want to tell it to me, that is? I am very intrigued and inspired.

It's good to know that my story inspires someone.

Angelo

Well, I am a bit tied up at work right now. Would you like to finish this conversation a little later?

Sure, I guess that wouldn't hurt.

Angelo

Great!
Talk to you later, Symone.

iMessage

Wait...did he just flirt with me? I questioned the ending of our text thread. I wasn't sure what I expected to come from the encounter, but I did not expect for it to **not end** after I said my thank you. I wondered why the man was so eager to follow-up and learn more about the dark situation that I had shared with him. Even more puzzling, I wondered what "talk to you later" meant. *When would he text me back? Would he call instead? Shit! What if he called back while I was with Jay? That would not be good. Why on earth did I agree to speak with this man again?* I was a bit confused by the way I naturally and openly welcomed the idea of speaking with the man again later today. The thought alone increased levels of anxiety to the max. Oddly, most of the emotions were feelings of excitement.

"I'm back!" I jumped up as Mr. Bricks made his entrance back into the firm.

"Hi, Mr. Bricks, you're back. Yes, you're back. How was lunch?" I shoved my phone in my pocket underneath the desk.

"Oh, it was lovely; I took a walk around the block and stopped for coffee and a sub. I sat on the outside bench to enjoy the crystal blue sky." Mr. Butler cheesed from ear to ear as he reminisced about his hour lunch.

"Wow, that sounds very relaxing."

"Indeed. Say, you should head out for lunch and enjoy the beautiful weather!" Mr. Bricks walked towards me with his hands in his baggy dress pants. His eyes were wide as he waited for me to accept his suggestion to go out and explore nature.

"Are you sure?"

"Oh yes! Things are pretty slow around here. I can certainly hold down the fort for an hour," he assured me.

"Sounds good, thank you."

Mr. Butler nodded towards me and headed back to his office. I immediately pulled out my cell phone and set up a quick lunch date.

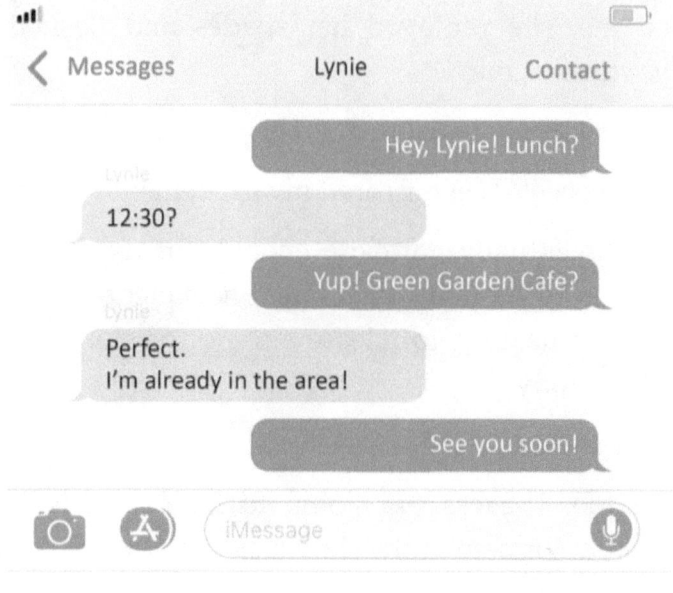

♦

I sat at the small table on the patio of Green Garden Cafe; the tall umbrella connected to the round table shaded off just enough sunlight to make it possible for me to look out into the day without being blinded by the sun's rays. I enjoyed the perfect breeze that raced through my hair as I nibbled on my chicken Caesar salad and sipped on a naturally handcrafted lemonade.

I spotted Lynie in the distance as she strolled her way through the lunch crowd and towards the cafe. I could see the huge, fashionable sunglasses that sat on her face, right above her bright red lips. Her walk was always strong and confident. Each step she took was with purpose. The yellow sundress that hugged her body paired well with the nude heels that snuggled her pretty feet. Once Lynie spotted me, she removed her shades and flashed her pearly whites at me.

"Lynieeeeee!" I screamed out of pure joy.

"Monieeeee!" She mirrored my excitement.

Lynie eventually got close enough for us to embrace one another through a warm hug. She squeezed me tight and exhaled heavily, to release a ton of tension from her cozy, thick body.

"I missed you, girl," she sighed.

"Me too. I guess I'm going to have to schedule a weekly appointment at the shop just to see my best friend on a consistent basis."

We both giggled as we took our seats at the table.

"So, what's been up? Last time I saw you, you were running out of my shop to pick up Court." Lynie's eyes were wide, eager to receive my updates.

"Oh yea," I chuckled. "I was just a little late picking up Courtney from school and I was freaking out."

"So, what happened?"

"Nothing, really. I got to the school building, picked up Court, went home and carried on with my day." I was getting tired of being dishonest with Lynie, but it was necessary.

"That's good. It could have been worse."

"Sure, could have," I exclaimed as I swallowed the last of my lemonade. *If you only knew.*

"And I take it that work is good?"

"Same ole, same ole." I nodded.

"And Court?"

"Just as beautiful as she can be." I beamed as I visualized my gorgeous baby girl.

Lynie's facial expression dropped and became stiff. "And that Jonathan?"

I took a deep breath and looked Lynie in her eyes. "Things are actually good between us. We sat and talked the other day and decided to start over. I'm excited for this new journey." I was proud at how convincing the statement sounded as it left my mouth.

Lynie cocked her head sideways and dug her index finger into the side of her cheek as to be in deep thought. She took a dramatic moment before responding. "You know what, if this makes you happy and you feel *safe*, I support you. All I ever wanted was for you to be happy, Symone. That's it. And since you are choosing to give that knuckle hea—I mean, that man—a second chance, I guess I can *try* to do the same." Lynie rolled her eyes at the thought of making amends with Jay.

I giggled at the disgusted look on her face. Lynie tried to remain serious but could not help it and cracked a smile.

"Anyhoo," she began. "So, I was glad that you reached out and asked to meet for lunch. There's something I wanted to share with you, but I know it's a sensitive topic for you and so I wanted to share it with you in person." I waited for her to continue. "I was online last night, just scrolling through different social media posts. And out of the blue, I saw a repost from a mike_bake_ account. I clicked on the username...and it was Michael."

My heart dropped. "How do you know it was Michael? *Michael* is a common name..."

"Symone. It was *him*. It was Michael. His profile picture was very clear," she quickly disrupted my doubt.

"But, what's the coincidence?" I thought out loud as I processed this new piece of information.

"I know. It's a big ass coincidence, but I took it as a sign from God himself. I'll send you a screenshot of his page and then you can sit with it and decide what you would like to do. I just wanted to do my part and relay the information to you." Lynie immediately pulled out her phone.

DING!

Seconds later my phone notified me of her text message. I held my breath for as long as I could, hoping to suppress the emotions that rushed through and began to quickly overflow my heart. I managed to utter a sentence without revealing my raw emotions in front of Lynie.

"Thank you. I really appreciate this information, I uh...I will be sure to look into it."

Lynie nodded her head. She reached her arm across the table and rested her hand on top of mine. "Take your time with it."

I exhaled sharply. "I will." I smiled at Lynie.

"Excuse me? Miss?" Lynie waved her hand to get the waitress' attention. The waitress stopped in her path to answer Lynie, and I took that moment as an opportunity to wipe my face and pull myself together.

"Yes, ma'am. What can I get you?" The woman pulled out a pen and pad from her white apron pockets, prepared to take Lynie's order.

"Yes, I would like to order the black bean burger meal with a classic margarita." Lynie glanced at me with a devilish grin on her face. "Actually, make that *two* classic margaritas...and make them real stiff!"

"Coming right up," the woman seemed excited to serve the strong alcoholic beverages that Lynie requested.

"Listen here," I pointed a finger at Lynie. "The last time I drank with you, I was late picking up my daughter from school." I joked.

"Ah shit, Monie. It was only two drinks," She laughed out loud as she brushed off my concerns. "And besides, you shouldn't live in the past. It's a brand-new day!"

"Yes, it's a brand-new day! But we have to learn from our past mistakes. And trust me, I'm not day drinking with you anymore." I was half-way kidding.

"Well, it's not my fault you're a light weight!"

"Oh, whatever," I scoffed silently as I transitioned into a different subject. "So? Have you been on any dates lately?" I grinned and treaded lightly into Lynie's love life.

"Damn, Monie. Why are you all up in my personal business?"

"*Personal business*? Excuse me? You stay all up in my personal business. Since when are boundaries a *thing* for you?" I was suspicious.

"Since *you* started asking me questions about my life. *I* ask the questions, and don't you forget it," she mocked me.

"Come on, Lynie. Fill me in," I insisted.

"Well, I actually went out to dinner with a special someone last week...someone that I have been seeing for some time now." Lynie stared down at her fidgeting fingers.

"Ohhh, look at you! Must be a special someone, got you all in front of me blushing and what not."

"Yeah, it's been a long time since I actually bonded with someone, you know? Like, this person really likes me, for *me*." Lynie's eyes became moist.

"Wow, Lynie." I was shocked. I could not remember the last time Lynie had been head-over-heels for a romantic partner. "When can I meet this mystery man that has you all in your feelings, *huh*?"

Lynie hesitated. Just as she opened her mouth to answer, the waitress returned to our table.

"Here is your fresh black bean burger meal and two homemade classic margaritas with a little extra loving." The waitress winked at Lynie before prancing off towards the back of the cafe. I instantly grabbed the margarita, completely dismissing my promise to *never day drink with Lynie again*. I began to slurp up the drink while continuing my praise for Lynie's new love interest.

"Girl, I am so happy for you. I've always looked forward to the day when you would find your better half. You are always so busy with LBR and I can only imagine how difficult it is to find a man when you spend most of your time in a beauty salon full of women," I giggled as I continued my rant. "I can imagine your wedding now! I can't wait to stand next to you as you read your vows to the man you are going to spend happily ever after with. Oh! And once you get pregnant, I can throw you a bomb ass baby shower!"

Lynie was silent.

"Okay, I know I just jumped the gun a tad bit. I'm just happy for you, girl."

Lynie sighed as she slowly and uninterestedly chewed on a fry.

"What's wrong?

"There will be no baby showers and certainly no wedding with a groom."

"Well, not right away but maybe in the future? Right?"

Lynie shook her head "No."

"Aren't you in love with him?"

"I'm not in love with *him*," she stated sharply. Lynie looked straight through my eye sockets and said, "I'm in love with *her*."

I gasped. Tears swirled down Lynie's cheeks. She took a deep breath before the next four words left her lips. "Symone...I'm a lesbian." She bit down on her lip to hold back the emotion that quickly brewed up inside of her. I stood up and hurried over to Lynie's side. She laid her heavy head against my small chest as I held her in my arms.

"It's okay, girl. Love is *love*."

Lynie sobbed in my arms. "You just don't know how difficult it has been. I feel so relieved now that I have broken the ice. My God, I didn't think I could do it."

"Oh, you are so strong. You know I've always admired you for that. You are brave, you will get through this and you, my friend, is one sexy lesbian heffa!"

Lynie burst into laughter as she pushed me away and wiped her tears.

CHAPTER 7

TEARS OF A SHIFT IN DESTINY

"I wondered if his smile was as big and bright as I imagined his heart to be. I wondered if he wore his hair short, thick, and natural. I wondered if each strand of hair was healthy and pure, just like I imagined his soul to be."

I was awakened by the weight of Jay's body on my back. His dry lips began to scrape my neck. I looked over at my phone on the nightstand to check the time. It was 6:32 a.m. and his unwanted sexual advances did nothing but motivate me to get out of bed.

"I should get going," I murmured.

Jay ignored my statement and kept at it. His hand crawled around my waist, slithered underneath my night shirt, and squeezed my breast. I laid still, hoping to communicate with him through my stiff body language. *I do not want to have sex with you,* is what my body screamed at him as he continued to unravel my clothes.

"Trust me, it won't take that long," his hot breath pressed against my eardrum and clogged my hearing. "And besides, isn't this part of starting over?"

I did not want to fight with him more than I did not want to have sex with him. I gave in and my body went limp.

He guided me into a position so I was lying on my stomach, facing away, with my hips raised towards him. I planted my knees under my waist in an attempt to find some type of comfort. I could feel Jay's hard shaft aiming towards my opening, ready to strike. I held my breath. Jay grasped my panties and forced them to the side to make room for himself. His hands were cold. He tightly gripped the side of my thighs and proceeded to penetrate me from behind. I watched my phone on the nightstand, praying for an interruption—hoping to be saved by a ring. Oh, how I wished Angelo would call and save me just like he did that one night. *Mhmm ahhh!* Jay's moan after each thrust sounded more like a growl. *Mhmm ahhh!* The droplets of sweat from his hot pores landed on my back and melted my flesh. *Mhmm ahhh!* I gritted my teeth together as I continued to focus on my phone. *Mhmm ahhh!* I wondered why Angelo had not reached out. It had been two days since our short-lived, awkward, yet comforting text conversation. *Mhmm ahhh!* Part of me was afraid the call I so desperately longed for would come at the wrong time. I cringed at the hypothetical idea of being at the dinner table with Jay and Court as my phone screamed from my pocket. I could picture Jay leaning towards me, demanding to see my phone so that he could inspect my call log. I was very aware of the risk that came along with Angelo contacting me at any moment. *Mhmm ahhh!* Still, the other part of me waited anxiously for him to show back up in my text thread. I fought myself every time the thought of reaching back out to this stranger crossed my mind. *What would I say? If he didn't think I was a creep before, he definitely would after I contacted him a second time.* I could not understand why I was so desperate to connect with this individual. *Mhmm ahhh! Mhmm ahhh!* I clenched the edge of the bed as Jay's thrusts became harder and deeper. *Mhmm ahhh! Mhmm ahhh! Mhmm ahhh! MMMMMM, AHHHHH…* Jay softened and exited my body at once. I could feel his evidence of satisfaction drizzle down my inner thighs. I glanced back over at my phone on the nightstand. The time was now 6:37 a.m.

"Wow. That was amazing," Jay flopped his heavy body down on the bed beside me. *Wow. That was horrible*, I thought to myself. I slid out of bed and made my way to the master bathroom. My night clothes dropped to the floor right before I stepped into the steaming shower.

♦

"Mommy?" Courtney's sweet voice called out from behind me.

"Yes, baby?" I took a quick peek in my rearview mirror to analyze my daughter's vibe as she sat safely, strapped into the car seat.

"Do you love Daddy?"

I redirected my attention to the road in front of me, scrambling my brain and searching for an honest, yet gentle answer for Courtney. I sprinted down memory lane, looking for reasons to love my husband. During my run through my past, I came across vivid scenes of blood, tears, screams, regret, disappointment, sexual assault, belittlement, and extreme sacrifice. My recollection of our time together was a warzone. It was a miracle that I was still standing...but how? Was I bulletproof? Was I destined to survive? I walked across the dark, cold, and muddy battlefield, searching for glory. Looking for any reason to be proud of this journey, and suddenly...it hit me. Courtney's spirit appeared and overshadowed any and all evil that Jay inflicted onto me during the passive battle we called marriage. Somehow, his demonic cells were able to produce something so pure, something so beautiful and something so a part of me...someone that I could not separate from or give up on. Even if it meant the daily endurance of pain from her co-creator.

"So, do you? Mommy?" I glanced once more at Court through the rearview mirror. Our eyes locked as she waited for me to respond. I pulled in and parked my car in her school parking lot, spotting Ms. Brown at the front door, ready to welcome Courtney in. She waved at me with great enthusiasm once she spotted my vehicle. I removed my seatbelt and turned towards Courtney. Her eyes were wide and filled with a splash of concern.

"Baby, I love you with all my heart. You are my greatest gift. And, because your dad helped me to create such a flawless being, I will always love him for that."

"So, does that mean you *do* love Daddy"

I smiled at Court's innocent, confused expression before simplifying my response for her five-year-old brain. "Yes, I love your dad."

Court's eyes instantly lit up after I confirmed what she already thought to be true. I wondered what created the sense of doubt inside of her. Deep down I knew she was very in tune with the energies that flowed throughout our home. She knew when things were bad. She often showed up right after a heated or physical argument to do nothing more than wrap her arms around me. She gave me the dose of strength I needed to move on each day. She was something like a guardian angel, always showing up at the right time.

"Okay, darling. Let's get going. Ms. Brown is waiting for you."

"Yay! I'm so happy, Mommy." Court beamed through her caramel skin. "Guess what? School is gonna be fun! Mrs. Greene said we're gonna paint today!"

I walked around to free Court from her seatbelt and let her out of the car. I bent down to hug her tiny frame tightly. "I love when you're happy. Sounds like your teacher has an exciting day planned. Have a wonderful day at school!" I surveyed the area to make sure there were no moving vehicles. I gave Court the *okay* to run towards Ms. Brown. "I will be by to pick you up after school, honey," I yelled after Courtney, and loud enough for Ms. Brown to hear. The woman winked at me and waved goodbye to assure me that she received my message and that Court was now in good hands. I gratefully re-entered my car and proceeded towards my place of work.

◆

The door swung open and a pleasant aroma rushed into the office and filled the room with a masculine smell from a top shelf cologne that I had not experienced in a little over a week.

"Welcome back, Mr. Butler," I blurted out.

The tall, dark man walked into the firm with a serious look on his face. "Good morning, Mrs. Michaels."

"Um...so, how was your vacation?"

Mr. Butler paused for a second to think over the last seven days. "You know, it wasn't that bad actually. Maybe a little too long for my liking."

"Really?" I pretended to be shocked, but I was not surprised at all.

"Yeah, it's just not worth feeling overwhelmed and so far behind once you return to work." He shrugged.

"Ahhh, understandable," I empathized.

"Mrs. Michaels, when you are fully settled, can you please bring me all of the files that accumulated from last week when I was out?"

"Coming right up, sir."

Mr. Butler flashed his perfect white grin towards me as he disappeared into his office. I was not shocked that his first priority upon returning to the office was diving right into open cases. Mr. Butler took his job very seriously and hardly ever took a break. I could count on one hand the amount of times I witnessed him take an actual lunch. He often ate a simple meal on the go, completely refusing to interrupt his workday for a full hour, *only* to relax and consume a nutritious mid-day meal. Nonetheless, I always admired his work ethic. Oftentimes, I found myself sort of blushing at his *good mornings* and him calling my name across the office when he needed my assistance. Most days, I struggled to suppress the obvious crush I had on Mr. Butler, but it was very difficult to hide the bubbly butterflies that danced within me every time I interacted with him. Whenever I found myself googly eyed over his natural charm, I was sure to quickly snatch myself out of the trance and fast. I remember feeling guilty at times. It was almost as if I was cheating on Jay by mentally drooling over the thought of being with someone like Mr. Butler, or who I perceived him to be.

There were times during our bi-weekly staff meetings when I would undress him with my eyes. I imagined his skin to be warm and soft, and his chest to be firm, wide, and solid. I pretended my finger pressed against his plumped lips and glided my hand down his rich brown skin, past his chest, and past the protruding muscles in his stomach, all the way down to his stiff, thick shaft. I held it in my hand, barely able to cradle it with just one limb, and started to massage it. Each stroke resulted in his male part growing longer and longer. Before I knew it, I was down on my knees, holding the beautiful slab of flesh against my cheek. It provided a sense of comfort and ignited a strong sexual urge throughout my vagina. I looked up at him and he smiled, as if he were feeling the same desire I was experiencing. I was mesmerized and slowly moved my warm, moist mouth towards the tip of his manhood. He anxiously bit down on his lip, ready to receive what I was preparing to give him. I grew more aroused and wanted nothing more than to taste his magical wand. I opened my mouth and...

"Hey, Symone? Could you also bring me a copy of the call log for reference?"

"Uh, yes, Mr. Butler. Be there in a sec." I shuffled around my desk, hoping to appear normal and look as if I were *not* once again daydreaming about an X-rated fantasy that starred my bottomless supervisor.

Symone, get it together, I chastised myself as I made copies and continued gathering documents for Mr. Butler. I took a deep breath in an effort to collect my hormones and lock them away as I prepared to enter his office.

"Mr. Butler? I have your files and a copy of the phone log right here for you." I leaned in to quickly place the paperwork on the corner of his long and wide chestnut desk. I stepped back and folded my hands behind my back, trying my best to hold my shaky body still. He spun his tall, black leather chair around to face me and observe the material he requested.

"Good, good. This is exactly what I was looking for," he mumbled to himself as he went through the files.

"Great, did you need anything else?" I asked as I glanced away to avoid eye contact. Mr. Butler's office was neat and spotless. He avoided clutter at all costs and used the last fifteen minutes of his shift to clean and organize his office each day. He kept his window shades low and lit a lamp in three of the four corners of the room instead. The environment was both inviting and relaxing, and would entice anyone that walked in. The place reeked of his strong and beautiful masculine odor. It was no wonder Mrs. Blair was so adamant about meeting with Mr. Butler instead of Mr. Bricks.

"No, actually I think I'm good for now."

"Sounds good. I'll be at my desk, let me know if you need anything el—"

"Mrs. Michaels?" He called out to me right as I was getting ready to leave his office. I let go of the doorknob and slowly turned back towards him.

"Yes?" Mr. Butler removed his reading glasses from his perfectly round bald head.

"You know, I've been meaning to tell you. I have noticed you and I'm impressed with what I see."

"You...you noticed me?" *Gulp!* I swallowed hard.

"Oh, most definitely." He leaned in towards me. "I've been witnessing your confidence and how you move around the office and...I like it." Mr. Butler stroked his chin and smiled. "I like it a lot."

I clenched my thighs together to catch the waterfall that was brewing in my silk panties. "Thank you, sir. I appreciate that."

Mr. Butler stood up from his chair and walked around to the front of his desk. He stood right in front of me, placed his hands in his pocket, and halfway sat on the edge of his desk. "I really like you and I want to show you just how much I do." He paused for a second and then whispered, "And I believe we have both been thinking the same thing." The man stared at me with his rich brown eyes as the words left his moist and juicy lips.

"Really?" I was stunned. Whoa, this can't be true! Has he been fantasizing about screwing me, too? No way! Mmmmm...I can only imagine how luscious his kisses will feel as I hold his head between my hips, pulling him in closer and drowning his face in my lustful river right before I clim—.

"Of course. Mr. Bricks and I talked it over and we want to grant you a raise."

I was stuck. "Oh. Yes. Yes! That would be fantastic!" I tried to portray pure enthusiasm through my facial expression but failed miserably.

He cocked his head sideways to assess my reaction from a different angle. "Is everything okay?"

"Yes, I'm sorry, I'm just shocked. Trust me, I am *delighted.*"

Mr. Butler looked concerned. "Are you sure? You know, Mrs. Michaels, I know you have been deserving of an increase in your hourly rate for some time now, and I'm sorry it took so long. I am more than happy to sit with you and discuss what an appropriate amount for your promotion would be."

"No, no, Mr. Butler, it's not that. Seriously, everything is perfectly fine." I started to slowly walk backwards towards the door to make my way out of the office, in hopes of fleeing the awkward and embarrassing situation as fast as possible. "I'm just beginning to feel a little ill. I think I need to go sit for a while."

"Okay, yes please take care of yourself. And, let me know when you are available to discuss your pay increase," Mr. Butler called out as I scurried from his office.

"Sure thing." I quickly shut Mr. Butler's door and slammed my back against the closed, thick slab of wood.

Wooooo. I closed my eyes and exhaled heavily. *Lord help me.*

"Good morning Mrs. Michaels," Mr. Bricks' greeting startled me as he pranced past me, across the lobby, heading towards his office.

"Uh...yes, good morning!"

"I take it Mr. Butler shared the good news with you?" He stood proud, grinning at me through the side of his face.

"He did! I am so excited, thank you so much!"

"Oh, it was no problem at all. My pleasure," he blurted out before happily skipping into his office and shutting the door behind him. The firm went silent.

I walked over and flopped down at my desk. *Woosah.* I took a moment to calm my jumpy nerves. After a brief moment of reflection, I was able to actually appreciate the thought of an increase in my pay. The truth of the matter was, I had always relied on Jay financially. He made great money and took care of the mortgage, utilities, groceries, medical expenses, and anything else that we needed as a family. After getting married and having a baby, I didn't get the chance to fully put my degree in organizational leadership to use. I always dreamt of financial independence; I prayed for the day when I would be able to support my daughter and myself without the assistance of Jay and his money. I even researched ways to receive government assistance until I was able to get on my feet but could never comprehend the security in such programs, and was afraid of leading my daughter down a path of uncertainty. Perhaps it was one of the many reasons I chose to stay in the brutal marriage for so long. I made great strides in landing a part-time job at the firm and convincing Jay that it was a good idea for me to work. Since then, I had been able to earn enough to maintain my physical appearance to my liking, engage in social activities with my daughter, do lunch dates with my best friend, and save a small amount of cash for rainy days. Now, I was sure this raise would not lead me to entire financial independence, but it was a start in the right direction.

RING!

"A and B Law Firm, this is Symone speaking. How can I assist you?"

"Monie! Good morning!" The woman on the other end was very loud, I could hardly recognize the voice.

"Hello? May I ask who I am speaking with?"

"Oh, you can cut out all that code-switching mess! Relax the muscles in yo' face, sis. It's *ME*! Ya girl!" Lynie exaggerated the level of Ebonics in her sentence to get her point across.

"Girl!" I rolled my eyes and looked around to make sure both of my supervisors' doors were still closed before fully responding to Lynie. "Don't be calling up here, disturbing my work with your shenanigans," I teased.

"Now you and I both know you're not working," she laughed out loud.

"Excuse me? I'll have you know that I have been *very* productive this morning," I quickly defended myself against Lynie's accusation.

"Yeah, I'm sure you were busy…" she blurted out sarcastically. "Busy checking out that fine ass supervisor of yours."

"Shhh!" I looked up nervously, checking for a second time and making sure there were no open ears around. "I'm at work and you are super loud, Lynie," I whispered through the phone as loud as I could. "Are you trying to embarrass me on purpose?"

She giggled at my mini panic attack. "Chill girl, he can't hear me through the phone. And what if he did? What do you think he'd do? Bite you?" she mocked.

"That wouldn't be so bad." I blushed, covering my mouth and giggling to myself.

"Look at you. Someone is feeling themself today, I see! Girl, you might as well take this new energy and ask this Benjamin Butler character out on a date."

"*Tsk*! Now you know I can't do that, he's my boss. Besides, I am a *married* woman, remember?" I reminded both Lynie and myself. "I told you that Jay and I are starting fresh and I'm giving it a fair shot."

"You *are* married, aren't you?" she asked rhetorically.

"Yes, I am, but…" I decided I would enlighten Lynie on a new situation that I came across.

"But, what?" she was intrigued.

"Okay, I'm going to tell you something, but this stays between you and I."

"Duh. Who am I gonna tell? Your husband? I don't even like him," she was blunt, per usual.

"And *please*," I emphasized. "Do not make this a big deal. It's really not a big deal and is just a weird thing that happened."

"Yeah, yeah okay, got it. Now, get to the point girl, what's up?" Lynie was anxious.

"Lastly, this is a no judgement zone, you hear me?" I scolded her.

"Girl, the other day I confessed to you that I was a full-blown lesbian. Of *all* people, who am I to judge? Wait," she paused for a moment. "Are you gay, too?"

"What?"

"Oh my God, you are about to tell me you like to partake in pum pum too, aren't you? I knew it! We can be lesbian besties and I can show you around to all of the LGBTQIA+ friendly spots in the city. Ohhh! Wait until I tell bae. We were just talkin—"

"*Lynie!*" I yelled as loud as I could without interrupting the rest of the office. "Snap out of it. I'm not *gay.*"

"No? Well tell me, what is it?" she was completely oblivious and grew even more anxious.

I was still stirred up about Angelo and how the entire situation came about; I yearned for him to contact me once more. I literally waited by my cell phone, hoping a text message from him would show up, and did not understand why I felt so connected to this stranger in such a short amount of time. I thought maybe it was simply because of his unexpected call that stopped me from making an irreversible and regretful mistake. It was like he showed up at the exact time I needed him to, and I wanted to experience that divine connection again. The only thing I could do to fill that void was discuss and relive the moment with a trusted confidant.

"Okay so, there's this guy…"

"A guy?" she screamed.

"Shhhh!"

"A *guy?*" she whispered.

"Yes, a *guy.*"

"Hold on, let me grab my popcorn." She was dramatic. "So, who is he?"

"His name is Angelo, and the crazy part is, I don't really know him at all."

"What do you mean?"

"I mean, he just sort of popped up out of the blue."

Lynie was silent.

"Hello? Lynie, are you there?"

"I'm here. I'm waiting for you to fill in the blanks to this unfinished ass story you just told me," Lynie blurted out impatiently. She was half-way joking and half-way serious.

I knew I could not tell Lynie the *entire* truth regarding how I came in contact with Angelo. She was familiar with my abusive marriage and unhealthy relationship with the *healing tool* I kept stashed away in my home. If I told her I had a fight with Jay and was in the middle of contemplating slitting my wrist and ending my life for good when Angelo interrupted me by somehow dialing the wrong number...that would trigger her, and she would only focus on the fact that Jay hit me and I was cutting, once again. I decided that a portion of the truth would be good enough.

"Okay, here's what happened. The day I left your shop, I picked up Courtney and headed home. When we got home, we ate dinner and chilled out for the rest of the evening," I lied. "Jay decided to go out with his friends. Moments later, I got a text from a random man asking if I was still at the restaurant waiting."

"*Huh?*"

"I know right?"

"Why was he expecting you to be at a restaurant?"

"Basically, this man was set up on a blind date with a woman by the name of Mariah and —"

Lynie quickly interjected, "How do you know her name?"

"Well, after I ignored a few of his text messages, he decided to call me!"

"He *called* you?"

"Girl, *yes*," I continued. "He kept referring to me as Mariah. By this time, it was late, I was already in bed and was annoyed with all of the interruptions from his text messaging and phone calls. So, when I finally answered, girl, I let him have it."

"Oh, no you didn't! What did you say?" Lynie was eager to hear more.

"I said some things along the lines of, I'm not Mariah, you should accept the fact that you were obviously given the wrong number and are being stood up."

"Damn!"

"I know, girl. The next day when I woke up, I felt so bad. This man was stood up on a blind date and here I go making his night much worse."

Lynie offered justification to my behavior. "Well, it *was* late, and he *clearly* needed direct guidance on what was going on and why he was unable to contact his date."

"True, but I still empathized with him and wanted to at least apologize for the way I approached the situation."

"Don't tell me you called him back?" I imagined that Lynie's eyes were wide as she waited for me to answer.

"You see, what had happened was..." I began to dilute my actions. "I waited a day or two and simply sent an apology text."

"*Girl*! You called that man's phone acting desperate for attention?"

"*Shhh*! No, I didn't *call* his phone. I texted him. And there was nothing *desperate* about it."

"*Mmhmm*. So, what happened after that?"

I ignored her judgment. "We actually had a nice short conversation before he got distracted at work, and he asked if we could continue the conversation later when he was free, and..."

"And?"

"And that was like two days ago, girl! He still hasn't called or texted. You think, he thinks I'm weird?"

Lynie mumbled to herself, "Shit, *I* think you're weird."

"I heard that," I scolded Lynie once more through the phone.

She laughed obnoxiously, overshadowing my short period of irritation. "Okay, no seriously," she began. "I think you got a whiff of a generally nice man, outside of your marriage, and enjoyed the brief interaction that you had with him. You're simply looking forward to experiencing this pleasant gentleman once again. There's no harm in that."

"Hmmm." I digested her words slowly.

"I also think that's why you are sort of infatuated with your boss," she quickly added to the conversation.

"I wouldn't say *infatuated*. It's just a phase, I'm sure it'll pass...hopefully." I looked over to Mr. Butler's office and cringed at the thought of shaking the silly crush I had.

"Maybe it will, maybe it won't."

"It has to," I quickly added.

"Well, what are you hoping to get out of this interaction with Angelo?" she was curious.

I sighed into the phone, frustrated that I didn't have an answer to the simple question. "I'm not sure, Lynie. It all happened so fast and is just *weird*. But like I said, it's no big deal. I'm sure this is *also* a phase and before I know it, I will be back to my regularly scheduled program."

"And is that what you want to watch for the rest of your life?"

I was silent.

"Because it sounds to me like you're ready to change the channel," Lynie interjected before I could reply. "You're just afraid to pick up the remote."

"Okay, that's enough, Life Coach Lynie," I blurted out in an attempt to lighten the mood. "I do not have time for any of your deep messages this morning, *ma'am*. I am still at work. You're not about to have me in one of these corners crying my eyes out." We both laughed hysterically.

"Don't shoot me," Lynie chuckled. "I'm just dropping some gems, hoping one day you'll finally decide to pick one up."

"I'm just moving at my own pace," I thought out loud.

"I know, honey, but I think it's time to pick it up and put the pedal to the metal. Sis, it's time to roll out," she fussed at me playfully.

"Oh, hush," I fussed back.

"Speaking of moving at your own pace, when are you going to reach out to Michael?"

I paused for a moment. The sound of my brother's name numbed me for a second. Both excitement and worry flooded my vital organs as I danced with the idea of reconnecting with him. I missed him dearly but was afraid he did not feel the same about me. It had been years since Michael and I had spoken, and I could only imagine the amount of blame he placed upon me; holding me responsible for our failing relationship. What was even more frightening was that I did not have a valid reason for why I stopped reaching out and looking after him. *Life just got in the way*, is what I told myself each time

I started to fall into the guilt trap. Perhaps, I was just pacifying my spirit and avoiding self-accountability. Or perhaps it was the truth. Life *did* get in the way. Either way, I felt it was time to face my fear of the unknown.

"I'm actually planning to reach out to him later today," I stated as confidently as I could.

"Good. I really think it would be nice for you to have a close relative in your life, again." I could feel Lynie's warm smile radiate from across the city.

"Yeah, I think so, too," I reciprocated her energy.

"Hey, Mrs. Michaels, did Mrs. Blair complete her invoice from last week?" Mr. Bricks startled me as he yelled the question from his doorway.

"Not yet, sir! She mentioned that she was planning to send in a check later this week," I assured him.

Mr. Brick shot two thumbs up before going back into his office and gently closing the door behind him.

"I guess I should be getting back to work," I whispered into the phone.

"Okay girl, talk to you later!"

"Okay, love you, sis."

"Love you, too. Bye!"

◆

The office was still, due to the quiet and slow workday. Thoughts of Michael rang out loud in my head, loosening and stirring up old, compressed emotions within me. I pressed the back of my head against the leather headrest that connected to my sturdy office chair. I tried to push all of the worry and fear out of my body, through the narrow nostrils of my thick nose. I wanted so badly to end the agony of fear. *Time to rip the Band-Aid off.* At that moment, I decided I would be bold and contact my brother by sending him a message on his social media account. I took a deep breath and quickly grabbed my phone from my desk.

DING!

Before I could unlock my cell phone, it chimed loudly and vibrated in the palm of my hand. I proceeded to enter my password into the device and quickly clicked on the message icon to read the incoming text.

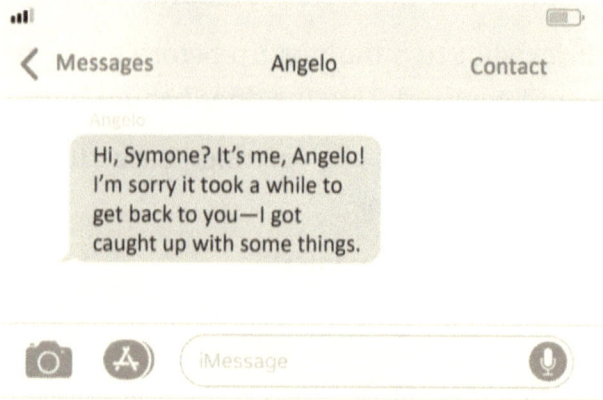

My heart began to pound fiercely through the flesh that covered my chest. The fingers on my sweaty hands went numb, making it difficult to type a reply, even though I desperately wanted to. *He finally texted me back.* I was beyond ecstatic. The excitement that ran through my body made it nearly impossible to focus on the letters that made up the words constructed by Angelo, but somehow, I managed to read over the sentences several times before replying.

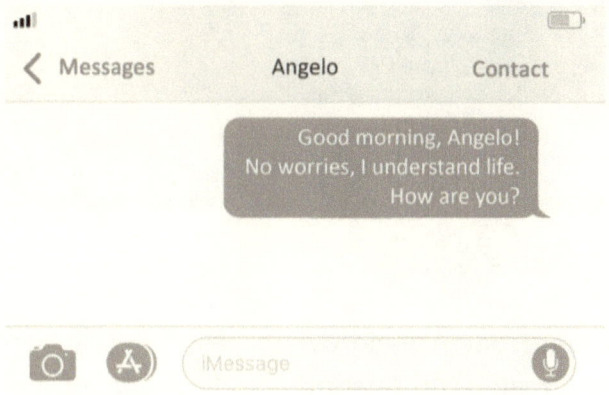

I tried to *"play it cool"* in hopes of disguising the fact that I had been waiting for his call since our last encounter.

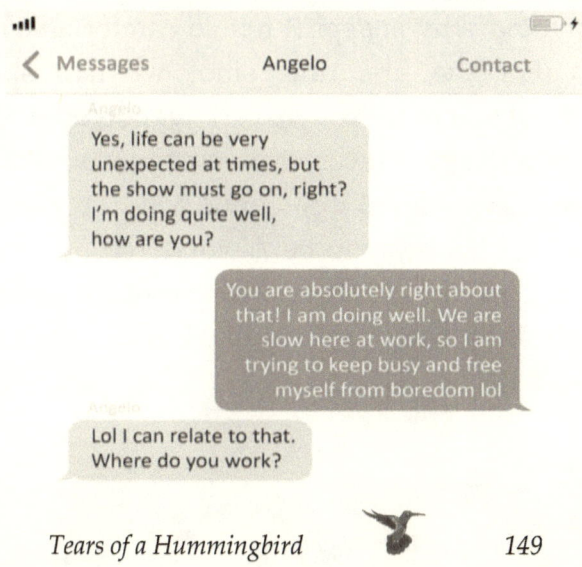

> I work as an Administrative Assistant/Secretary at A&B Law Firm downtown Boston. And you?

Angelo

> Interesting! I pass that building on my way to work each morning! It's the brick building with the tall windows and sign that reads, "A&B Law Firm" in black bold letters, right?

> Yes, that's where I work! Such a big, but small city!

  iMessage

Learning that Angelo drove past the law firm every morning created flutters on the left side of my chest. Suddenly, he seemed that more reachable—that more *real*. Perhaps our energies had already intertwined with one another during our daily commutes to work. Maybe this was the reason I felt I was already connected to him in some way and why *my* spirit felt so comfortable dancing with *his*. For the first time since we had spoken, I imagined what he looked like. I wondered if he was covered in a deep, rich caramel complexion with vibrant brown eyes. I wondered if his smile was as big and bright as I imagined his heart to be. I wondered if he wore his hair short, thick, and natural. I wondered if each strand of hair was healthy and pure, just like I imagined his soul to be.

 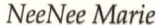

ᴵᴵᴵ   ▭ ⚡

< Messages   Angelo   Contact

Angelo

It is! What a coincidence lol I
serve as a Coordinator for FADA.
Our main office is located in the
middle of the city, near the
senior high school.

FADA?

Angelo

FADA is an acronym. It stands for
Fighting Against Domestic Abuse.
We're a non-profit organization.

Wow, very interesting! I
never heard of FADA.
Organizations like this one
are so very important.

Angelo

It really is, which is why I committed
myself to this type of work.

So, do you serve the high
school students in that area?

Angelo

I am assigned to the high school
students in that area, yes. But
FADA serves all populations
from the youth to the elderly.
From the rich to the poor. Each
coordinator is assigned to a
specific area and/or population.

  iMessage

‹ Messages   Angelo   Contact

> That's awesome! So does FADA serve the entire city of Boston?

Yea, pretty much! Though we're constantly growing and hoping to expand even more.

> Dope! What type of services do you provide?

Well, as you can imagine, we work closely with all social work agencies, including child protective services. We go into schools and community centers to conduct domestic violence awareness presentations for all ages and grade levels. We also work with victims and those affected by domestic violence directly. We provide guidance and support with the assistance of professional mental health counselors.

> Wow, that must be emotionally heavy work! I'm glad that we have brave individuals like yourself that get up in the morning to serve our community by fighting against domestic abuse.

  iMessage

Messages   Angelo   Contact

Angelo

Very heavy work. You wouldn't believe the stories I come across working with teenagers. I know they need me to fight for them, so that's what I do.

Oh, trust me, I can imagine what those poor babies are experiencing. Just sad! Especially if they're going through troubled times alone.

Angelo

The sad reality for most of these young folks is that they are dealing with these issues alone.

Aw man, it's devastating to think about.

Angelo

It's devastating to watch. I just worked with a young man earlier this week. His alcoholic stepdad literally beat his mom to death.

Oh my God!

Angelo

Yeah. His mom is deceased, his stepdad is in jail, charged with her murder and he is in the process of being placed into foster care.

Oh no! Does he have any other family members that can take him in?

iMessage

Angelo

During the intake appointment, he mentioned that he has an adult sister that lives down south with her husband. Sounds like he doesn't have a close relationship with her anymore...not sure, yet. I'm hoping to assist him in getting in contact with her.

Aw this breaks my heart... I hope he can connect with her.

Angelo

Me too! Otherwise, he'll be in the system with no family or loved ones to look after him. And that's what I am trying to prevent.

Damn... This all seems like Deja Vu. Sometimes the universe has a way with pushing us to do something that we've been hiding from.

Angelo

What's wrong?

Oh everything is fine. It's just that your story about the young boy made me think of my little brother. We kind of lost contact over the years and I've been meaning to reach out to him.

Messages   **Angelo**   Contact

> Angelo
>
> Is everything okay? If he's experiencing a crisis, I would be more than happy to provide FADA resources and assist in any way that I can... it's kind of what I do for a living.

> Thank you, but I'm hoping that he's fine. Besides, he still lives back home in Cleveland. And our crisis already happened... we lost our mom to suicide some years ago.

> Angelo
>
> My God. I am so sorry to hear that.

> It's okay. I've found different ways to cope over the years.

> Angelo
>
> I understand. I also know that emotions are easily triggered by many different things, such as holidays and anniversaries. So, if you, or even your brother, need someone to vent to during these times; I'm here to help.

> Hmmm, that may explain why I have been a little more emotional these days. My mother's death anniversary just passed and I've been thinking about Michael more lately.

  iMessage

Messages   Angelo   Contact

Angelo

Michael?

> That's my brother's name.

Angelo

Got it. Well, yea, the death anniversary of a loved one can definitely be difficult to get through. Like you said earlier, you just have to find different ways of coping that work for you. And the way you cope may change over the years. Just know that is normal and perfectly fine.

> I never thought about it in that way.

Angelo

I'm not sure how you usually get through this time of the year, but it sounds like this time around, you are wanting to connect with your brother. Perhaps, it may bring you comfort to be in the presence of someone who is also dealing with the same loss. Perhaps you two can grieve together.

> Exactly! It's like this time around, I have the strong urge to console him and just make things right between us. The fact that he may be suffering in the dark alone really bothers me.

Angelo

Sounds like you have a flight to Cleveland to book, ma'am :-) .

  iMessage

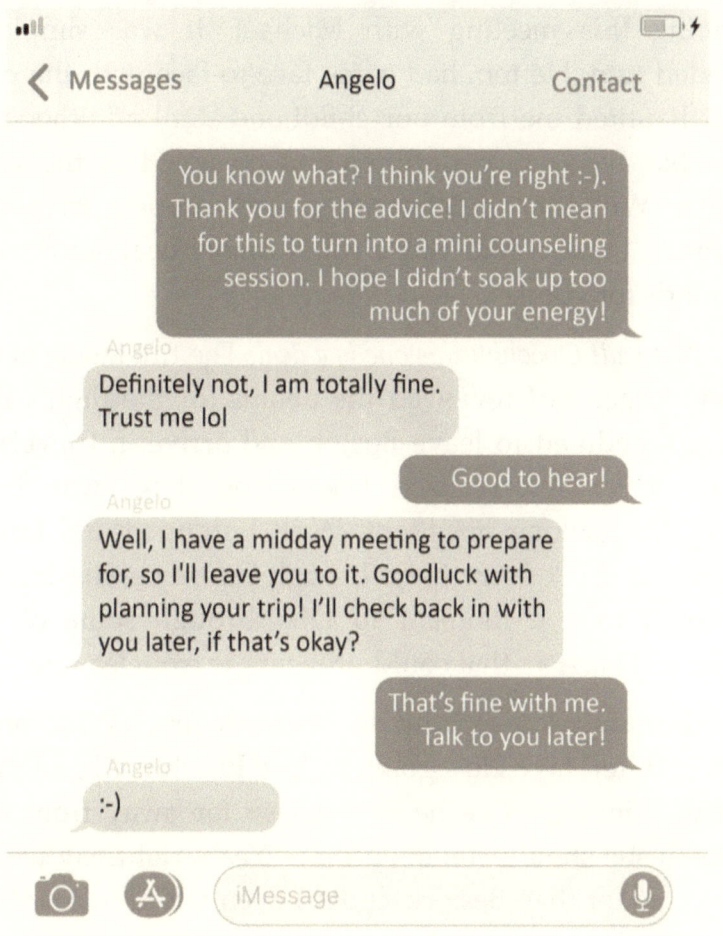

The short conversation with Angelo ignited a fire within me. I quickly logged into my work computer and browsed through different airline websites, searching for the most affordable roundtrip ticket to Cleveland, Ohio. I was more than willing to dig into my savings to fund a quick visit to reconnect with my brother. At that point, I did not care what it would take to see him in person. Angelo was able to help me to understand why I was craving this meeting with Michael. It was simple: I needed him. He too, had come face-to-face with the pain that haunted me from our childhood until adulthood. It was like we were both bitten and poisoned by the same snake. With the understanding and support from one another, I was confident we could finally heal our ancient wounds for good.

Not bad! Oooohhh this one is a deal. The fire inside of me grew larger as I reviewed the details for the flights that were scheduled to leave Boston and arrive in Cleveland that weekend. I realized I was one click away from officially booking my flight. *Wait!* I stopped and forced myself to think everything through before purchasing my ticket. I took a moment to talk through some of the potential barriers that could prevent me from leaving.

Shouldn't I reach out to Michael, first? What am I going to tell Jay? He's going to lose his shit! Oh, and my baby, Courtney! I've never been so far away from her. Maybe she should come with me? Yeah, right. Jay would never go for that. Besides, could I even afford to cover the cost for the both of us? Shoot! Can I even cover myself? Let's see... I would need a roundtrip ticket, a rental car to get around, a hotel, food, and extra cash just in case some unexpected emergencies come up during my stay. Hmmm...if I am very intentional with my spending, I can make this work.

Thinking through all of the large and minute details that could stop my urge to travel home, brought even more confusion and uncertainty of how I was going to execute this plan. However, it did not dim my determination and drive to proceed with purchasing my airline ticket. I felt a strong wave of adrenaline that began to build up in my body, starting in my feet and quickly finding its way up through my legs, past my thighs and abdominal area, then straight through my fingertips. Before I knew it, my hand was cradling the computer mouse tightly as my index finger clicked around viciously for about thirty seconds and...*done!* Just like that, my flight was booked with the confirmation message already sitting in the inbox of my personal email account. I sat back in my chair and took a deep breath, looking over and gazing out through the tall, thick windows of the law firm. The bright sun and blue sky seemed more vibrant than ever before. The view brought a strong sense of peace upon me and provided comfort as I began my new healing process. I slowly exhaled through the faint smile that occupied my face, eager to start the new journey to discover true healing.

◆

"You did *what?*" Jay stood at the countertop with his hands buried in a large bowl of seasoned raw fish, cornmeal, and flour. The grease on the stove behind him sizzled quietly in the cast iron skillet, signaling it was ready to receive the fish that Jay was preparing.

"Jay, I need to see my brother. This is very important to me; I am just asking that you offer a little understanding and support." I stood in the doorway of the kitchen as I pleaded for Jay's approval. Courtney and I had just walked in from work and school only moments ago. I saw that Jay was prepping dinner, which usually meant he was in a good mood. I decided to take advantage of his easygoing vibe and spilled the beans about my scheduled trip to visit Michael.

Jay continued to massage the seafood into the breading mixture as he looked through my eye sockets. "Symone, we are married. We have a daughter. You don't make these types of decisions without discussing them with your family, first. Did you even *consider* Courtney and I when you decided to book a flight all the way to Cleveland? That flight leaves in less than two days, Symone."

"Jay, Cleveland is my *hometown*, and Michael is my *brother*! I have not spoken to him in years. He's the closest living relative that I have. I'm his big sister; I *need* to be there for him."

"Why *now*, Symone?" Jay twisted his face up towards me.

"I don't know; it just felt right." I knew it would be difficult to explain to Jay where my motivation came from without mentioning the conversation I had with Angelo. Bringing up *anything* about conversing with another man through text messaging would lead this conversation down to the pits of hell.

"It just *felt right*? You *don't know*? Yeah, right! I bet that damn Lynie put you up to this. Is she going with you? Is this some type of secretive girls' trip the two of you have planned?" Jay was stiff as he glared at me, waiting for a response.

"Secretive girls' trip? What? *No!* Lynie doesn't even know anything about this trip."

"So why are you going alone, huh?" I could smell Jay's suspicion radiating from his body.

"Jay, if it would make you feel better, you are more than welcome to travel with me. I have nothing to hide!" In the back of my mind, I knew that Jay would be unable to take time off from work with such a short notice. The truth of the matter was that I did not want him, Lynie, or anyone else to travel with me—it was something I needed to do alone.

"Now you know damn well I can't leave work and abandon my business for the weekend all because you decided to plan a trip without warning. I would have to give proper notice, you know? Because that is what responsible people *do*." The sarcastic statement rolled off of his hot tongue as he began to lay the lightly battered fish into the hot grease sitting in the black pan.

At that point of the discussion, I felt it was the perfect time to use Jay's own words against him in hopes of winning the disagreement. "Jay, you said that you wanted for us to start over, right?"

"Yes, Symone, but what does that have to do with this situation?" Jay was irritably confused.

"Well, in order to truly start from a clean slate, I will need to also work on myself individually so I can be the best version of myself for our marriage. I can't give my all to you if pieces of me are still broken."

Jay clenched his jaws tightly as he watched the fish in the frying pan, avoiding eye contact with me.

I continued, "You know I have struggled with coping with my mother's death, in addition to completely losing contact with my brother. No, I can't change the fact that my mother killed herself. But I can restore my relationship with Michael and that would be healing for me and essentially bring me happiness."

Jay was slow to respond as he took his time to check on the pan of macaroni and cheese that he had baking in the oven on three hundred and fifty degrees. He proceeded to a different part of the elongated kitchen counter where there were two bunches of fresh broccolis sitting on a wooden cutting board. Jay calmly removed the largest butcher knife that we owned from the knife block. The sharp screeching sound created as the knife was pulled out of its stainless-steel holder made my teeth tremble. *BAM!* He quickly chopped off the roots of the raw broccoli, causing a loud noise that echoed through the entire house.

"You know what?" Jay began as he sliced the remainder of the broccoli into manageable sizes, small enough to steam on the stove top. "Sometimes, I honestly believe deep down in my soul, that you say things to purposely piss me off. So, you're telling me that you need to climb your jolly ass on a plane and travel to another state in order to be happy? As if Court and I are not good enough for you?"

"I'm coming right back," I was frustrated with his inability to think outside of himself for once. "Jay, I never said you and Court were not enough for me." It was clear that no matter what I said to Jay, he would make the entire ordeal all about him.

"Well, it sure as hell *sounds* like it. And the fact that you booked a flight before thinking about how it would affect the functioning of this household just baffles me. What were you thinking?"

"For crying out loud, I told you I needed this for my personal healing; this has **nothing** to do with you." I said in the politest way that I could.

BANG! Jay slammed the butcher knife down on the marble countertop with, what seemed to be, every single ounce of force he carried in his right arm. He looked towards me and blurted out, "Since when is marriage all about one person, huh? We're supposed to be in this together and here you go thinking about no one but your damn self."

"Jay, I just—"

"You know what, fuck it. I'm done with this. If you want to leave this weekend, then go right ahead." Jay quickly grabbed a spatula out from one of the kitchen drawers and flipped over the crispy fish that was sizzling away in the grease. He then walked towards me with his index finger leading the way. Once he was just two inches from where I was standing, he pushed his finger deep into the flesh on the middle part of my nose. "But Courtney is staying here with me, and that's final." He stared down at me until I acknowledged his statement.

Once I nodded my head in agreement, Jay yanked his finger away from my face and walked back over to where he was preparing supper.

◆

I walked upstairs to Courtney's room, where I found her at her mini desk, coloring on the homework sheet Mrs. Greene assigned to her kindergarten class.

"Hi, baby!"

"Hi, Mommy! Do you want to color with me?" Courtney's beautiful eyes looked up at me, making it impossible to say *no*.

"I'd love to!" I kneeled down next to Courtney so that we were eyelevel and able to look into each other's face.

"Here you go, Mommy." She handed me a purple gel pen. "You can color the grapes and I will color the rest."

"Sounds like a deal! But first, I need you to tell me how many grapes are in this bunch?"

Courtney leaned over and used her tiny finger to count each grape. "One... two... three... four... five... six... and seven!"

"Good job, baby!" I praised Court as I began to fill in the black and white printout of a grapevine.

"Thank you, Mommy, but that was too easy. This looks like it should be for a four-year-old kid. Mrs. Greene took it easy on us today," she said with a serious face.

"Easy, huh?" I laughed out loud at my daughter's direct critique of her teacher's homework assignment. "Well, maybe she was just giving you all a break, you know?"

Court shrugged her small shoulders up to her ears. "Maybe, I guess."

We colored in silence for a few moments before I spoke. "I wanted to let you know that Mommy is going out of town this weekend."

"Where is out-of-town?" Her facial expression made it apparent that she was unable to comprehend and process my sentence.

"Well, it just means that I will be leaving the city where we live for a couple of days and will return Sunday night," I clarified.

Court gasped. "Are you getting on a spaceship and going far, far away to see the aliens?"

I chuckled at her innocence. "No sweetie, but close. I am going to get on an airplane to go visit my little brother in Cleveland. Cleveland is the city that I lived in when I was a little girl, around your age."

"You have a little brother?"

"Yes, remember I told you about Uncle Michael?"

"Oh, yes! I didn't know Uncle Michael was your little brother," Courtney placed her hand on her forehead, appearing to be in deep thought and trying to make sense of the family structure.

"Yes. Michael and I have the same mommy. I was born first, and then he was born about seven years later, so I am his older sister, which makes him your uncle."

"Ohhhhhh!"

"Make sense?"

"Yes! So, can I come with you? I want to see Uncle Michael too," Courtney's mouth and eyes were stretched wide open as she was full of excitement.

"Not this time, baby."

"But why not?" She pouted.

"Well, Uncle Michael and I have some serious, grown-up things to talk about. But, I promise, next time you can come along. Or, who knows, Uncle Michael may come down to Boston to visit!" I gently rubbed Court's back, hoping she would accept my deal.

"Okay. I can't wait until next time."

I smiled at Courtney. "Me either baby. But guess what? This weekend, you get to spend quality time with your dad, just you and him."

"Yay! We're going to have fun."

"Sure is! And you know what else? If you want, you can ask to go over Auntie Lisa's house to play with your cousins for a little while." I looked deep into Court's eyes and watched her face glow from pure enthusiasm.

"Oh my gosh! We could have a kiddie party with snacks and games!"

"I'm sure Auntie Lisa would be up for that." I winked at her.

"Oh, yea! We're going to have so much fun this weekend!" Courtney hopped out of her chair and began dancing around her room.

"Baby girl, dinner is ready! I got your favorite," Jay's voice traveled from the kitchen all the way to our daughter's room on the second floor.

Court stopped in her tracks in disbelief. "This is the best day ever!" She instantly took off running towards the staircase that led to the first floor as she started to chant, "Mac and cheese! Mac and cheese! Mac and cheese! Mac and Cheese!" Her words eventually fainted away completely as she got further and further away.

I remained kneeling on Courtney's floor, leaning forward onto her desk for extra support. *Okay, just one more thing.* I pulled out my phone and proceeded to open my social media app. I clicked on the search bar and typed in @Mike_Bake_. Once I arrived at the profile, I saw that Michael did not have many pictures posted. The ones that were there only showed parts of his face. Even still, I was happy to see pieces of him. My heart fluttered. I went to the messaging option and created a new message.

To my surprise, I received an instant reply. I was so happy to hear from Michael directly and in real time. Reading his message, though it wasn't much, validated that all of it was worth it and would be beneficial for the both of us. I experienced a sense of relief as I replied back.

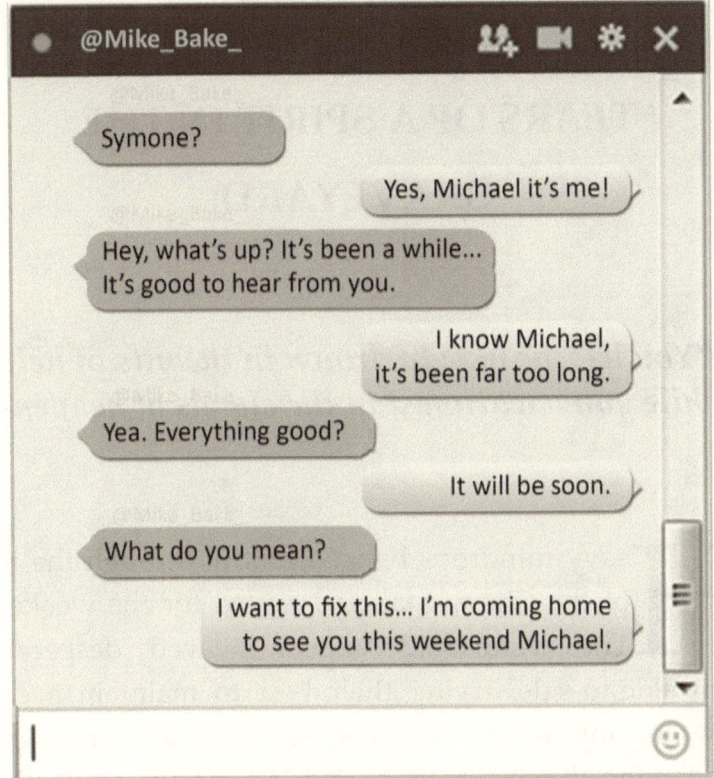

@Mike_Bake_

Symone?

Yes, Michael it's me!

Hey, what's up? It's been a while... It's good to hear from you.

I know Michael, it's been far too long.

Yea. Everything good?

It will be soon.

What do you mean?

I want to fix this... I'm coming home to see you this weekend Michael.

CHAPTER 8

TEARS OF A SPIRIT IN THE GRAVEYARD

*"You left me here to drown in the pits of hell
while you vacationed in the clouds of heaven."*

Heavy raindrops banged loudly through the roof of the Chevy Malibu I rented for the weekend. The windshield wipers swayed desperately from side-to-side, trying their best to maintain a clear view for my wide eyes. The sky was a murky gray, swallowing the sun entirely and leaving the atmosphere below the full clouds, dark and foggy. Huge, tall trees stood high above the streets, drenched from the rain that had evaporated from the shallow waters of Lake Erie and fell upon the city of Cleveland.

It was only 5:10 p.m., but the gloomy vibe of the day made it feel much later in the evening than it actually was. My car crept the wet roads slowly as I struggled to read the street signs through the thick rainstorm. My hometown felt like a foreign environment. I was no longer able to navigate the neighborhoods that were once so familiar to me. I remembered moving through the city effortlessly; I now found it difficult to direct myself from I-90 towards River Way cemetery...where my mother was buried. I continued through the west side of the city, knowing that deep down inside I was close to my destination. However, I was still lost. I pulled the car into a nearby gas station and parked next to a gas pump, pulling out my phone to re-read Michael's instructions for our meet-up.

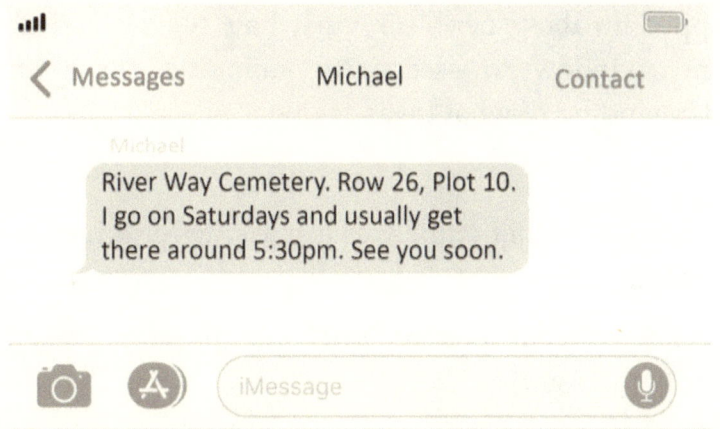

Reality pressed heavy on my nerves. The time was near; I was just moments away from being face-to-face with the one person that knew the true depths of the pain that rooted from my past. I was unsure if this meeting would bring peace or discomfort. The fine hairs on my neck stood strong and stiff. I took several deep breaths to calm my body and prepare to see Michael. *I wonder what he looks like in person now. My God, he probably has facial hair and a deep voice,* I chuckled to myself as I pictured my baby brother with a beard.

I looked up and caught a glimpse of a young, slim Hispanic woman walking out of the gas station where I was parked. I quickly lowered my driver's window to catch the woman's attention.

"¡Hola, señorita! Can you tell me donde es River Way Cemetery? Por Favor?"

The woman looked confused by my broken and far from perfect Spanish. She adjusted the umbrella that was propped up above her black, curly hair. She walked closer to my window to escape the rain and get a better understanding of what I was asking.

"Excuse me?"

"Sorry to bother you; I was just asking for directions to River Way Cemetery?"

"GPS on your phone? No?" her question reeked of friendly sarcasm.

"I think the weather has my service and connection all screwed up." I lifted my phone towards the woman so that she could verify my inability to connect to my GPS application.

"Ah, okay." The woman immediately lifted her arm and began pointing in various directions. She spoke fast in her thick accent. I tried my best to keep up and focus on her verbal and physical instructions. "So, we're on Pearl Road. You want to turn out this way and make a left. Once you get three lights down, make a right. That road will turn into West twenty-fifth street, yea?"

"Oh, yes! West twenty-fifth—I remember that street."

"Good. Take West twenty-fifth *all* the way down and pass the freeway. Once you pass the freeway, River Way Cemetery will be on your right."

"Oh, now I see where I went wrong, *tsk*! When I got off of the freeway, I went the wrong way! Dammit," I cursed myself in front of the woman before turning my attention back towards her. "What's your name?"

"I'm Daniella."

"I'm Symone. Thank you so much for your help!" I gave the woman a warm smile as I restarted the engine of the car, anxious to follow Daniella's instructions before they left my memory bank for good.

"Symone?" she called out to me just as I was getting ready to drive off.

"Yes?" I pressed on the brakes to stop the car.

"Next time, just ask for directions in English," Danielle shrugged and winked at me as she laughed and politely waved me off.

"Yes, ma'am," I laughed, waving back at the woman.

◆

I slowly drove into the entrance of the cemetery. The front gates were black, tall, and heavy. They were grand and sat wide open, allowing visitors to come and go as they pleased. I felt small as I passed by the gates and entered, cruising carefully on the narrow path, looking for row twenty-six. The rain had not let up and reading the small signs was a challenge. I squinted my eyes as much as I possibly could and managed to make out one of the signs: *Row 8*, it read. *Looks like she's further in the back.* I sped up a tad bit and drove towards the rear end of the muddy cemetery.

I passed a few cars were parked on the side of the skinny path, making it nearly impossible to drive around and continue my journey towards my mom and Michael. I glanced over the graveyard and saw a sporadic amount of umbrellas, balanced on the shoulders of grieving individuals. Some of the weeping eyes were close and some were far out, deep into the cemetery. I read the names on the tombstones that lined perfectly in the front row and along the path that I was traveling, thinking about the type of life the souls lived while on earth and how they perished from their physical forms. Perhaps it was their time to go. Some of the birth-to-death dates made it obvious that many of them were gone too soon. There were large spaces in between several of the tombstones. I assumed these empty plots marked the graves of spirits whose family could not afford a tombstone for their loved one. Or more devastating, maybe the remains of the person buried six feet under the bare grave had no one that cared enough to stamp their last resting place. Maybe there was no one left to honor them.

My thoughts continued to wander as I made my way further down the road, and began to feel a flutter of ice-cold butterflies at the pit of my stomach. A thin chill raced through my body. *I think I'm close.* I stopped once more to read the next sign that appeared. *Okay, I've made it to Row 25. So, Row 26 has to be right over ther –* . I stopped mid thought as I looked up and observed a shadowy, hooded figure in the row next to where I was. The individual did not have an umbrella, instead they soaked up all the rain with the loose clothing draped from their tall, slender body. I watched through the heavy rain as the figure kneeled down in front of a tombstone and bowed their head. *Michael.*

I carefully drove closer to row twenty-six and parked the wet car about ten feet from where Michael was. My shaky hands reached over to the passenger seat to grab my large, black umbrella. I pushed the driver's door open and pointed the umbrella out to inflate it. I stepped out of the car. My legs felt numb; I looked ahead, unsure of how I would make it over to Michael. The thick, black boots on my feet carried me through the puddles and mushy mud that covered the grounds. Before I knew it, I was standing just inches behind my brother. Michael remained in a squat position with his head bowed towards the grave in front of him. He wore a black hoodie and dark brown pants with splashes of dried paint on them. The small splatters of gray and white paint continued down onto his brown boots. I stood silent until his moment of prayer was complete.

Annie L. Baker. July 13, 1972 - January 22, 2013. Fly Free, Beautiful Soul. My mother's tombstone stood tall with bold black letters engraved into the rich gray marble. I remembered my brother reaching out to me after the funeral. He was very quiet on the phone; slow to voice his reason for the call. I didn't mind sitting with him in silence, as I knew we were both grieving ...just in different ways. After ten minutes, he finally began to speak. He explained that he picked out a tombstone for Mommy. He placed the order and picked out the format of the literature. *Fly Free, Beautiful Soul.* Michael recited the words to me over the phone. Picking the lasting quote for her grave meant so much to him. Towards the end of the call, he mentioned that he was short on the cost. *"They're asking for $200 for a down payment. I won't have that until next pay. Can I borrow –"* I cut him off immediately. *"Send me the payment information for the entire amount and I will pay for it in full."* Michael was still a teenager at the time and working part-time at a fast food restaurant. There was no way I was going to let him carry the financial burden alone. I trusted him with the honor of choosing how our mother should be remembered, and didn't ask to approve the design or layout he chose. It was my very first time viewing the beautiful stone and poignant words in person and it was simply breathtaking.

"You know what's interesting?" Michael's bold voice startled me a bit. I had no idea he was aware of my presence from behind. He remained facing away from me and at eye level with our mother's tombstone as he replied to his own rhetorical question. "I have been coming up here every weekend for the past seven years, and it has not rained during my visit. Not one time, until today," he paused for a moment. "Sometimes it rained right before I arrived and then stopped once I got inside of the cemetery. Other times my visit was dry as a desert, and the minute I left, it would start to pour. I remember praying for rain, you know? To disguise my tears and whatnot. I always felt like Mommy would keep the rain away when I was here. Like the rain was her tears and she didn't want to cry in front of me." Michael stood up and looked up into the sky. "But today, it's like the whole city is crying hard. And Mommy can't hold back her tears this time," he glared over his shoulders towards me. "I wonder what she's so sad about."

The thought of my mother still being unhappy in her afterlife tugged at the soft tissues in my heart. I walked up so I was beside Michael, seeking out warmth in the cold moment.

"I can think of a list of reasons why she was sad when she was here. I just pray that those things are no longer a burden on her resting soul."

Michael looked over to me and into my eyes for the first time since I arrived. His eyes were light brown mixed with a hint of sorrow. Random small patches of kinky knots covered his chin and lower jawline. His mustache was just thick enough to cover the skin above his upper lip. Michael's facial hair was a chocolate brown and matched the color of his tight curls that made up the tiny 'fro that peeked from underneath his hoodie. The brown sugar tone on his skin shone bright through the foggy weather.

"What's on your list of reasons?" His look was sharp.

"Well for starters, she didn't have the healthiest childhood and I don't think she fully recovered from those traumas. A lot of that pain followed her into her adult life. I believe she tried to suppress the hurt that she carried, but she was triggered at certain points in her life."

"Triggered? In what ways?"

"Triggered from the toxic marriage. Triggered from the obsessive drinking. I just think those things were a gateway to her alcoholism and depression, which led to her...you know," I could not bring myself to utter the word *suicide*, in front of Michael. I still pictured him as that five-year-old boy I tried my best to shelter from the harsh realities of the world.

"I know her and Derrick had some issues and yes, they would argue sometimes. But name a married couple that didn't have disagreements sometimes. I mean, you're married. I'm sure you and Johnathan bump heads on a few things here and there, but that doesn't make you want to just out yourself and leave your daughter behind!" I hid behind my silence as Michael carried on. He exhaled. " Sure, marriage is hard, and I know Mommy didn't have it easy. I just never understood how *that* could voluntarily lead her to *this*." Michael gestured towards the grave.

"Michael, there was a lot going on and you were just too young to understand," I looked into his eyes.

He scoffed and snatched his gaze away immediately. "Why hide the pain I was going to feel in the long run anyway, hmm? You know, maybe if someone was honest with me, I would have learned to cope better and not be so emotionally fucked up like I am now.'"

"I was trying to protect you."

"Protect me *how*? By running away to a new city, with your perfect new husband and your perfect family?" Michael's words stung.

"Michael, it was not my intention to leave you here wit—"

"Well you did, Symone! *What*? You think the foster care system raised me while you were away living your best life? Well think again! You left me here to drown in the pits of hell while you vacationed in the clouds of heaven." His nostrils widened as a result of the anger that pushed through his face. The heat from his rage began to boil my blood.

"I did not just *leave*, Michael, there were reasons for why I did what I did."

Michael walked closer to me until he was only centimeters away. He looked down at me. "Oh, word? Well now is your chance to explain."

I shook my head in disbelief that this moment was really happening. I was actually being confronted about why I mustered up the courage to remove myself from a dangerous environment. "Things were complicated."

"Complicated like, *how*?" his level of agitation began to increase rapidly. "You keep giving me these meaningless bullshit-ass answers like I'm still a kid. I'm twenty-two years old, Symone, I'm a grown ass man out here! I been out here on my own ever since I was sixteen, in case you hadn't noticed," he ended his sentence in a nasty sarcastic tone.

"Well how long do you have because explaining the shit that went on in that house could take hours!" His frustration was contagious.

"The floor is all yours," Michael folded his arms across his chest and planted his eyes onto me, waiting for me to begin. I was annoyed with the fact that he had come into his own person and was using this maturity and stability to pressure me into clarifying our unstable childhood. However, I knew he deserved answers and I was clearly the only person that was still alive and able to provide him with the truth.

"Mommy and Derrick did not just *argue*, okay? He *beat* her. Often and badly."

Michael remained in his stiff stance, waiting for more. I could barely see his face, as the rain continued to pour and make it difficult to see his features.

"The first time he put his hands on her, you were three years old. You were in the living room on the couch, not too far away from where they were standing. They were having an argument, which was the norm at that point. I was in the kitchen attempting to wash the dishes. I was standing on a crate so I could reach the kitchen sink. Suddenly, I heard a loud **CLAP!** I ran into the living room and found Mommy on the couch next to you. She was curled up, holding her face. I looked up at Derrick and he stared me down in a daring manner. I ran towards Mommy to see if she was okay. I was scared. My trembling hands tugged at her, hoping to get a response. When she finally removed her hands from her nose, I screamed at the site of blood splurging down and out from her face. I was in a state of shock; I just could not move. It was like my feet were super glued to the floor. Your precious cry was the only thing that was able to snap me back into reality. I grabbed you and led you upstairs to my room where I thought we would be safe. Michael, I was only nine years old. I was *traumatized.*"

I could sense that the story made Michael uncomfortable. He adjusted his posture and clenched his jaws together. I thought about stopping there and not giving more examples of the hell pits that we inhabited, but there was something inside of me that urged me to give him the full truth.

"You know, one time he broke her jaw with his bare hands. She told everyone that she fell down the stairs," I scoffed, "I never understood how anyone ever believed that. It was as if they did not care enough to dig for the truth. Every day, him and Mommy would drink until they were sloppy drunk. So intoxicated they would forget to prepare dinner sometimes. I would make us cereal, noodles, or bologna sandwiches on nights like that."

I could hear Michael sigh aggressively through his tightly closed lips. It was apparent that my words were painful for him. Still, I kept going.

"One night, I thought he was going to *kill her*. It was a school night and we were both in bed asleep when I heard commotion from the backyard. I tiptoed downstairs to see what was going on. There was something in my spirit that led me to believe this was not an ordinary argument between the two of them. I guess they got into a fight outside that led to Mommy's face being busted open, yet again. She ran in the house to get away from him. I was standing behind her as she struggled to lock the back door before he was able to follow her inside. A few moments later, Derrick threw a large brick into the kitchen window. It landed right at my foot, barely missing me. I immediately grabbed you and carried you upstairs to our safe spot. After making sure you were safe, I left the bedroom to check on Mommy. Michael, what I saw next would haunt me forever," I took a moment before continuing. "Derrick somehow pulled Mommy through the shattered window, and through the sharp pieces of broken glass. She was stuck. There was a sharp piece of thick glass that surged through her abdomen and cut deeper each time Derrick yanked at her body. I could hear her life slipping away as she urged me to call the police. Thankfully, the ambulance came just in

Tears of a Hummingbird 182

time and was able to save her life. Of course, by the time they arrived, Derrick was nowhere to be found. I was sure that Mommy would give him up, you know? I just knew she would give the authorities his name...but she didn't." Michael looked confused. "She fabricated another story about getting too drunk and somehow slipping and falling through the window. It was fucking ridiculous. She was actually willing to criminalize her character in order to protect him. I was angry! But I kept quiet and just followed Mommy's lead."

He shook his head before uttering, "just fucking unbelievable." The words from the painful memories pieced together and flowed from my mouth so effortlessly. *Okay, that's enough,* I thought to myself for a second. But the relief that came along with releasing some of the compressed weight from my heart and onto Michael felt so freeing.

"I cannot begin to explain the hurt I felt when she let him back into the house only weeks later," I gritted my teeth as I re-experienced the emotions from that day. "I came home from school and heard his deep, grimy voice traveling from the living room. I was sick. I did not understand why she would put us all *back* in harm's way. Even at that very young age, I knew our mother was completely neglecting our safety. I was afraid...and then the worst began." He twisted his face down at me as to think, *what the hell could be worse than what had already happened?* I knew Michael was completely oblivious to the secret that I was getting ready to reveal to him next. "One night, a couple of months after he returned to the house, Derrick came into my room and..." I stopped to hold back the flood of raw feelings that started to consume me. "He, um...he raped me, Michael," I could no longer resist the tears. "And that was the first of many times," I bit down on my bottom lip to distract from the disgusting and hurtful memory.

"What the fu—. Are you **SERIOUS**?" Michael's eyes widened. "Why didn't I know this, *huh*? This is fucking sick!"

"I was a kid."

He grunted loudly. "*So was I*! I was left in the dark about this demon that I once called a stepdad, you understand? Playing ball, doing homework, laughing, and sharing space with a man that was beating my moms by day and molesting my sister at night!"

"Imagine how I felt! It was a vicious cycle—brutality that never ended for me." Heated chills raced through my body.

Michael took a step back. "So, you mean to tell me he did all of this and that muthafucka is still walking around breathing? Why the *fuck* is my mama in the grave and not **HIM**?"

"Yea, well you know he always had a way of escaping the consequences for his cruel actions." I was sick.

"Well, did you tell anyone what he was doing to you? Did you call the police?"

I shook my head. "Again, I was a *kid*. And as cliché as it sounds, I was afraid and didn't think anyone would believe me."

"What about Mommy? Did you tell her?"

My lips began to tremble, and my voice cracked as I gathered up the energy to respond. "And that...hmm. That was the *worst* part about everything."

"What do you mean?" he was curious.

I took a deep breath and exhaled all of the fear out from the pit of my being. I dug deep inside of me and grabbed the forbidden words that I buried so long ago. For the first time, I said the words out loud to Michael.

"She didn't believe me," I sobbed through a slow, high pitched cry. Suddenly, a bright bolt of lightning struck the sky above us, followed by a tense roar of thunder. The rain slammed down faster and harder.

"No, Symone, fucking *NO*! Mommy would *never* do that," Michael walked up to me, staring deep into my pupils, looking for the hint of dishonesty that did not exist.

"*What*? Why do you think I left, huh? Six years! For *SIX, long, agonizing* years I was being raped by that monster and she turned the other cheek each time. I had to save myself. Or else...I wouldn't have made it this far. College was my way out, Michael. I applied to all types of universities and chose the college that was the farthest away from *THIS PLACE*."

"And you left me here in this whirlpool of dark chaos to *drown*? I was alone! When you went off to college, I was left to pick up the pieces by myself! I was left with an emotionally unstable drunk, and an abuser turned rapist," Michael punched through the cold rain. "Why didn't you take me *with you?*"

"Michael, I was eighteen. I didn't have any money, stability, nor a solid plan. I just went with the flow of things, just hoping things would be better. I could not just bring you with me. And to be quite frank, I took care of you since the day you were born, but you were not *my* child. It was time for me to live my life for me," I yelled over the roaring weather.

He sarcastically nodded his head in agreement. "Yeah, you're right. I'm sorry I was such a burden on you, but the least you could have done was send for help."

I was stuck. He was right. I was unable to produce words, so what escaped my tongue at that moment was a pitiful cry. "I know Michael and I'm sorry that I left you here. I should have come back for you. I beat myself up every day for muting your cries in the same way that Mommy did to me when I was in the midst of suffering." The thunder grew louder. "I've always felt that you hated me and my fear of reaching out to you may have created this large gap between us. I ran away and never looked back. I should have saved you, Michael. Forgive me," I pleaded with him.

Michael's head and shoulders dropped simultaneously. He seemed tired from the tug-of-war discussion between us. He sat his bottom on the muddy grounds adjacent to our mother's tombstone.

I continued my emotional plea. "Although Mommy ignored my cries for help, I still loved her, Michael. My heart ached for her. I knew she was just afraid of the truth. So, when I left Cleveland, I didn't call for help because I was scared it would hurt her. Looking back, damn right I regret not sending for you and Mommy. Had I been brave enough to do so, she may still be alive today!" The pace of the rain increased and intensified. I threw my umbrella down and walked over towards Michael. His head drooped between his knees and his body weighed down to the ground from the heavy information that was placed upon him. He was quiet.

I sat on the ground next to my brother, connecting my hip with his. His strong sense of despair reached me. I wrapped my arms around him tightly to relieve some of the pain.

"Michael, I'm sorry that I left you. I'm sorry that you were alone when you found Mommy's lifeless body. I'm so sorry that I wasn't there for you."

Michael hugged me back. I could see the veins in his neck begin to extrude from his skin. His body was stiff and hot under the cool storm that took place right above us. He buried his face in my shoulder and dumped his dense tears into my coat. I squeezed him tighter as he wailed uncontrollably.

"I promise that you'll never have to be alone again. I'm here for you brother," I laid my head on top of his.

We cradled each other and whimpered to ourselves for several minutes. No words, just our on-and-off again sobs. My hair was drenched with the salty rain and stuck to the side of my face. My lips trembled from the intense sentiment in the air. Our soft cries echoed throughout the cemetery as mother nature continued to weep along with us.

Moments later, the dark clouds began to separate to expose a chunk of a vibrant blue sky. The rain gradually let up and eventually came to a complete stop. I looked up and admired the pale rainbow that began to form not too far from where we were sitting. The sun peeked from behind the foggy atmosphere, revealing a piece of itself. Michael picked his head up to examine the new clear skies.

"Simone?" he asked while still observing the bright environment that had emerged through the dark.

"Yes?" I turned towards him.

"Was the grass greener on the other side? You know, when you moved to Boston?"

I took a couple of seconds to reflect on my time in Boston and the horror that I had endured since marrying Jay. I realized that I left one toxic environment and slid right into another. I realized that my mother and I had a lot of unhealthy habits in common. Our stories were painfully similar and dramatically aligned with one another. I decided that I did not want the same outcome. I did not want Courtney to be left alone with nothing but hurt and questions for why I left her behind. I wanted to live. I realized it was not too late to break the generational curse.

I looked back up at Michael. "I'm still watering the lawn."

CHAPTER 9

TEARS OF A REVIVED SOUL

"The closer I get to you, the more you make me see, by giving me all you got, your love has captured me."

"He said *all* of that to you?" Lynie stood wide eyed with both of her hands buried in a head full of thick, curly hair. Lynie's client sat still in the salon chair with her eyes closed as Lynie massaged her scalp and moisturized each strand of hair with her homemade mixture of natural, pure oils. Lynie wore her sparkling apron that was all black, outlined in rhinestones with large, bold letters that read, *Lynie's Beauty Retreat*. The apron barely covered her fresh blue jeans and snug white t-shirt that she complimented with her new white tennis shoes.

"He sure did," I cheesed out loud.

"And you think that's cute? *Tsk!* I would have given *my* baby brother an old school ass whooping. Right there in the middle of that cemetery."

I laughed hysterically at Lynie's reaction. "You see, it wasn't even like that. I mean, it was, but I understood where he was coming from. I understood his pain." I paced back and forth on the shiny floors as I recalled my visit with Michael. "He was so angry. He yelled at me from the top of his lungs. I screamed back. Then, we eventually collapsed down to the muddy ground, held each other and cried our eyes out. Oh Lynie, it was so *beautiful*!"

Lynie's face was screwed up as she observed my unexpected excitement. "You okay?"

"I feel better than ever!" I flopped down in an empty chair not too far from Lynie. "It feels like a boulder has been lifted from my chest! I feel free as a bird!"

It had been five days since I returned from my trip to Cleveland and I was still surfing the emotional high that lingered from my visit with Michael. I barely got to express my excitement with Jay, all because of his personal insecurities in regard to my connection with anyone other than him. Therefore, I contained most of my joy for his sake and watered down the time I had with my little brother.

Business had picked up unexpectedly at Lynie's beauty salon. With two of her stylists out on vacation, she found herself filling in at LBR for long days, and unavailable for our frequent girl chat sessions. I took it upon myself to pay Lynie a visit in person, right in the middle of one of her hair appointments. With the okay from Mr. Bricks, I left the office an hour early so I could check in with Lynie before picking up Courtney from school.

"Oh, and look," I jumped right back up from my seat and rushed over to Lynie's side. "We took some selfies!" I snatched my phone from my pocket and shoved the device in Lynie's face. "Do you think we look alike?"

Lynie quickly grabbed the phone from my hand to get a closer look at the photos. "Damn girl, I didn't know Michael looked like this," she proceeded to point the phone towards her client. "Girl, look at her brother. He fine as hell, ain't he?" The two women squirmed and giggled amongst each other for several seconds.

I reached over and collected my phone from Lynie's hand. "*Aht, aht*! My innocent little brother is off limits! I will not let you hungry women devour my precious Mikey, Mike. Besides, I thought you were..." I stopped and leaned in towards Lynie and whispered in her ear. "You know...gay?"

Lynie rolled her eyes and whispered back at me, "Girl, I would change my whole sexual orientation for that sexy young thang you call baby brother!"

"Yuck." I was mildly disgusted.

"Besides, Michael is a grown ass man, now. Whether it's me or some other woman, you better believe that *somebody* is riding that pony."

"Okay that's *enough*," I waved off Lynie's accusations. "Just know it won't be you." I sat back down in the chair and looked through my pictures with Michael for what might have been the hundredth time. I swiped through the photos and smiled harder and harder as I browsed through the camera roll.

"Wow," Lynie looked over at me with her hand on her hip and a wide grin on her face.

I slowly looked up from my phone. "What?"

"Nothing," she chuckled. "You just look...*happy*." Lynie turned her attention back towards her client's hair as she continued conversing with me. "I like it!"

"Yeah. I guess you're right. I do feel happy," I continued through the pictures on my phone.

"So, how has your friend, Angelo, been?"

The sound of Angelo's name mentioned out loud in a public place startled me, at first. When I looked at Lynie, she shot me a glance that reassured me that the coast was clear and it was okay to discuss my *friend*, Angelo.

"Oh, he's been good."

"When was the last time you spoke with him?"

I gave Lynie an aggressive and side-eye look.

"Well if you *must* know. I spoke with him this morning. He happens to send me daily good morning texts."

"Is that so?"

"Yep," I blushed to myself. "Because that's what *friends* do, right?"

Lynie nodded to herself. "Hey, Shante," she called out to the back of the salon. "Can you please take Miss April to the dryer?" She carefully helped the woman up and out of her chair and pointed in the direction where Shante was standing. The woman slowly wobbled towards the section of the salon where the dryers were. Lynie walked over towards me and sat in a chair next to me.

"You seem really excited about Angelo," she stated.

"Yea, he's cool," I replied, still fixed on my phone, swiping through pictures.

"So, what is this little thing you got going on between the two of you?"

"Little *thing*? It's not a *thing*. He's just a friend. That's all." I was slightly offended.

Lynie raised her palms towards me to defend herself. "Don't shoot me now, I'm just asking."

I continued glancing through my phone. There was a brief moment of silence between us before Lynie interrupted.

"So, umm. Does Jay know about your *friend*?"

I looked up from my phone. "No."

The one word response was enough for Lynie. She nodded her head to signal her understanding of the complicated situation that suddenly unfolded in my life.

"Well, my friend. As always, I am here for you no matter what, and you know I will always have your back." She looked into my eyes, "I just want you to be *careful*."

"Dammit, Lynie," I threw my face into my hands. "You always do this." My words were muffled as they sang out from my sweaty palms.

"Do what?"

"This!"

"Listen, I am just being straightforward with you, Monie. I am not here to sugarcoat anything, what good will that do? It's obvious that you like this guy. I just want you to be careful because we both know that damn Jonathan is a monster, and I swear to God if he lays one more finger on you—"

"He's not! I told you that we are in a different place, Lynie."

She cocked her head to the side and scooted at the edge of her seat so she was a few inches closer to me. "Oh yeah? In a better place until he finds out you are having an—"

"Don't you dare say it."

"*Affair*! Symone, if you don't get a hold of this situation, that's exactly what it's going to turn into."

I rolled my eyes and exhaled all my frustration out into the air.

"Why don't you just *leave* him?"

"Lynie, we always have these conversations and the answer remains the same." My head dropped between my shoulders. "It's not that simple."

"I never said it would be simple, but wouldn't it be worth the hard work? At least you'll be happy, right?"

I shook my head viciously. "I can't risk losing my daughter in a custody battle with Jay. The thought alone is too much to digest. If I don't have my baby with me, I could *never* be happy."

"Why do you think you would lose her?"

"Lynie, I barely have anything without Jay. I would lose the house, the car, and all the belongings he purchased. I have no money! I'm working part time at a law firm with very little savings. I have mommy issues and fresh scars on my wrist. Any court in their right mind would choose Jay as the custodial parent."

"Not if you are honest and upfront about his abuse," she quickly interjected.

I exhaled sharply. "And what would that do for Court, huh? Not being able to see her dad would devastate her. Besides, it would completely destroy life as we know it. Our family would be torn apart and, honestly, I am not sure how or if I could survive without him."

"You call this surviving? Symone, you're holding on by a thread. You have to know that Courtney would want the best for you because she loves you," she firmly pressed her index finger against my chest. "Believe that in your soul. You can't allow her to continue living this lie and pretend that everything is okay...like the *both* of you are not in harm's way," she paused for a fraction of a second. "Isn't that what your mom did to Michael?"

I shot up from my seat and turned towards Lynie. "You don't know everything, Lynie. You've never been married; you don't know sacrifice. You don't have children; you don't know how far a mother would go to protect her young! My mom did her best and that's *exactly* what I'm doing."

Lynie stood up from her chair. "Oh yeah? Well, I don't have to be married to have common sense! And where did your mother's *best* lead her to? Look at the long-term effect *her best* had on Michael. I'm sorry sis, but you have to get real with yourself and get real with life. I'm sure your mother wouldn't want you to go down the same path she did. Don't you think she would want better for you?"

I stared deep into her eyes, refusing to answer her question, but taking in every word she spat out through her thick lips.

She continued. "Seeing you genuinely excited about something, like a picture you took with your brother, or a *good morning* text from a friend, reminds me that you deserve to feel happy, loved, and important. Symone...don't allow him to continue to rob you of your joy."

I took a large gulp to swallow the buildup of sticky emotions that plagued my narrow throat.

Lynie gripped my arm. "Symone, I will help you every step of the way; just say the word," she pleaded.

"*I can't,*" I snatched my arm away. "I'm not ready to completely throw a wrench in my marriage and shake up my little girl's world." I used both hands to smooth out my shirt that had gotten slightly wrinkled from Lynie's grip. I turned around and grabbed my belongings from the chair and slung my purse across my right shoulder. I felt heavy as I dragged myself to the door, preparing to exit the salon. I looked back over at Lynie, who was standing with her hip poked out at one side and her arms folded across her chest. She softly shook her head and carried a great deal of sorrow in her warm eyes.

"You sure know how to ruin the moment," I hissed at her before leaving out the door.

◆

I sat in my parked car in the salon's parking lot to collect myself before driving to pick-up Courtney from school. I looked down at my watch and was happy to know that I had a few moments to stay put as I calmed my nerves. I knew Lynie made valid points, but even the right information at the wrong time could be ineffective. I closed my eyes and sighed to myself, praying for peace of mind.

DING!

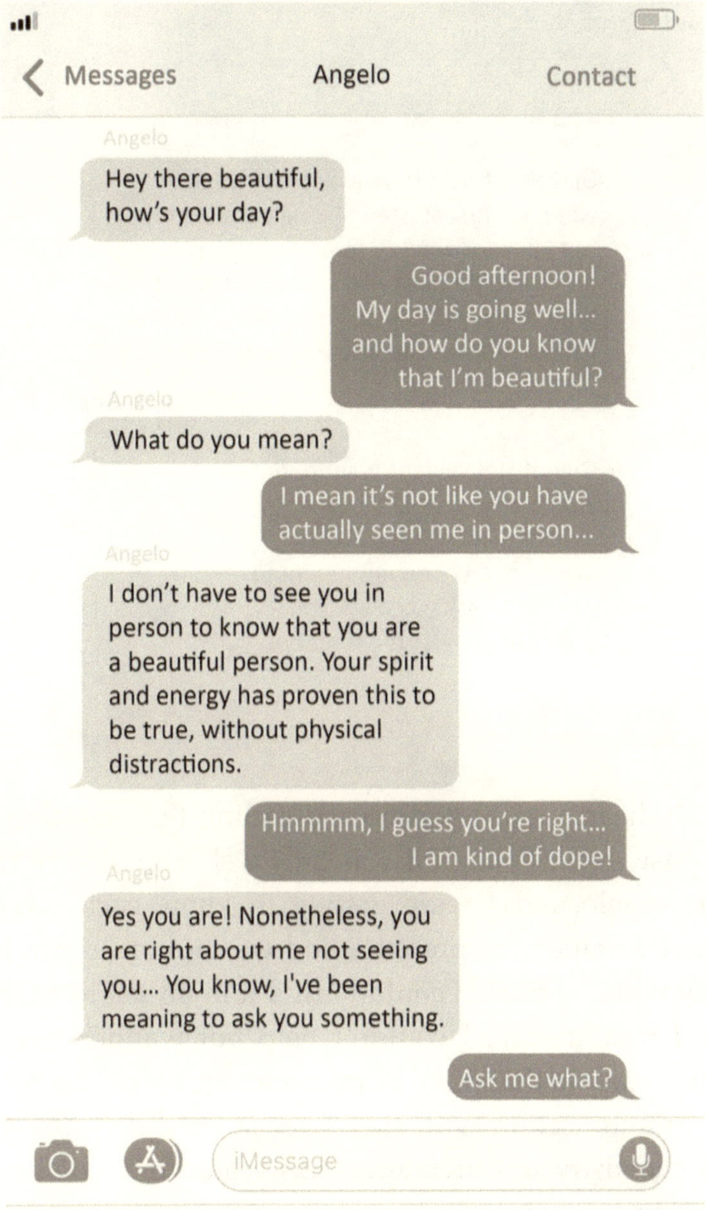

Messages   Angelo   Contact

Angelo

Hey there beautiful, how's your day?

Good afternoon! My day is going well... and how do you know that I'm beautiful?

Angelo

What do you mean?

I mean it's not like you have actually seen me in person...

Angelo

I don't have to see you in person to know that you are a beautiful person. Your spirit and energy has proven this to be true, without physical distractions.

Hmmmm, I guess you're right... I am kind of dope!

Angelo

Yes you are! Nonetheless, you are right about me not seeing you... You know, I've been meaning to ask you something.

Ask me what?

iMessage

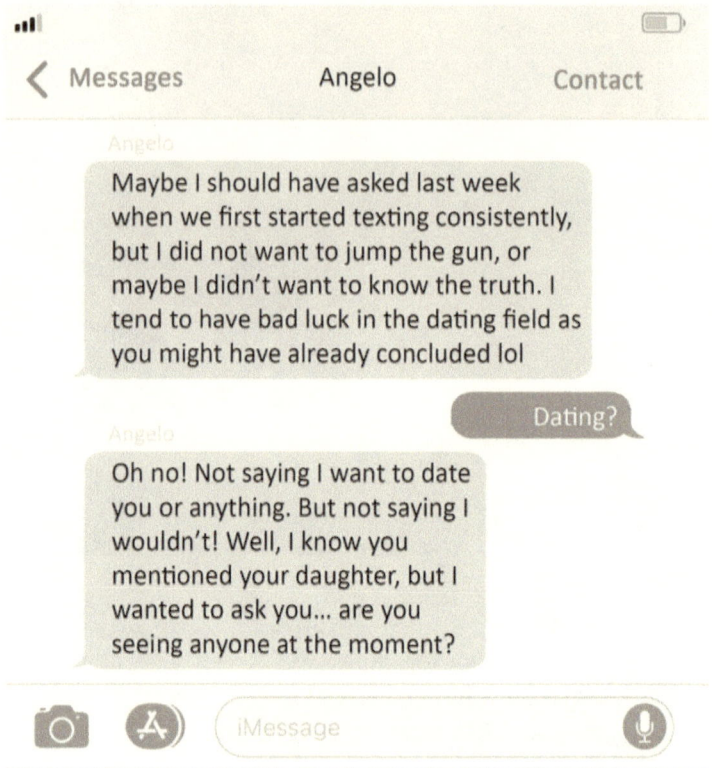

My heart sank. I had been dreading that question for the past week. Though it was only a short period of time that Angelo and I were getting to know each other, I honestly valued his presence and was afraid I'd run him away with the truth. I couldn't find it in myself to tell him that I was *married*. I couldn't help but wonder how he would react to that piece of information. Would he cut off all communication with me? Even if he didn't, the vibe and chemistry of our interactions would most definitely shift, and I was no shape or form interested in that happening.

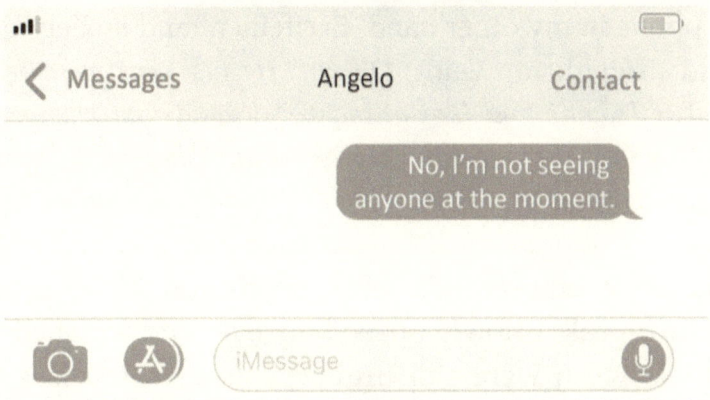

I felt bad about not being honest with Angelo, however I didn't think the truth was worth losing our connection. There was something about the odd and strange way we found each other that made this growing friendship divine and meant to be. I did not want to jeopardize that.

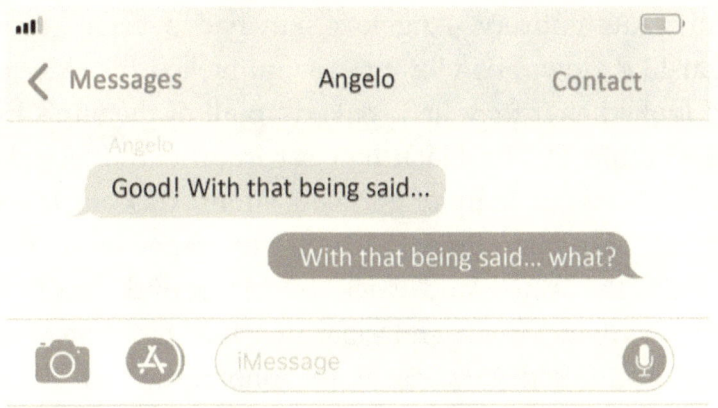

As soon as I sent the text, I received an incoming image that began to download automatically. *Gasp!* As soon as I caught a glimpse of the picture sent by Angelo, I slapped my free hand over my eyes, while still holding the phone in my other hand. Excitement and anxiety both raced through my veins. *Oh my! He just sent me a selfie! What if I don't find him attractive? Would that change the vibe? Ahhh! I'm scared to look! But, what if he's more physically appealing than I could ever imagine, or as Lynie would say, sexy ass hell!* I went back and forward in my head for several seconds before finally convincing myself to take a peak. I slowly opened my eyes and widened my fingers, which were still firmly planted on my face. By spreading my fingers apart, I was able to peep through the spaces and analyze the picture.

Good God! My heart dropped once more but was caught by the butterflies that lived at the pit of my stomach and quickly carried my heart back up to my chest. I snatched my hand from my face and bought the phone closer so I could appreciate the beauty in human form in its entirety. Angelo's skin had a bright brown sugar-like glow. His vibrant eyes mimicked his skin tone and looked as if they had soaked up all of the sun's light and vitamin D. His black hair sat in an extremely short afro that was made up of gorgeous, tight Afrocentric coils. His hair was complimented by a neat taper haircut that covered the sides and back of his round head. His eyebrows were thick and rich, just like his moist, pink lips. I continued to stare at the photograph as Angelo smiled back at me with his pearly white teeth through the picture. As I examined the photo further, I noticed the royal purple polo shirt with the acronym FADA printed across the right shoulder.

Messages   Angelo   Contact

Angelo

This has been the longest five minutes of my life... am I that ugly? Lol

Oh, you're alright... Nice work shirt, though! Lol

Angelo

Hahaha very funny, Ms. Symone!

I'm just kidding! No, you are... simply a beautiful man.

Angelo

Wow. I don't think any woman has ever referred to me as 'beautiful' before. I like it.

Really? Hmm. They must have been blind.

Angelo

Maybe so! I can't wait until I can also compliment you on your physical features...

Is that your way of requesting a picture from me?

Angelo

Only if you're comfortable with doing so.

Lol... I am. One moment...

  iMessage

I reached over to open the glove department and grabbed for the hairbrush and lip gloss that I kept in my car. I looked up and unfolded the sun visor to reveal the small mirror and dim courtesy light that lived on its surface. My hair was still straightened from a couple of nights before, so I just used the brush to flatten out the few flyaway hairs that sat wild at the crown of my head. I quickly twisted the cap of the lip gloss and removed it from the long, clear tube. I proceeded to glide the shiny gloss over my wide, firm lips. *There, much better.* I picked up my phone and clicked on the camera icon, ready to take a picture for Angelo. I stretched my arm out straight in front of me, as I shifted back and forward in different positions, attempting to capture the most natural light in my frame. I looked into the camera and took a deep breath before snapping away. *Click! Oh no, this one looks horrible! Click! Ooooo this one is sexy...perhaps a little too sexy? Click! Nah, I look desperate. Maybe I should smile! Click! Okay, maybe I shouldn't smile. Click! Let's show some teeth. Click! Ugh! How did I get food in my teeth? Click! Yes, this is a great angle! Now, just look natural. Click! Perfect! Yes, this is the one!* After choosing the selfie I was the most satisfied with, I sent the image to Angelo.

Ahhhhhhh! I felt a bit nervous about what his reaction would be, and hoped he would be equally as attracted to me as I was to him. I sat anxiously and waited for his response. My foot made music as it tapped loudly on the stiff gas pedal, causing a rhythmic tune. I suddenly became very warm as sweat began to gather and exit the opening of my pores. *Woosah.*

DING!

The text notification was loud and vibrated through my entire being. I immediately unlocked my phone to read the incoming text message.

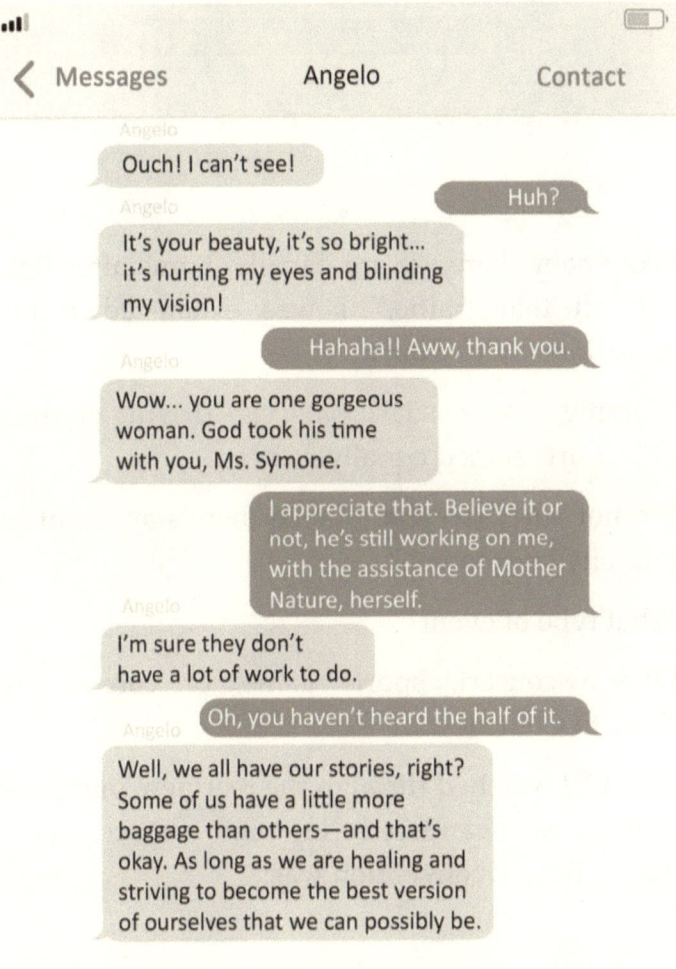

Tears of a Hummingbird

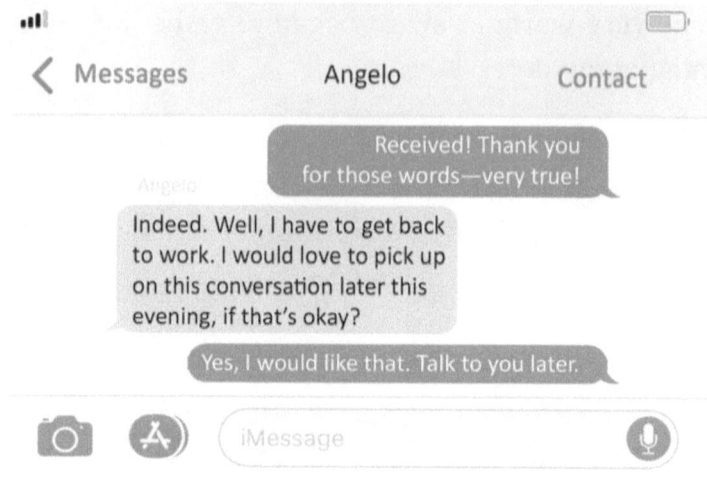

"Okay baby, here we are. Finally, home after fighting through all that traffic," I was exhausted from my commute home with Courtney.

"Mommy, why was it *so many* cars driving on the road today?" Court seemed equally as beat.

"I'm not sure, sweetie. Maybe there's an event going on in the city later today."

"What type of event?"

"Like a concert, sports game, or convention," I explained to Courtney.

"Ohhh," I watched through the rearview mirror as her innocent eyes wandered off into space, perhaps wondering what a convention was.

I parked and completely turned the car off, signaling to Courtney that she could now unfasten her seatbelt. I walked around to the rear of the car to let her out. As soon as I opened the door, she jumped into my arms, completely cradling me with her entire body. Her arms hugged my neck tightly and her small legs squeezed my thighs as hard as they could.

"Oh, you want to play, huh?" I teased my daughter. Her laughter egged me on. I instantly wrapped my arms around her tiny frame and spun around in circles as fast and as safely as I could. The sun shined down on our melanated flesh as we screamed and laughed out loud. Before I could help it, we had literally fallen to the grassy ground near the driveway. Courtney rolled away as I made my way towards her with all ten of my fingers moving in slithery motion, indicating that I was going to give her a nice tickle as soon as I got a hold of her.

"Mommy, no," Courtney cried out when I finally caught her and gently, but firmly vibrated the sides of her torso with my hands. She laughed uncontrollably, showing her bright grin as her giggles escaped her mouth. "Okay, okay," she pleaded as she called truce. "You win again, Mommy!" She picked herself up off of the ground and dusted her school clothes off while catching her breath.

"Yay! I'm the champion," I struck a fake warrior pose with my chin held high.

"Not for long. Last one to the door is a rotten egg," the sweet little voice behind me called out as she dashed towards our home.

"No fair! You had a head start," I yelled after Courtney as I trailed behind her.

"Mommy, you know it's okay to lose sometimes, right?"

I giggled to myself as I jogged fast enough to compete, but slow enough to allow Courtney to beat me to the door.

"I win," she screamed out of pure joy.

"You sure did! Maybe I'll practice my footwork so that I can win next time." I softly pinched her cheek.

I took out my ring of keys to unlock the door and slid the house key into the keyhole, but before it could connect, the front door swung wide open.

"Ladies," Jay beamed as he greeted us at the entrance.

"Daddy," Court hugged his leg and shot her father a kiss before running past him and into the house.

"Don't forget to wash your hands and do your homework, baby girl. Dinner's almost ready," Jay called after our daughter before turning his attention back towards me. "Hey baby, how was your day?"

I was still standing outside of the door. Jay placed his hands in his pockets and leaned against the doorframe with his left shoulder, slightly blocking my pathway into the house.

"My day was good! Typical workday for the most part."

"Really?" he bit down on his bottom lip and closed his eyes before responding. "That's interesting because I called up to your job earlier and Mr. Bricks said you requested to leave work early."

"Oh yea. I forgot, I left work a little early to stop by the shop and see Lynie. Just to catch up."

"Just to *catch up,* huh?" Jay stared deep into me.

"Yes, I was there for no more than an hour, Jay. It was nothing." I could sense his mistrust.

He continued to look at me with an emotionless expression plastered on his thick, pale face for several seconds before eventually lighting up the tense moment with a wide smile. "Right, right. I know it's hard finding time to chat with your bestie and all. Come on in baby; why are you still standing out there?" Jay motioned for me to come inside as he cleared the doorway for me to enter. I instantly smelt a strong and pleasant aroma of onions and peppers; I walked towards the dining area and saw that Jay had the table set for our small family.

"What's this?"

"*Aht, aht!* Remember what happened last time you asked that question?" Jay laughed alone, as I did not find his sarcastic comment funny at all. "Oh baby, I'm just playing with you. You know we're passed all that," he pacified.

I ignored his statement. "You cooked a family dinner?"

"I sure did. It's sort of a pre-celebration for our anniversary," he said as he walked away and deeper into the kitchen.

Anniversary? Fuck! Is it that time of year already?

Jay continued to converse with me from the kitchen, though he could not see me. "I figured we have dinner tonight with Courtney and tomorrow on our actual anniversary date we can do something more exclusive and maybe a little more romantic. My sister already agreed to keep Court for us."

Tomorrow? I panicked quietly to myself.

"I'm sorry it's kind of last minute. I know it's my year to plan the festivities for our big day, I've just been so damn busy, you know? But don't sweat too hard, I have a nice date planned for us tomorrow."

Whew! I was relieved to remember that it was Jay's turn to plan our anniversary, because Lord knew I had not prepared *anything.* "It's okay. I understand you've picked up extra shifts to help the company. I'm okay with a low-key celebration."

I heard the clashing of pots and pans in the kitchen come to a sudden stop. Shortly after, Jay walked out to the dining room with a confused look on his face. "Really?" he asked.

"Yea, I just don't want you to stress yourself out about it," I assured him.

"Huh...that's interesting. I just remember our anniversary always being a big deal to you. Why so nonchalant about it now?"

"It *still is* a big deal to me, Jay. The fact that we have remained married this long means a lot to me. You know I cherish our union and family unit. I'm just trying to ease some of the pressure for you," I managed to produce a lukewarm grin.

"You've always been such a considerate person," he smiled back. "Listen, why don't you go get yourself and Courtney freshened up and ready for dinner. Meet me back here in, say, twenty minutes?"

"Sure thing. We'll be back down shortly," I said as I made my way up the stairs.

◆

I went to my bedroom to quickly undress and throw the grass stained clothes into the laundry. I let the shower run in preparation for a quick cleaning. After shoving my shower cap onto my head and drenching my body in soap and hot water, I dried my skin and moisturized it carefully with natural oils and lotion. I decided on an outfit that was comfortable, yet appropriate for the pre-anniversary dinner that Jay had planned. I dressed myself in black leggings and a rich Monroe colored, flowy blouse that hugged my waist and drooped just inches passed my buttocks. The top of the shirt was a perfect v-cut that did not reveal too much of my cleavage. I slipped my fresh feet into my favorite black and fluffy slippers.

"Mommy, can I wear my new pajamas to dinner? Please? Please?" Courtney burst into my room, already wearing the PJ's that she was asking to wear.

"Well baby, I think it's a little too late to ask if you're already wearing them," I chuckled. "Come here, let me at least wipe you down." I grabbed Court's hand and led her to the bathroom. I took a fresh washcloth and saturated it with warm, soapy water. I cleaned her face, hands, and feet until they appeared to be spotless.

"Ladies?" Jay's baritone voice traveled up to the second floor of our home.

"Coming," I replied back. I looked down at Court as I held her face in my hands. "Are you excited to see what your dad has waiting for us?"

"Yea!" she shouted.

"What do you think it is?" I asked only to prolong staring into her lovely face.

"An octopus!"

"An *octopus*? I sure hope not!" We both laughed out loud as we began to migrate downstairs to the dining area.

Jay had already filled our plates with food. We were served thick grilled salmon fillets with a sprinkle of crushed herbs, lumpy and creamy mashed potatoes topped with fresh chives and vibrant green asparagus. My stomach grumbled at the site of the delicious meal. Next to each plate was a tall glass of dark red wine. Courtney's dinner was half the size of ours. Her salmon was cut up into small pieces paired with a scoop of mashed potatoes and three perfect pieces of asparagus. Next to her small plate was a clear plastic cup shaped like a miniature wine glass that was half-way filled with a dark and purple liquid.

"Don't worry; it's grape juice," Jay said to me as he helped Courtney into her chair.

I chuckled. "That's so cute, I like it."

"Daddy, it's not grape juice, it's kid's wine," our daughter shouted out as I took my seat at the table, directly across from her.

"There's no such thing, baby girl," Jay set at the head of the rectangular table with Court to his right and me to his left.

She frowned her face up towards Jay, but didn't say anything.

"This looks and smells so good, Jay. Thank you," I smiled towards him.

"It's only the beginning, you just wait and see," he pointed his fork towards me right before stabbing it into his juicy salmon.

"I can't wait," I pretended to blush. I picked up my fork and used it to cut through the pink, flakey fish. The tender meat melted in my mouth and left a satisfying trail of intense flavors. The potatoes were warm and seasoned to perfection. My first bite of the asparagus was an even balance between crunchy and chewy. We were quiet as we enjoyed our meal—the sounds of silverware clinking against the glass plates was the only thing that could be heard.

"Court, do you know what tomorrow is?" Jay asked.

I took a sip of my wine as I curiously waited for Court to respond.

"Saturday!" She threw her hands high in the air, expressing her excitement for the weekend.

"It sure is! But it's also your mom and I's wedding anniversary."

"What's that?"

"Well, it basically means that years ago, we decided to be husband and wife; we chose each other. We had a grand wedding, which was basically a huge party to celebrate our decision to marry," Jay explained to Courtney.

"Wait a minute, Daddy! Are you telling me that you and Mommy had a big party without *me*?" She frowned.

Jay laughed at Court's pouty face before clarifying. "Well baby girl, you were not even thought of at that point. Another two years would go by before your mom and I found out that she was pregnant with you."

"Hmmmm, okay," Court seemed to be satisfied with her dad's answer and resumed eating her dinner. Jay continued his explanation on marriage and what it meant. He slightly shifted his chair to Courtney to hold her attention as he spoke.

"So, like I was saying, Mommy and I chose to commit to each other, which is a beautiful thing. There are billions and billions of people in the world, and somehow we found one another to love and to love *forever*." He looked towards me. "We decided we would be together until death do us part."

I smiled and nodded back at Jay as I took another gulp of wine. He said nothing else as he sat back up in his chair and finally began eating away at his mashed potatoes.

DING!

My heart shriveled as my phone screamed from my pocket. I was afraid to open the message with Jay just inches away from me—it could have been Angelo resuming our friendly conversation from earlier. I also did not want to employ a guilty look by not opening the message. Jay looked over at me, waiting for me to acknowledge my phone. I cursed myself in my head for not programming my phone notifications to silent as I read the message to myself.

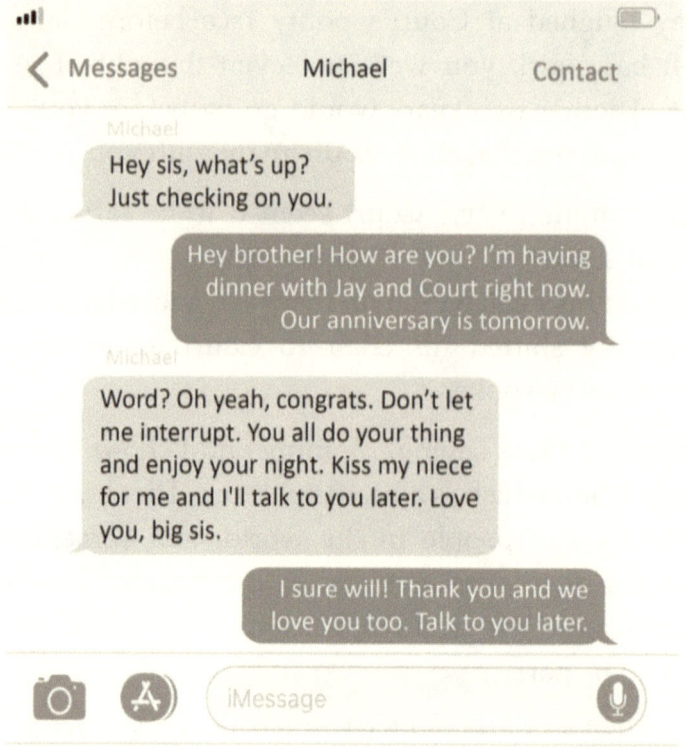

"Awwwweee, it was Michael. He was just checking in. He said happy anniversary and that he loves us all," I paraphrased.

Jay smoothly brushed off the message I delivered and continued stuffing his face.

"Mommy, when are we going to see Uncle Michael?" Court asked.

Jay did not look up from his plate, but I was sure he was listening and waiting for a response. "That's a great question, baby. Umm...I'm not sure. Maybe one day he'll come to visit us."

Jay suddenly cleared his throat excessively but did not verbalize any words.

"But, if that happens, it would probably be a long time from now," I quickly added. "Uncle Michael is very busy with work."

"I can't wait to see him."

"It will eventually happen, sweetie," I reassured Courtney.

"So," Jay began, "Are you excited for tomorrow, babe?" He looked at me through his wine glass as he took a sip.

"Yes, I'm so excited. It's gonna be nice to spend some quality time tog—"

DING!

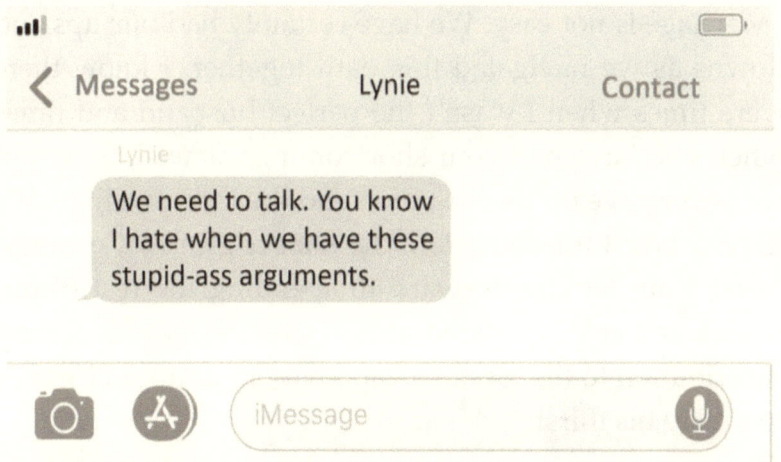

"Oh, sorry. It's Lynie. I'll just talk to her later." Jay rolled his eyes. I quickly stuffed my phone in my pocket and carried on with the conversation. "Umm, yea I'm looking forward to tomorrow. How should I dress?"

Jay thought for a moment. "Just wear something very classy, but also bring an overnight bag with comfortable clothes." He winked at me.

"Ahhh, sounds very adventurous," I said as I guzzled down the last of my wine.

"There's more where that came from." Jay grabbed the bottle of wine from the middle of the table and poured more into my glass.

"Daddy can I have more, too?" Court grabbed her empty cup and pointed it towards Jay. He quickly reached under the table to grab a bottle of grape juice to fulfill her request for a refill.

"I would like to make a toast," Jay raised his glass. "Marriage is not easy. We have certainly had our ups and downs as we navigated this path together. I know there were times when I wasn't the perfect husband and times when you have had your shortcomings as well, however, we never gave up on our union and the love we share. We have a beautiful daughter," he shot a grin at Courtney. "And I am looking forward to spending the rest of our lives together." Jay glared at me, seeming to wait for my contribution to his toast. I scraped my brain to find words to satisfy his thirst.

"Umm, I am also proud of how far we have come. I am grateful for our beautiful daughter. I can't wait to see what the rest of our lives will look like," I paused for a few seconds to think of more bubbly things that I could possibly say about our troubled marriage. Jay continued to stare through me as I continued. "I...uh, I know that we have been through a lot, but have faith that we will — "

DING!

"Dammit Symone! Would you tell that damn Lynie that we are in the middle of something?" Jay yelled out from the head of the table. "And here's a tip," he said sarcastically. "No one will be able to interrupt us if you place your phone on *silent*."

I bit my tongue as I pulled my phone out once more, irritated by Jay's sarcasm.

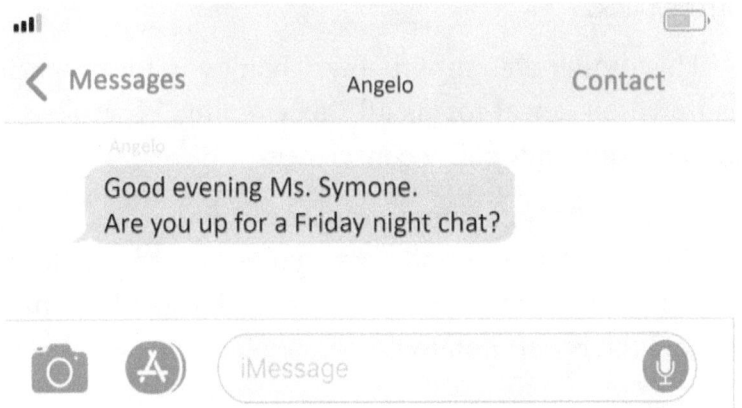

My heart pounded through my chest the minute I read Angelo's name on the screen of my phone. I immediately closed out of the messaging app and programed my phone to silent. I placed the device out of site, on the empty chair next to me, and took another quick sip of my wine to help calm my outraged nerves.

"We weren't finished toasting, Symone," Jay rumbled.

"Oh, yea. Sorry. As I was saying, I know we have been through a lot, but I have faith that we will remain united and stronger than ever. I believe in us and will do anything to protect the love that we have for one another." I lifted my glass towards Jay. "Cheers to *us!*" I buried my face into my glass, once again, hoping that I fed Jay enough of what he wanted to hear.

"Cheers to Mommy and Daddy!" Courtney's sweet voice called out.

"Thank you, babygirl." Jay reached over to lightly rub Court's back.

"This dinner was superb, Jay. Thank you for preparing this nutritious meal for us all this evening," I stroked his ego to disguise my guilty conscience.

"Thanks, baby. I knew you would like it and picked out the salmon especially for you. I even made the mashed potatoes from scratch because I know how much you hate the boxed potatoes."

"Boxed potatoes are not potatoes. They're flakes that turn into creamy slop that is *oddly* referred to as mashed potatoes," I shot back in a joking manner.

"Yea, I've heard that a million times throughout this marriage," he chuckled as he scrapped up and ate the last of his homemade mashed potatoes.

RING!

Jay's phone rang loudly from his pocket. I looked at him with a half-twisted smile, calling out his audacity to not take his own advice. Slightly embarrassed, he snatched his gaze away from mine and answered his phone.

"This is Johnathan. **What**? No, not tonight. I'm with my family. Where's the new hire? *He quit*? You gotta be kidding me!" Jay stood up and walked away from the table to finish his conversation in private.

Courtney's eyes were heavy. "Mommy, I'm sleepy," she murmured across the table.

"I know, baby. Go upstairs to potty and get into bed. I'll be up to tuck you in shortly. Court disappeared from the table before I could even finish my sentence. I digested the remainder of my food as I eavesdropped on Jay's conversation. I listened to his end of the phone call as he paced back and forth in the living room area.

"So, you're telling me there's nobody else that you can call in to produce and process the rest of the product? I can't afford to lose money on this order, man! *Fuck*! Listen here, tomorrow is my wedding anniversary; don't you dare try to pull this shit after today. FIX IT!" He ended the call.

"Everything okay?"

"I'm sorry, but I have to fill in tonight at the office. One of our workers dropped out unexpectedly." He walked over to me and kissed my cheek.

"That sucks. Good thing we will have tomorrow to ourselves," I tried my best to appear disappointed.

"I promise tomorrow will be beautiful. No distractions. No work. Just you and I." Jay grabbed his hat and jacket from the coat hanger along with his keys. "I'll see you in the morning," he said as he scurried out of the front door.

As soon as I heard Jay's truck screech out of the driveway I jumped out of my seat and ran to the front door to secure and engage both locks. I eagerly skipped up the stairs, leaving the kitchen and dining room with unwashed dishes and partially filled wine glasses. I convinced myself that I would get to them after checking on Courtney and talking to Angelo. I carefully pushed Court's bedroom door open and popped my head in.

"Courtney," I whispered. She was silent. I tiptoed over to her bedside and pulled the blanket over her resting body. The light snores that whistled from her slightly opened mouth were soft and innocent, like music to my ears. I eased out of her room and made my way down the hallway and into my room. I slid my house shoes off right before flopping on top of the thick comforter that spread across my bed. I propped myself up in a cozy position with my back resting against the fluffy pillows. I immediately pulled out my phone to reply to Angelo's text message.

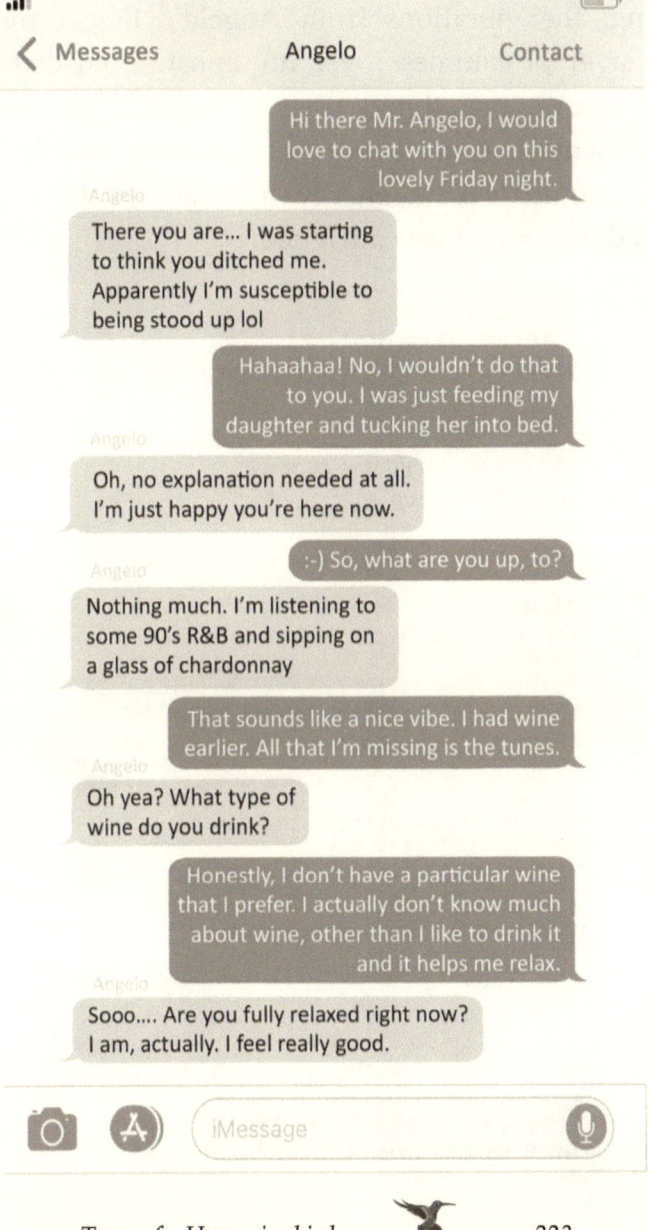

The wine that I gulped down during dinner had finally penetrated my bloodstream, causing a warm and sensitive sensation throughout my body. I felt open and inviting; the vibrations from Angelo's tone brought a thick layer of calmness over my spirit. I blushed as he asked about the things that I enjoyed doing, and complimented my taste in music. As we texted back and forth, I could feel his energy from across the city and yearned for more. I was intrigued.

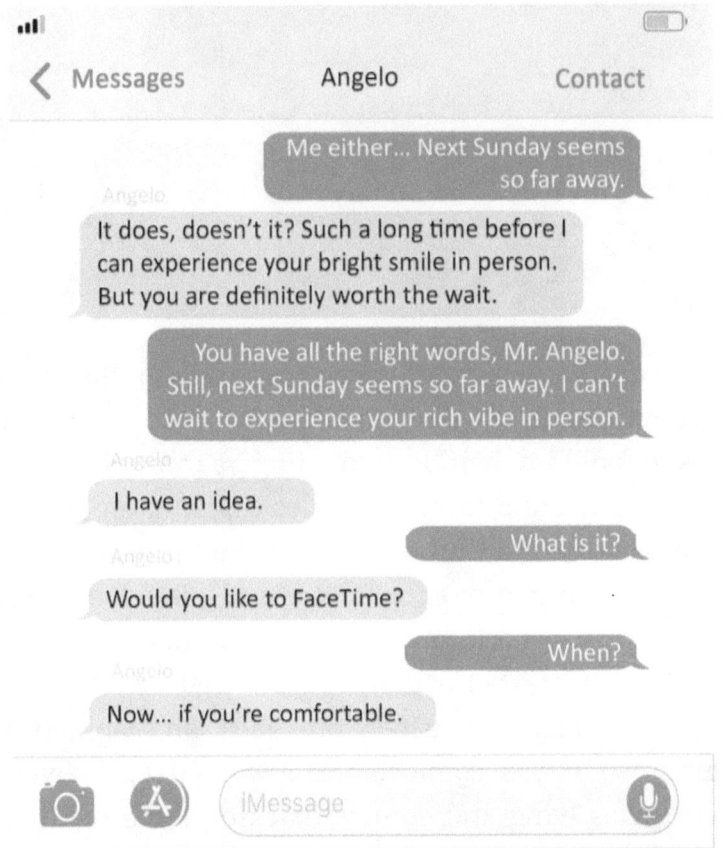

The thought of speaking with Angelo on FaceTime at that very moment triggered a burst of excitement inside of me. I was floating on cloud nine and refused to come down. For the first time in a very long time, I was making choices that made me happy and it felt good. In the back of my mind, I knew that going on a date with Angelo in public could have great consequences. But, for some odd reason, the emotional high I was coasting on would not allow me to care about the risks for too long.

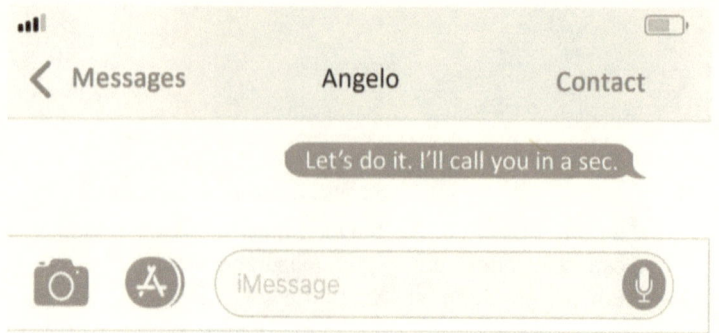

I jumped out of bed and ran over to the master bathroom, looked in the mirror, and used both of my hands to mold my hair. I ran my fingers through the roots to create shape and form while also utilizing my palms to flatten some of the flyaways. I dug the tip of my fingers into a jar of organic cocoa butter and glided the cream across my face, neck, and arms. The butter moisturized my skin and created a golden glow that beamed along with my smile. I adjusted my shirt and shifted my leggings so I was comfortable. I walked back over to where I was lying and climbed back onto the soft bed. I grabbed my cell phone and took a deep breath. *This is really happening,* I thought to myself as I began to dial Angelo's number on FaceTime.

"Well hello there, beautiful," Angelo smiled at me through my cellphone screen. He looked even better in real time. His lips were plumped, and his skin was flawless. I could tell that Angelo was also propped up on pillows in his bed. A fresh white t-shirt hugged his broad shoulders. I watched him in awe as his gorgeous brown hands gripped a glass of wine that he placed to his lips periodically.

"Hi there, handsome," I replied back.

Angelo chuckled and blushed to himself for a moment. We examined and looked at one another without words before he finally said. "Man, you seem so perfect. What's the catch?" We both giggled.

"I was thinking the same about you. You're crazy or something?" I teased.

"Naw, not at all. But I guess you can describe me as a hopeless romantic. I guess that's the catch."

"I think it could be much worse," I assured him.

"Well, what about you?" he asked through a friendly smirk.

"Ummm," I thought out loud before responding. "I believe I still have some childhood trauma that I'm still working through. It may be the cause of some of the demons that I am fighting as an adult."

Angelo was both empathetic and curious. "I understand how difficult it can be to navigate childhood trauma. You know there are resources in the community available for you. Have you thought about seeking professional guidance?"

I thought about my one-time session with Ms. Rita-Fray. "Yes, I have tried it once."

"How was it?"

"Frightening."

Angelo nodded his head in agreement. "True. It can be scary at first."

"Very. I think sitting in a room with a stranger and revealing your deepest, darkest secrets, memories, and emotions can be intimidating. But if I'm being honest, it helped me to realize that many of the suppressed feelings and resentment from my early years are weighing me down. Though it was uncomfortable, it was necessary. I think I would like to go back to learn how to let go of the things that are weighing on me and causing me pain."

"I'm glad that you see the benefit of therapy and counseling. The best part is, you can take your time and go at your own pace," Angelo encouraged me with his soothing voice.

I sighed through a relaxed smile on my face as I took in his words.

"Also," he continued, "You know, there are activities you can do on your own to relieve frustration and stress as you transition and until you are ready to take on professional guidance full time."

"What type of activities?"

"For me, I get very anxious when I'm stressed. So, I exercise with weights for about a half an hour to alleviate some of the tension."

"Okay, I see."

"And after my workout, I feel so much better and relaxed. It's a miracle," his eyes widened as he expressed his passion for self-care. "You may choose a different activity. Maybe it's drawing, cooking, or cuddling with your daughter. It could be taking a safe drive around the city, reading a book, or..." Angelo stopped before finishing his thoughts.

"Or, what?" I asked.

"Or physical and intimate pleasure."

"Physical and intimate pleasure?"

"Yes. Like sex; anything that can safely bring you to a powerful orgasm, which is a great way to release stress."

"Really?" I was mildly embarrassed. "Well that explains why I have been stressed out lately," I mumbled under my breath.

"Is that so?" he asked.

I looked away and chuckled, surprised that the conversation was going in this direction so soon.

Angelo took my silence as an answer. "You know that's not healthy, right?"

"What's not healthy?"

"Being sexually frustrated."

"I looked into my phone with a little harmless sass in my tone. "Well sir, not all of us have the luxury of experiencing hot, steamy, satisfying sex whenever we are ready and wanting it."

Angelo twisted his face up at me. "But why not?"

"For starters, it's not easy finding a partner that you are sexually compatible with."

"See, that's your first mistake. Why wait for someone else to sexually satisfy you, when you can sexually satisfy yourself? You can have hot steamy sex with yourself."

"You mean, like masturbation?"

"Exactly."

I was shocked. "Well I haven't done that since my late teenage years."

"Well, that explains why you have been stressed for so long," he mocked me.

We both laughed.

"But, seriously," Angelo continued, "You gotta take care of yourself," he licked his soft lips, causing a sudden tingle in between my thighs. Angelo and I shared another moment of staring at each other without words. I could feel his eyes checking me out through the FaceTime call as much as the tiny screen would allow. I observed his rich skin and luscious lips, and imagined what the rest of his body looked like. I wondered if his abs were hard and if his arms were strong like his shoulders appeared to be. I wondered if his manhood took up most of the space in his fresh, gray jogging pants. The more I fantasized about

Angelo, the more sensitive the pearl in my underwear became. I used one of my decorative pillows to rest my phone so I could free my hands. I placed the cell phone and pillow next to me and at an angle where Angelo could see my entire upper body and face.

"You know, I can assist you," he said.

"With what?"

"Re-discovering self-pleasure," he smiled at me.

Rivers instantly started to form and flow from in between my hips and slowly landed in the bed of my panties. "And how are you going to do that?"

"Well, I can walk you through a guided session."

I gazed deep into his eyes and fixated on the warmth that stared back at me. I felt secure and safe. "What do I have to do?"

"Just close your eyes and listen to my voice. Follow my lead."

"Okay," the words left me in a seductive whisper.

"Let me guide you. But stop me if it ever starts to *not* feel right," Angelo made sure the last part of his instructions were clear. I nodded and closed my eyes, resting my head on the pillows behind me.

He began. "Relax as much as possible. Let your body become one with the bed. Take a few deep breaths and try to let go of any tension that you may be holding in your shoulders, your back, your arms, your hands, your hips, and anywhere else. Just let it all go."

I took a moment to inhale and exhale, even though I already felt relaxed and comfortable.

"Now, take your hands and use them to explore your body."

I slowly glided my fingers up my thighs, stopping at my hips. I gripped the meaty flesh on my hips before continuing up to my stomach. I used my fingertips to lightly brush across my stomach, causing a tickling and calming sensation. Not long after, I moved my hands up to my B-cup size breasts. I held my right breast in my hand as I used my other hand to massage the left one. My nipples were firm and tender underneath my shirt and bralette.

"How are you feeling?" Angelo's voice ignited my ecstasy.

"I feel good," I whispered.

"I'm glad that you are enjoying yourself...literally," he chuckled lightly. "Now, when you are ready, remove any article of clothing from your body. The choice is yours."

I immediately began to slip my shirt up and above my head, quickly tossing it to the floor beside the bed. I reached behind my back to unfasten the lace bra to free my breasts. I exhaled as they fell graciously into their natural state, and slowly inched my way out of my skintight leggings and black lace bikini cut underwear.

The moisture from my womanhood had completely soaked both items of clothing, leaving them sticky and no longer welcome on my body. Before I knew it, I was completely naked. I quickly flipped the bed cover back so that I was now lying on the fresh blue bed sheets. I felt Angelo's warm eyes resting on my petite physique.

"You are gorgeous; every part of you."

I remained silent as I took in his compliment, eager for the next steps.

"You ready?" he asked.

"Yes," I bit down on my bottom lip.

"Okay, now slowly lick and slurp on your middle and index finger."

I giggled without judgement on the inside, as Angelo revealed his lustful side. It was rich and raw and everything I needed to fuel the sexual fire that I had burning inside of me. I inserted my fingers into my mouth, completely saturating them both with my thick saliva.

"When you're ready, take your wet fingers and place them anywhere on your body that will feel good. Think about parts of your body that you would want a partner to touch — to kiss. Think about your hotspots," he caressed me with his words.

I pressed my fingers against the left side of my neck, pretending that they were Angelo's lips. Soft whimpers of pleasure escaped me as I enjoyed my vibrant imagination while repeatedly dipping my fingers into my mouth and rubbing them against the sensitive spots on my neck. Next, I traced my fingers towards my belly button, running them down the middle of my breasts and eventually to my pulsing vagina. I outlined my thick, juicy vaginal lips with a light brisk of my fingertips. I carefully caressed the soft flesh, increasing the blood flow around my pearl. My body was screaming for stimulation and I was ready to answer its request. I placed my two fingers on my warm, moist clitoris—a shock of pure delight ran through my body with every stroke. I couldn't stop. My hips naturally rotated from side to side, up and down as I caressed the top part of my vagina in a firm, circular motion.

"How do you feel?" Angelo's voice turned me on even more.

"Oh, I feel so fucking good," I moaned.

"You should always feel this fucking good. You deserve it."

I continued to grind my clitoris hard against my fingers. *Mmmmm. Ahhhhhh. Yessss.* I sang out loud. The euphoria feeling became more intense and more pleasurable each time I stroked myself. *Ahhhhh.* The sensation took over me entirely. *Mmmmmmmm. Ahhhhh.* I moved my body in synchrony of the energy that flowed through me. *Mmmmmmmm. Mhmmmmmm. Ahhhhh.* Soon, I felt an unbearable wave of satisfaction and pleasure develop in my vagina and vibrate throughout my entire body. ***Ohhhhh yesssss! Mmmmm!*** The orgasm was strong and bold. ***Ahhhh, yessss!*** My juices squirted from in between my legs, onto my thighs, the bedding, and anything else that was within two feet of my throbbing vagina. I continued to caress myself until the climax had come to an end and the comforter underneath me was soaked.

"Well done. I'm proud of you."

I opened my eyes and looked into Angelo's smiling face, giving him an exhausted smile back. "My God. That was everything. I haven't had an orgasm in about two years."

"*Two years*?" He seemed to be both shocked and mortified.

"Unfortunately, yes. But don't you worry. You just reminded me that there is so much power in an orgasm. I feel like I just released a ton of bricks," I said as I carefully found my way underneath the cover on my bed without disturbing my cellphone, which was still propped up on one of my pillows.

"Yea, I guess sometimes you need people to come into your life and remind you of all the buried treasures in your own backyard. I mean, you could literally masturbate everyday if you wanted to. The best part is, it's safe and you don't need anyone outside of yourself to get it done," he winked at me.

"You're right about that. Even though, I am not sure I would have gotten through that without your professional lead," I laughed.

"Hey, maybe you're right. But you're a pro now. My work here is done," he joked.

"You were amazing," I closed my eyes and smiled as I pulled the cover up to the bottom of my chin. I was light as a feather as I floated on clouds of peace.

"You were amazing to watch," Angelo whispered. He took another sip of his wine right before shifting his body to a more comfortable position. He stretched out, lying on his stomach, and folding his arms underneath him. He looked into my heavy eyes, flashed his teeth, and gently winked his joyful eyes at me. He began humming a familiar R&B tune and eventually started to sing the words. *"The closer I get to you...the more you make me see...by giving me all you got...your love has captured me..."*

I quickly jumped in and proceeded to sing the next verse in a light, yet exaggerated tone. "Over and over again...I tried to tell myself that we could never be more than friends...and all the while inside I knew it was real...the way you make me feel..." I laughed after giving a short dramatic performance from my bedside.

"Look at you," Angelo seemed to be caught off guard. "I heard a couple of solid runs in those vocals you just blessed me with."

"I got a few tricks up my sleeve," I smirked at Angelo.

"What do you know about Donny Hathaway and Roberta Flack?"

"Uh! You mean Beyonce and Luther Vandross?" I asked sarcastically.

"Oh, so you're one of them types of people, huh?"

After a few moments of laughter, our giggles simmered down slowly, ending in a warm and peaceful state between the two of us. I watched as Angelo stared into my face once more. I tried hard to remain conscious so I could look into his eyes forever...or as long as I could. My eyelids became heavier as seconds went by. Angelo restarted his calm humming, singing more of the song lyrics. *"Lying here next to you...time just seems to fly... Needing you more and more...Let's give love a try..."* Each of the beautiful words hugged my eardrums one by one, sending me off into a soothing sleep.

CHAPTER 10

TEARS OF A HUMMINGBIRD

"Looking at you right now...in the state he left you, is like watching a hummingbird cry. Only a monster could hurt something so precious, harmless, genuine. Only someone evil enough could kill something so beautiful and hurt someone so worthy."

"Symone! I've been calling you all morning. Why the hell is your phone going straight to voicemail?" Jay's voice ripped through me. "And why are you still in bed? It's nine a.m., and you're usually up around this time." The early morning sun nearly blinded my sight as I tried to regain consciousness and make sense of what was going on. I partially sat up, lifting myself from underneath the covers and pillows I was buried in. I put my right arm over my eyes to block the sunlight so I could see Jay clearly and completely wake up my discombobulated brain. As I sat up, I remembered that I was nude underneath the covers, but it was too late. My naked boobs were already exposed in the broad daylight.

"What the *fuck*?" Jay was furious as he walked to the foot of our bed and quickly snatched the cover from the mattress and flung it across the room. "Why are you naked? Huh? You *never* sleep naked! What the hell is going on, Symone?" I hugged my arms around my breasts and pulled my knees to my chest to cover myself as much as possible. The guilt inside of me made it difficult to respond to Jay's question before he carried on his rant. "See! I *knew* you were up to no good! I should have followed my first mind and said something instead of giving your trifling ass the benefit of the doubt!" His gaze suddenly fell to the floor where my clothes, panties and bra laid out across random parts of the carpet. "Wait...did you have someone in our bed?"

"*No*! I would never!"

"Then explain yourself," Jay walked around to the side of the bed so he was closer to my shivery body. I looked up at him, once again, afraid to speak. Jay looked down at the royal blue bed sheets underneath my bottom. He cocked his head to the side with a disgusted expression on his face. I looked down to see what had caught his attention. My heart sank as I realized that Jay had observed the dried-up vaginal juices that leaked from my womanhood after my session with Angelo. As I continued to examine the sheets along with Jay, I noticed that my orgasm fluids had squirted across the entire bed. I could see that the small droplets of white stains traveled far ahead of me, leaving evidence of my DNA on the sheets. "YOU LYING BITCH!" The heat from Jay's rage sliced through my flesh. "You fucked another man in our bed, in our home, while our daughter was nearby in the other room?"

"Jay, no," I pleaded. "I would never bring someone in our home! This is not what it looks like. This is all from me. There was no one else here, I promise!"

"So *where* did these stains come from? It sure as hell didn't come from us! *What*? You made this mess all by yourself?" he scoffed. "I know your body better than you! You don't even know what to do with your body; I'm not fucking stupid!" He was outraged.

"Jay, I know my body well enough. There was no one else here," I reiterated, hoping that he would believe me.

"***Fuck you***! Who is he?" he yelled.

"*Who*?"

"The guy that you had sex with last night while I was out working late to make sure our family was good!"

"I told you, I *didn't* have sex with anyone."

"Tell me, is he the reason you never want to have sex with me?"

"Jay. There was no one else in our bed. Why is that so hard for you to believe?"

"Did you use protection? Do you love him?"

"What?"

"Did you put his dick in your mouth?"

"Jay, *stop it!*"

"Were you going to kiss me with that filthy ass mouth of yours?" he continued to pound me with degrading questions, completely dismissing my plea of innocence. As thoughts raced through my mind under the intense pressure of the moment, it was the first time I admitted to myself that things may have gotten a little too deep with Angelo. *Lynie was right.* I may have not made the best choices when it came to Angelo's friendship. I could have been more open and honest with myself, Angelo, and Jay. Although I knew that I wasn't *completely* innocent, I also knew I was not fully guilty of what Jay was accusing me of. My daughter's safety and wellbeing had always been my number one priority and I was not going to allow Jay to convince me otherwise.

"*Hello?*" Jay waved his hand at me to regain my attention. "Don't have anything to say for yourself? What? Did his penis damage your esophagus? Can't talk?" he taunted me.

"I *said*, I slept with no one. I was here by myself, Jay." Anger radiated inside of me as I became fed up with his insulting remarks.

"You know, I never knew I married a lying, cheating, *whore.*"

"That's enough. I will not allow you to keep talking to me like this!"

"Oh yeah? Well, what the fuck are you going to do about it?" he mentally challenged me with his bold words.

I'm going to leave you, is what I wanted to say but could not muster up the courage to do so. "You're not perfect," were the only words that left my lips.

"I **never** claimed to be! But at least I am upfront about my shit. You, on the other hand, are nothing but a sneaky and nasty slut. I never stepped out on you! How could you? I've loved you with my whole heart," his voice cracked in between his screams.

"Well it doesn't *feel* like love," I was shocked at my own words, but the wave of fury within me would not let me stop. "I don't feel safe when I'm with you! I feel fear, uncertainty, and regret. I feel resentment...*I resent you*! How could you love me and hurt me in the same breath?" My heart beat through my chest viciously as I stared up into Jay's wide eyes.

"We all have shortcomings, Symone! And don't you dare try to flip this around on me. You always throw this up in my face when you know I have been working on stabilizing my mental health so the physical fights between us don't happen agai—"

"Not every shortcoming deserves mercy or a second chance, Jay," I interrupted. I knew he was quick to lead me to a pity party when it came to the topic of abuse, and I was not in the dancing mood.

"You ungrateful bitch! After all I have done for you, and you don't think I deserve patience? You *resent* me? Are you fucking kidding me?" he punched through the air, putting emphasis on every other word. "I work my ass off, night and day, to build a life for our family. I pulled your ass from the gutter; you would have **none** of this without me. Had I not taken you in, you'd be back living in the ghettos of Cleveland. You have no career, no sustainability, no credibility. Nothing at all! You think that part-time job at the law firm is something? Huh? That's just to keep you busy...that job ain't shit! You couldn't take care of yourself with what they're paying you down there. You're like a hamster on its wheel: not going anywhere."

"I'm capable! I'm smarter than you think, I'm stronger than you think, and I can pull myself from the mud. I don't **NEED** you, Jay! And I *will* show you better than I can tell you."

"And what the hell is that supposed to mean?" he asked through his closed teeth.

I took a deep breath to prepare myself for what was next. I looked him straight in the eye. "I want out of this marriage." The words slithered out of my throat and left me numb. I waited for Jay's response, but he was silent. I could hear his breaths becoming increasingly more rapid. It was as though I could hear his blood boiling through his flesh and then eventually overflowing and oozing out of his pores. Once he reached the point where he was no longer able to hold in the inflaming emotions that had brewed inside of him, he transferred most of its toxic energy to his dominant right hand and projected it on to me by striking me across the face with his wide, open hand. The force sent me flying across the bed and onto the floor. Shortly after landing on the carpet beside the bed, I heard Jay's heavy footsteps walking over to where I was. I tried to look in the direction of where he was coming so I could block my face with my arm, but my vision was still blurry from the slap that violated me seconds before.

"Please, don't do this," I cried out with my hands up above my head, hoping to block any other potential hits.

Jay's strong hands managed to slip passed my weak shield and landed firmly around my neck. He kneeled down on the floor with my naked body in between his legs. "You think you're going to leave me that easy, huh? And you got to be out of your rabid-ass mind if you think you're gonna take my little girl with you." He squeezed tighter. "You want to leave me? How about I give you what you want right now?" I tried my best to gasp for air, but his grip around my neck was way too tight. I used both of my hands to pry him off of me, but he seemed unphased by my weak punches. His hands overlapped one another as they continued to crush my throat. "I could end you right now and no one would question it. It'd be easily written off as another depressed woman who committed suicide, just like her mother. Way to keep the legacy alive, right? The hidden razors around the house...the cut marks on your wrists would be enough evidence alone to support a self-inflicted death." Tears streamed from the corner of my eyes, down my cheek, and landed on Jay's sweaty hands, which were still locked around my neck. "And there will be no one there to speak up for you. You think your bum-ass brother would have the common sense and courage to fight for you? Huh? Oh! You think Lynie would step in for you? Tell me, who is going to listen to that illiterate, ghetto, trash-ass bitch?" He pulled me in closer to his face by yanking his hands and my upper body so my nose was touching the tip of his. "You're done, Symone. You hear me? **DONE!**" My throat sat in Jay's fists as he squeezed them tighter and tighter. "Happy anniversary, *bitch!*"

I strained my throat, fighting for a brief opening so I could steal a quick breath, but I failed. My hits and punches became weaker and weaker. My cries became fainter as it became more apparent that *I wasn't going to make it out this time.*

My vision became blurry. My hearing started to fade and become distorted. I watched Jay grind his teeth together with all of his might as he proceeded to cut off my air pathways...*completely.* My body became hot. Then, cold. I was numbed. My eyesight was flooded by a bright light that overpowered me entirely. *This **is** it.* I felt my spirit end the resistance against Jay's force.

I thought about my life up until that point, and instantly wished I had smiled more, laughed more, and *just* enjoyed life more. I wished that I were more courageous and stood up for myself. *I wished I had not allowed myself to suffer for so long.* I wished I had set myself free long ago, so I could peacefully enjoy the glories of life.

I thought about Angelo and his beautiful smile, and the glee he had brought to me in such a short period of time. I thought about Courtney and her angelic face. *What will she think of me after I'm gone?* I wondered if she would live a life of resentment towards me, like I did when my mom passed on. *How would she cope?* I prayed that she would find healthy ways to grieve my death...I prayed that the cycle would not repeat itself, again. I broke on the inside as I wondered if she could ever forgive me for leaving her. For giving up.

NOOO! I can't leave her; I'm not ready! I screamed on the inside , hoping the higher power could hear me. *I'm not ready! Please! I have unfinished business with my daughter — she **needs** me,* I whelped to myself. Almost instantly, the bright light disappeared, and I was once again face-to-face with Jay, who was in the same position with his fingers still tight around my neck. I managed to gain some strength in my right leg. I bent my knee so it was firmly below Jay's groin area and used every bit of energy I had to force my knee up and deep into his testicles.

"*Ahhhhh*! You fucking bitch!" Jay released me from his grip so he could cradle his private area with both hands. He leaned against the wall as he cried out in pain.

I rolled over to my side, gasping for air uncontrollably. I took in deep breaths to nourish my body and replenish all of the oxygen I had lost in the last couple of moments.

Jay's footsteps limped and crept over to where I was curled up on the floor, still desperately inhaling air into my crushed lungs. Once he was close enough, Jay raised his heavy foot from about ten inches off the ground and rammed it into the side of my face. I felt the tip of his shoe crack through some of the delicate bones in my chin and jawline. I moaned and cried out for relief of the misery that Jay had cursed me with.

"You're *worthless*! You will be nothing without me," he yelled at me as he quickly made his way out the bedroom door, still securing himself with his hands. I could faintly hear his footsteps jog down the stairs, followed by a slam of the front door. Seconds later, I heard his truck race out of the driveway and into the far distance.

My heavy breathing continued as I grabbed on to the bed and pulled myself up off the floor and onto my knees. I knew I needed to leave before Jay returned. I rambled my hands through the twisted sheets and pillows on the bed, looking for my cell phone. After seconds of feeling around for my device and being unsuccessful, I became frustrated as I raced against time. *Ahhhhhh*! Finally, I was able to fully stand up. Once I was up on my two feet and completely off the ground, I grabbed the knotted sheet and shook it out with three large ripples that ran viciously through the blue fabric.

Thump!

My phone flew from the bed, through the air and landed on the floor near the bedroom door. I ran over and picked up the phone immediately. My fingers trembled uncontrollably, making it difficult to input the code to open my lock screen. I paced back and forth, cursing the air, and stomping the floor at the same time. I was growing more and more impatient with my slippery fingers. **UGH!** After a few failed attempts, I was finally able to remember and enter the correct code. I went straight to my most recent call history and clicked to dial Angelo's number via the FaceTime app.

"Well, well there. Good morning, sleeping Beau—" Angelo's wide smile melted away as he stared at me through the tiny screen. It was the first time I had seen my own reflection since the altercation that transpired between Jay and I. I looked into the small box on my phone to see what Angelo was seeing. My left eye was nearly swollen shut and the skin on my bottom lip was cracked. A thick line of blood trailed from my lip to the bottom of my chin and down my frail neck. The skin on my face was moist and red from a combination of sweat, smeared tears, and stressful tension. I lifted my chin slightly for a better view of the dark ring around my throat. The mark was bold and told most of my story before I had a chance too.

"*SYMONE!* Who did this to you?" Angelo yelled out.

I sobbed loudly at the site of myself.

"It's going to be okay, dear. We just have to get you to safety. Where are you?"

I tried to answer. But my cries continued without my permission.

"I'm so sorry that this has happened to you, but I need your attention, Symone, please. I need to know what happened and where you are, so that I can help and get you to safety as soon as possible."

"I uh…I um…Angelo, I…" I wrestled with myself to get the words out. I knew I had to be completely honest with Angelo before I could tell him what happened.

"It's okay, take it easy. Take a deep breath," he slowly inhaled and exhaled to demonstrate what he wanted me to do.

Woosah. I closed my eyes and breathed in as much as I could before completely letting go. "I'm married."

Angelo stopped in the tracks of his thoughts. He cocked his head slightly sideways. "*Married*? But you told me that you were—"

"I lied, Angelo. I'm so sorry. I just didn't want to jeopardize something that started to feel so special. I felt a bond that started to quickly develop between the two of us and it felt good; I wanted to protect it by any means necessary. I haven't felt this way in a *very* long time.

Angelo, I didn't mean to hurt you. I just knew that if I told you the entire truth right away, you would run away...and I couldn't stand the thought of letting the one strand of hope that I had, slip right through my fingers. The risk was too great," I stared into Angelo's spirit, searching for a hint of forgiveness.

Angelo's eyes were glossy and his cheeks were full of air and emotions that he fought to keep to himself. I could see the disappointment in his face as he processed the load of words I just dropped on to him. I wanted so desperately to reach through the phone to hug and console him; I watched as he took a seat on what appeared to be the edge of his bed. He was silent for several moments before speaking.

"Did your husband do this to you?" his voice cracked with sorrow.

"Yes," I sobbed.

Angelo's head dropped deep in between his shoulders.

"I wanted to tell you. Every time that we talked, I wanted to tell you, but...I was so *afraid*. It never felt like the right time to speak up," I pleaded through my cries. "I promise I'm not a bad person, Angelo. I guess I just got lost in between two worlds of good and evil. Your positive presence made life more manageable in the hell that I was experiencing within my marriage. You deserve honesty from me. You deserve the truth," I took a deep breath. "And the truth is, I have been married to my husband, Jonathan, for seven years. Our wedding anniversary is today. We met in college and fell in love. I chose to leave my hometown for good to stay in Boston with my husband. We have a beautiful daughter together and she means the world to me," Angelo looked up at me with pitiful eyes as he listened.

"But the deeper reality is, being married to Jay has been a nightmare. I understand that I'm not perfect, but this man has put me through *pure hell* and it has broken me over and over again! There were times that I didn't think I could take any more of his abuse and I just wanted out. Out of this mental prison that he had me caged in. Out of this marriage and out of this life for good," I wiped tears from my face as I continued. "The night you called my phone by accident...you saved me. I had my mind made up; I was ready to end my misery, and you intervened. It was almost like you were at the right place, in the right situation at the right time. Like...I was meant to be here."

Angelo's eyes began to flood as he slowly lost the fight against his tears.

I proceeded. "And so, you asked what happened today? Jay's jealous tendencies led him to suspicion of my loyalty. He came in this morning in a roaring rage because I slept in later than usual and missed his wake-up call. When he found me naked and discovered stains on the sheets, he accused me of sleeping with another man in our bed." Angelo closed his eyes and softly shook his head for a second once he realized how the stains got on the sheet and how such a beautiful moment between us led to a disaster. I carried on with the story. "I tried to explain to him what actually happened and that there was, in fact, no other man in our home, but he was furious and unwilling to hear me out. Instead, he attacked me," I wept uncontrollably. "He tried to kill me!"

"My God, Symone," Angelo murmured through his frustrated and trembling lips. I felt his heart break for me, completely dismissing his own pain that bred from the event. Suddenly, the focus was no longer on the lie I had told him. He quickly shifted the conversation to my emotional needs and safety. "Listen to me. *You* don't deserve this. *You* deserve better. You hear me?" he was stern and passionate.

"Yes," I whimpered.

"I'm sorry that you had to suffer in silence for so long. You are beautiful inside and out and should be cherished. You are delicate and sweet; you should be protected, not harmed. I'm sorry that he did this to you. He has to be fucking insane to batter and bruise your face, your body, your spirit...he doesn't deserve you, Symone. Looking at you right now...in the state he left you...is like watching a hummingbird cry. Only a monster could hurt something so precious, harmless, genuine. Only someone evil enough could kill something so beautiful and hurt someone so worthy," Angelo planted every word deep inside of me.

I was overcome with emotion and beyond grateful for his kind words. *Worthy.* I repeated the word to myself. The word danced throughout my body. It was not often that someone referred to me as *worthy.* His appreciation for me, his acknowledgment of my very existence melted me. I realized that I was in fact, *worthy.* And I was ready to live in my *worth.* I was ready to leave the house, the marriage, and brutal lifestyle for good. I was finally strong enough—mentally and physically prepared to break free and strive for freedom. "Angelo, I have to get out of here before he gets back."

Angelo stood up from his bed, seeming to quickly switch gears and turn up his sense of urgency. "Symone, I have a plan. Listen carefully. I need you to pack a small bag for you and your daughter. Just grab some essential items like comfortable shoes and clothes, but just a few outfits. Grab just enough hygiene products to hold you two over for a few days, but don't spend too much time looking for soap and toothpaste. I will make sure you have a steady supply later." I could tell that Angelo was in work mode as he advised me on my plan to escape. It was as though he was working with a new client in a crisis situation at FADA. Only this time, it was personal. "It's important that you pack your contact information and proof of identification, like birth certificates, social security cards, driver's license, marriage certificates, and anything else that may help in identifying yourself, and Courtney as your biological daughter. Don't forget to bring any cash, debit cards, credit cards, and bank account information that you may have. Oh! And any medication or prescriptions since it may be a while before you get settled. I'm going to make sure we get you food, but if you have any basic snacks and water that you can pack for the both of you, then perfect."

"Okay," I nodded my head in agreement as I mentally prepared myself to flee the only life I knew for the past seven years.

"Hey," Angelo caught my mind wandering and racing as I mumbled and recited his instructions over again to myself with fear and anxiety making it difficult to maintain focus. *Grab clothes, shoes, toothpaste, identification, and money. Don't forget snacks. Grab clothes, shoes, toothpaste, identification, and money. Don't forget snacks.* "Symone! You're going to be FINE. I promise," he reassured me before moving on to the next phase of our plan. "Once you are out of the house, stop at the nearest gas station to fill up your gas tank. Immediately after, I need you to meet me at a public place so that I can prep you for filing the police report."

"Police report?" I was taken back a little.

"Yes, Symone. You *must* file a report to officially document the abuse, to hold your husband accountable for his actions, and more importantly, to protect you and your daughter. Who knows, by going to the police you may even save another life, another soul from suffering in the way that you have once suffered," Angelo bought the phone closer to his face so I was staring deep into his eyes. "Don't you worry. I will be there with you every step of the way. You do not have to walk through this alone."

"Thank you," I whispered through a soft, subtle whimper. Going to the authorities was going to be a huge step for me but, with Angelo by my side, I felt that I was capable.

"You are more than welcome, you are deserving." He paused, seeming to give me a moment to take in his words. "Now, go! Let's not waste too much more time. I have to make a few calls to find temporary housing for you all. Say we meet in thirty minutes? Do you know where the Green Day Cafe is?" he asked.

"Absolutely. My best friend and I meet there for lunch every so often." I instantly thought of Lynie and longed for her support.

"Perfect. Let's meet there no later than ten a.m., but call me if anything out of the ordinary happens before then. If he comes back to the house before you leave, contact authorities RIGHT AWAY."

"Okay, okay. Ten-thirty a.m. Green Day Cafe. Call authorities. Got it," I repeated back to Angelo.

"Most importantly...be safe,." Angelo's eyes locked into my gaze.

"I will," I promised Angelo as I began to end the call so I could begin the first phase of our plan.

"Symone, wait," he called out and stopped me right before I pressed the *end call* button.

"Yes?"

"I love you," he said softly, but sternly.

My heart initially shrunk in resistance to the warm words that Angelo offered. I came up with every excuse I could think of for why I could not accept his love. *How could he love me so soon? He doesn't love me; he just pity me. It's not love, it's lust.* I was afraid. Still, the fear and doubt could not rule out or overpower the strong emotions I shared with him. It was that very moment that my heart fully opened up to him. "I love you, too."

Angelo exhaled, as if he had been holding his breath, waiting for my response to his confession of intense affection for me. We exchanged one last solid smile before hanging up the phone.

◆

10:01 a.m. I looked around the room as I adjusted back to reality; I was still nude from the night before. The room was messy and indicated that a struggle had taken place moments earlier. I caught a glimpse of my reflection in the bedroom window and my battered face clearly proved that I was in danger. I had no clue if and when Jay would return home. However, based on previous patterns, I was sure he would stumble his way back in the house with a drunken apology and weak excuses for why he assaulted me.

I quickly turned to my dresser and yanked open my underwear drawer. I grabbed the first pair of panties and bra that I could find and put the mismatched fabrics onto my body. I ran to my bedroom closet, slung the door wide open, and shuffled through the clothing items dangling from the wooden hangers. I sought out a fashionable jumpsuit gifted to me by Lynie about a year ago—the two-piece set was light blue with deep pockets in the loose pants and a wide hood attached to the jacket. I never wore the fit because it was far from my preferred style of comfort, but at that moment in time, it was perfect for the unfortunate occasion. I snuggled my way into the jogging suit, zipping the hoody jacket all the way up to the bottom of my chin to hide the bright purple bra that was underneath.

I looked up towards the shelf in the closet where I kept my old traveling duffle bag, which was big enough for both of our belongings. The black bag was clearly out of reach. I jumped up in an attempt to grip the tip of the strap that connected to the bag that was visible, so I could utilize gravity to pull the bag down from the shelf. On the third jump, I was successful in grasping the tip of the bag. It fell down from the shelf and onto the top of my head, then to the floor. Along with the bag, I spotted a small shiny object that hit the closet's doorknob on its way down to the bedroom floor. *BING!* Curious, I moved closer to the piece of rectangular shaped metal that laid on the carpet to identify it. *My healing tool.* I stared down at the razor as I remembered the significant role it once played in my life. When Jay discovered my secret stash underneath the bathroom sink, I hid more razors in new places throughout the house, including my clothing closet. I picked up the razor to examine it closely. It was sharp—ready to cut through my flesh and pretend to alleviate the pain that I was feeling. When in actuality, it never relieved any of my hurt; it never freed me from any of my demons. Instead, this healing tool prolonged my journey to peace while causing more scars. It was fraud. I felt ashamed that, for so long, I had relied on a destructive tool for comfort. How could I be so naive?

"*Ahhhhhhhh!*" I screamed out loud as I threw the razor across the room—out of mind and out of sight.

10:07 a.m. I shuffled through the drawers and closets in my room, frantically packing my bag with the essentials that Angelo mentioned during our phone conversation. I grabbed loose clothes, socks, toothbrushes, soap, lotion, a head scarf, and a blanket. I made my way out of the room, down the stairs, and into the living room area where we kept all of our important documents. At the bottom of the TV stand was a manilla envelope with our legal identification and certificates inside. I kneeled down and began flipping through the ragged pages. *Bingo.* I felt accomplished once I located Court's birth certificate and social security card, along with my own documents. I carefully looked through the stack of papers one last time to be sure I did not overlook anything that I would need in the near future. I stopped as I came across Jay and I's marriage certificate. *The state of Massachusetts legally recognizes the union of Johnathan Michaels and Symone Baker.* Who knew that just seven years later, I'd be fighting for my life and to end that so-called union for good? It took everything within me to not rip the marriage certificate into a thousand pieces, only because it might be needed at a later and more crucial time. I stood up and shoved the documents into an isolated compartment on the side of the travel bag. I made a mental note that my bank cards and other financial information were already safe and tucked away in my purse.

I jogged to the kitchen and collected a host of fruit, crackers, and bottled water for Court and I. I realized that I had no idea for how long the process would take and the next time we would get the chance to sit for a hot, home-cooked meal. I rushed back to where my bag was and shoved the snacks into an empty area on the other side. I looked upstairs towards the bedrooms; it was time to get Courtney dressed and into the car.

I swiftly bounced up the stairs and walked into Courtney's bedroom. She was still sleeping, snuggled, and tangled up in between her thick blanket. I decided to open her dresser so I could retrieve a few clothing items for her as we embarked on our brand-new life. I used my forearm to hold the growing pile as I added more and more of Court's clothes to it. *Socks, underwear, jogging pants, t-shirts, pajamas, hoodies, sweaters, more underwear, a pair of jeans just in case it got too cold, a pair of shorts just in case it got too hot, more t-shirts just in cas —.*

"Mommy?" the sweet, innocent voice behind me stopped me in my tracks.

"Yes, baby?" I slightly turned toward Court as she sat up in bed with one arm high above her, fully engaged in a stretch and the other viciously rubbing her still half-sleepy eyes. Her heavy eyes and the dark room prevented her from seeing my bruised face fully.

"Why do you have *that* on?" she pointed to the vibrant blue jumpsuit that I was wearing. Court knew that it was out of the ordinary for me and was obviously confused.

"It was a gift, honey," I said as I continued to gather the last bit of Courtney's things.

"What are you doing, Mommy?" her curiosity made me nervous.

"Just packing up some of your clothes." I held the bunch of clothes tight in my arm as I used my loose hand to close the drawers back shut.

"Where are we going?"

"On a road trip," I wanted to pacify her for as long as I could.

"Are we going camping?" she got excited before I could even respond.

"Hmmm, something like that, sweetie. I'd say more like an adventure."

"Yay! Is Dad coming, too?" I was silent. I realized that I could no longer hide the truth from Courtney. Why hide pain that I was going to feel in the long run any way, hmm? You know, maybe if someone was honest with me, I would have learned to cope better and not be so emotionally fucked up. Michael's words from the evening at our mother's gravesite lingered in my head. I did not want Courtney to suffer the same way Michael had suffered for so many years. I wanted to end the generational curse once and for all.

I placed the pile of clothes on top of Court's dresser to free my hands, walked over to her window, and yanked the thick curtains open, letting in the beautiful natural light to expose my ugly scars. I took a deep breath before turning around towards my baby girl. Her small face became stale and pale.

"Mommy! Your face is bleeding! Mommy!" She was frightened.

"It's okay, baby. Mommy is going to be okay; *we* are going to be okay. You hear me?"

Courtney slowly began to vent out a high-pitched cry as she continued to glance over my puffy eye and split lip. I walked over towards her and sat on the bed to comfort her. I placed my arm around her tiny shoulders and pulled her in close to me.

"It looks worse than it feels...It doesn't hurt *that* bad. Besides, I'm superwoman, remember? *Dun-dunna-dun*," I reached my hand out in front of me to mock the feminine superhero character.

Court's cries continued. I squeezed her tighter to console her as she drenched my hoodie with tears. After several seconds, she finally unburied her face from my chest and looked into the one eye that wasn't swollen completely shut. "Who did this to you?" she asked.

I froze. I scraped my brain for the correct and gentle way to break my daughter's heart once again. I struggled to find the courage to mouth the words to her. How could I tell her that her father, her protector, her first love, was the monster that had brutalized me?

DING! My phone rang out loud from my pocket.

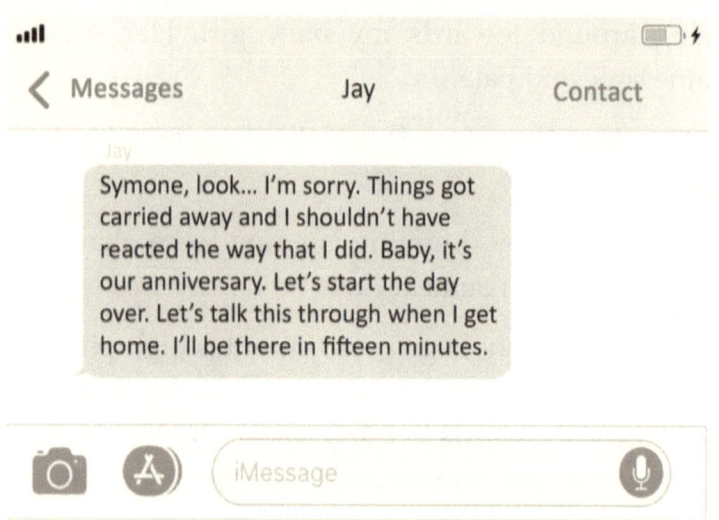

Messages   Jay   Contact

Jay

Symone, look... I'm sorry. Things got carried away and I shouldn't have reacted the way that I did. Baby, it's our anniversary. Let's start the day over. Let's talk this through when I get home. I'll be there in fifteen minutes.

iMessage

10:15 a.m. My body went cold and numb. I looked into Court's wandering eyes. "Come on, sweetie. We have to go, *NOW*." I jumped up from the bed and pulled Courtney up with me, swinging her on my hip.

"But Mommy, I still have my pajamas on," she called out.

I walked back over to the dresser and swooped up the pile of clothes with my free arm. "It's okay, honey. You'll change a little later."

My heart pounded at the beat of the clock as I raced against time. I hurried down the stairs towards the duffle bag that was now already overfilled. I sat Courtney down on the couch so I could use both hands to stuff her belongings into the bag. *Grrrrrr!* I struggled to keep all of the items inside of the bag as I zipped it closed inch by inch, little by little.

Finally! After eventually getting the travel bag closed, I grabbed Courtney's pink and white tennis shoes that were scattered on the floor nearby. "Here, sweetie." I stuffed her small feet into the shoes and double tied them tight. "Okay, come on baby, let's go. Come on, come on," I was breathless as I urged Court towards the front door. I snatched my keys from the key holder and my purse from the coat closet. Before opening the door, I squinted one eye to look out of the peephole, making sure the coast was clear. I knew that if Jay spotted us, he wouldn't let me leave...alive.

"Who are you looking for, Mommy?"

"Monsters."

Once I verified that the yard and driveway were empty, I slung my travel bag, purse, and all its heavy contents on to my shoulder, propped Courtney up on my hip, and sprinted out of the house with my car keys in hand. I ran across the yard towards my car as fast as I possibly could. The sun led the way as the birds chirped beautiful tunes and cheered me on. The cool wind guided me, providing me with an extra push as it carried some of the load, assisting me in making it safely to the black Audi that waited for us. I quickly strapped Courtney into the backseat and swiftly strolled to the trunk to dump our luggage inside. Shortly after, I hopped into the driver's seat, started the ignition, secured my seatbelt, and scurried out of the driveway. As I drove off, I watched in the rearview mirror as our home slowly became more and more distant. The further I drove, the smaller it became before eventually disappearing entirely.

10:18 a.m. I checked my fuel volume on the dashboard of my car and noticed that I had nearly a full tank of gas. *There's no need to stop for gas*, I thought to myself. I had just twelve minutes to make it to Green Day Cafe to meet Angelo and did not want to be late. As we cruised through the city, I looked around nervously, hoping that my car wouldn't be spotted by Jay as he made his way back home. My fingers tapped viciously on the steering wheel as we waited at a red light. I looked back at Courtney to access her mental state. She sat quietly, looking out the window, seeming to be curious about where our road trip would take us. I could tell that the wheels in her mind were spinning and I did not want to interrupt the start of her coping process.

I have to call Lynie. The last conversation between us ended with a heated disagreement regarding my fast-paced relationship with Angelo and how it could result in a violent response from Jay. *She was right.* She became agitated with my unwillingness to terminate the abusive marriage. I was frustrated that she would never let up and refused to join me in pretending that everything was okay. But now more than ever, I was glad she never gave up on me.

"Call Lynie," I called out to the vehicle's automatic voice response and Bluetooth system.

"*Now, calling Lynie,*" the system replied back.

The phone rang three times before she answered.

"So, I take it you're not mad anymore?" Lynie asked. Her voice was loud, vibrating through each and every one of my car speakers.

"Not at all...you were right," I confessed.

"Is everything okay?" I figured she detected a sense of sorrow in my voice. I looked up in my rearview mirror once more to check on my daughter. Her droopy eyes continued to gaze out the window as we passed through the Boston streets. I waited a few seconds before responding to Lynie, giving Court enough time to fall to sleep.

"I'm doing it," I whispered.

"Doing what?" Lynie was completely lost.

"Leaving," I tried compressing my emotions, but a few whimpers slipped out as I clarified to Lynie what was happening. "I'm leaving, Jay," I cried quietly to myself as I trembled with both fear and joy. "I'm *finally* doing it, Lynie."

"My God, Symone, did he hurt you? Where are you? Where are you going? Did you call the police?" she was mildly irate as she investigated the situation.

"Shhhhh," I shushed her as I peeped back at Courtney's sleeping face. The side of her head lightly rested against the car door and her mouth hung slightly open. She was peaceful, and I wanted to keep it that way for as long as I could.

"What's going on?" Lynie asked in a quiet yet concerning voice.

"Courtney and I are in the car headed to Green Day Cafe to meet Angelo…he's going to help me file a police report and get settled with housing."

"Whoa…back up. Look, I'm happy to hear that you are fleeing this marriage, but what brought you to this decision? Do you need my support? I'm not too far from the cafe myself. I can meet you up there in about five minut—"

"He tried to *kill* me, Lynie. You hear me? He tried to take me away from my baby girl. He beat me and nearly choked the life out of me," I covered my mouth and sobbed into my hand to muffle my emotions. "That is when I decided it was time to go."

"Symone, I'm so sorry," her voice crackled as she empathized with my hurt. "You deserve so much better and I am happy that you are still alive today, with another chance to seek out and live the life that you are worthy of. The both of you."

"Thank you for always being there for me, Lynie."

"I have always been there for you because I believe in you and because I love you. You're my sister. And you better believe that I'm going to be there for you during one of the most crucial times in your life. I am grabbing my shoes and keys, now. I will meet you at the cafe in five."

♦

10:28 a.m. I pulled into a parallel parking space directly in front of the cafe. There were only three other cars parked sporadically on the narrow street. I surveyed the vehicles, hoping to spot Angelo in one of the cars, but he was nowhere to be found. *Click, clack! Click, clack!* The sound of glasses of orange juice and oatmeal being served in white glass bowls traveled from the patio of my favorite cafe, intertwining beautifully with Courtney's soft snores that tiptoed from the backseat. I glanced over, wondering if Angelo was one of the individuals enjoying a late breakfast. I searched for his bright smile, smooth skin, and coily hair. However, all I found was an elderly couple sipping coffee, a mom feeding oatmeal to her toddler while cuddling her infant, a man in a suit reading the newspaper, and a young waitress bouncing back and forth between the tables to serve the hungry customers. *Where is he?* The longer I sat, the more anxious I became. I looked at my phone to see if I missed a call or text from Angelo. Nothing. I unlocked my phone so that I could call him and learn of his whereabouts. Just when I was getting ready to dial, I was interrupted by a massive voice that called out to me from across the street.

"Monie!" Lynie shouted towards me as she parked her white SUV on the opposite side of the street. *That was fast.* I thought to myself as I imagined Lynie speeding and running stop lights to get there. I watched as she hopped out of her automobile and hurdled across the concrete road and to the passenger side of my car. She immediately climbed into my car with a boost of energy, ready to get things done.

"My God, Symone," she placed both of her hands over her mouth to cover her outburst, but it was too late. Her eyes watered as she continued to inspect my swollen face. Slightly embarrassed, I looked down into my lap and then out of my car door window to escape her gaze. "That piece of shit! He's gonna pay for this," she cursed Jay under her breath.

"That's the plan," I said as a mysterious car crept up the street. *Angelo?* Through my side mirror, I could see a male driver, with glowing brown skin and roaming eyes.

Angelo! The car continued to creep and eventually got close enough for me to view the driver clearly. It wasn't him. The mom that I saw at the cafe just moments ago came hurrying from the patio with her arm around her toddler and a small baby on her hip. The woman led her children past my Audi and into the car of the handsome man that resembled Angelo.

"Symone? Snap out of it, honey. We have to get going!"

"We can't leave now; I'm still waiting for Angelo," I said as I continued looking around the perimeter.

"Well, where the *hell* is he?" Lynie was growing impatient.

DING!

"Here he is," I eagerly opened the text app to read the message. Only, I was wrong. It wasn't from Angelo.

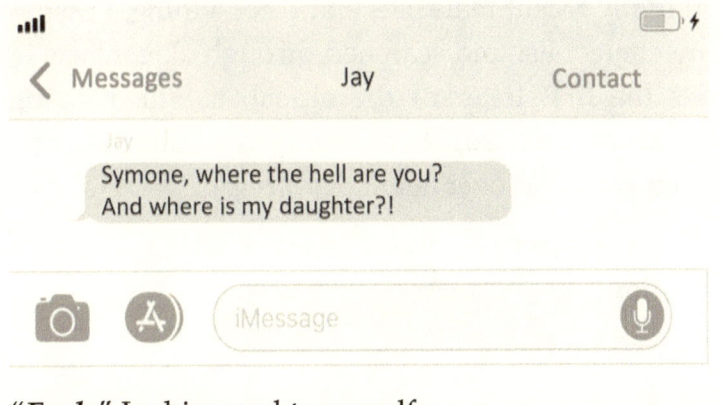

"*Fuck,*" I whispered to myself.

"What is it?"

"It's Jay…he's looking for me," I turned to Lynie, worried and startled by the text.

"That's it, we have to leave. **NOW.**"

"But what about Angelo?" I wept through my trembling lips.

"Symone, we don't have time to play hide and seek. This cafe will probably be one of the *first* places Jay looks to find you. We can't risk that."

"I need to at least try to call him before we just disappear, Lynie. After all, he constructed this *entire* plan to help me."

"Well, you need to hurry up because we don't have much time," she said as a matter of fact while looking around, making sure Jay's car was nowhere in sight.

I browsed through my call log to find Angelo's contact. *I just talked to him, where is it?* I was confused. I went to my recent messages and…not a thing. I then went to my contact list and searched through all contacts listed under the first letter of the alphabet. Still, no Angelo. Completely puzzled, I retraced my call history and contacts over and over again. **Nothing.**

"What's wrong?" Lynie responded to my twisted expression.

"I can't find him."

"What do you mean?"

"I can't find Angelo. He was just here. He was right *here*! He's not here anymore," I quivered out of uncertainty.

"*What*? That doesn't make any sense. Here, give me that," Lynie reached over and grabbed the phone out of my shaky hands. I watched her anxiously as she swiped through the phone, hoping she would find something that I may have overlooked. "How do you spell his name?"

"A-N-G-E-L-O."

"Did you save his name under a different contact name? Did you block his number by mistake? When was the last time you spoke to him on this device?

"No and no! I just spoke with him this morning, around 10 a.m. Do you see it?" I rushed her.

"Are you sure? Because I'm not seeing anything at all."

"*Yes, I'm sure*," I snapped. "We talked on FaceTime last night, we spoke this morning, and we literally text back and forth every day," I grew more irritable.

"Okay well just calm down, the messages between you two should still be there." Lynie opened the text messaging app to further investigate. Her large, bright eyeballs quickly raced side to side as she read through the pile of words on the screen. After a short while, I witnessed her spirit suddenly shrink and shrivel inside of her. Her body caved in and her shoulders drooped as she placed the phone face down in her lap. An epiphanic expression raided Lynie's face.

"What's wrong?" I was curious.

She was silent.

"*Lynie.* What happened?"

Her gaze dropped. She sighed deeply and looked up at me with pitiful eyes. "Symone... there's no Angelo."

"*What*? Where did he go? Did he text back? What did he say?" I reached over and attempted to grab the phone, but she quickly pulled it out of my reach. "Lynie, what the hell?"

She turned towards me and looked deep into my soul. "Honey, he doesn't exist."

"What the hell are you talking about? You are *crazy*!" This time, I snatched my phone from her lap.

"Look at the texts," she stated as I began to dig into my phone. "All of the messages that you thought you were sending to this Angelo character you were sending to yourself. You were texting yourself, Monie."

I trembled in anger. "That doesn't make sense! You're fucking delusional! He is no character: he is **REAL**! I felt him, I heard him, I saw him. Dammit, he is real!" I looked down at my phone to review the old text messages that Lynie was referring to.

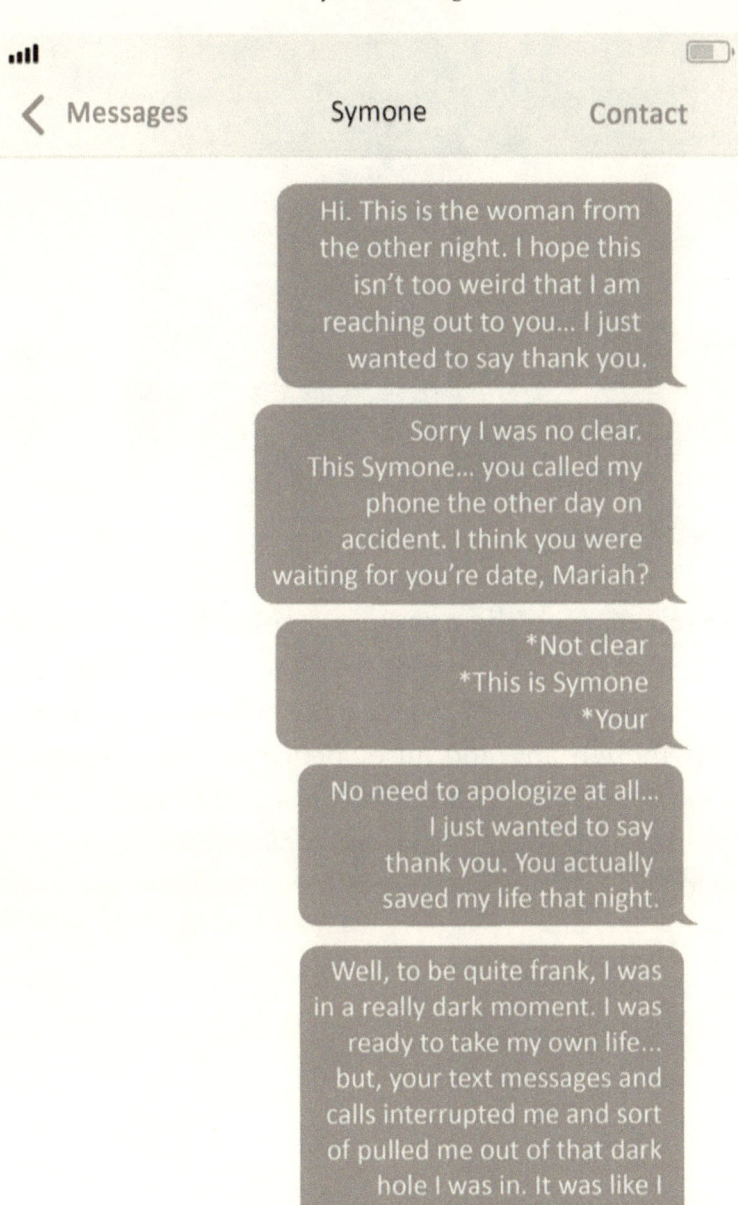

.ıll

< Messages   **Symone**   Contact

> Hi. This is the woman from the other night. I hope this isn't too weird that I am reaching out to you... I just wanted to say thank you.

> Sorry I was no clear. This Symone... you called my phone the other day on accident. I think you were waiting for you're date, Mariah?

> *Not clear
> *This is Symone
> *Your

> No need to apologize at all... I just wanted to say thank you. You actually saved my life that night.

> Well, to be quite frank, I was in a really dark moment. I was ready to take my own life... but, your text messages and calls interrupted me and sort of pulled me out of that dark hole I was in. It was like I snapped back into reality...

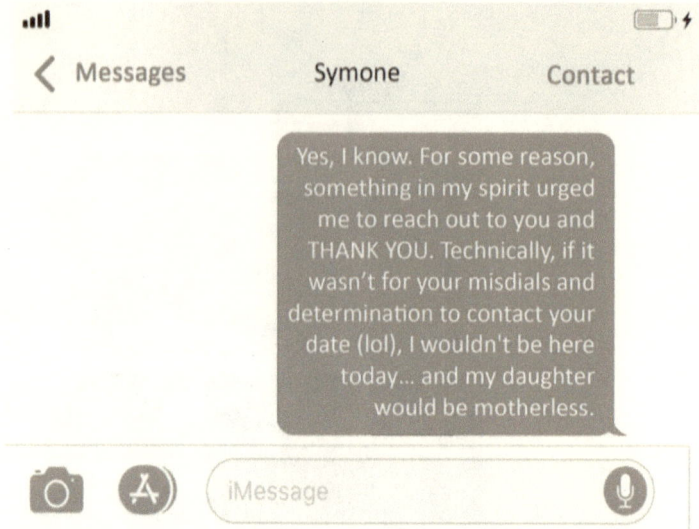

I read through the messages, baffled by the complete absence of Angelo's responses. They were gone. *How could that be? There had to be a glitch with the technology!* It was as though any and all evidence of him had simply vanished and disappeared into thin air. I continued to swipe through old messages, looking for a trace of Angelo.

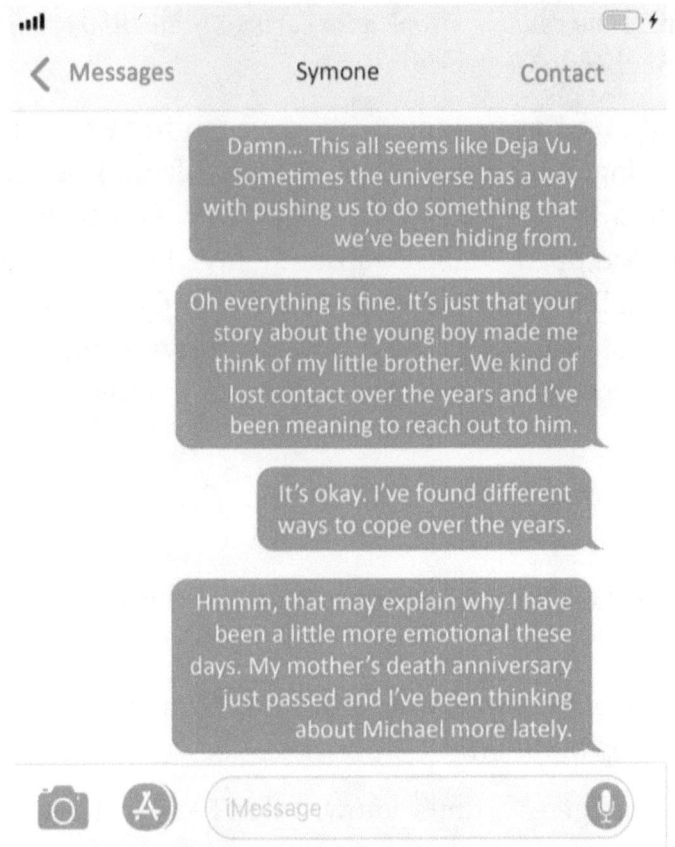

I wept to myself as I began to place the pieces together. My fingers frantically swiped through call logs, FaceTime history, and texts as I desperately searched for proof that Angelo *did* exist. Still, I came up with nothing. *Could I have fabricated his entire being? But **how**?* I thought about all of the things he helped me with since he came into my life. He intervened during my suicide attempt and was the reason I gained the courage to reach out and reconnect with my brother. Angelo reminded me that I could achieve true happiness and instilled hope into my future. *How could someone with such an influential spirit be so far from reality?*

I allowed my phone to slip and fall from my fingers, not caring at all about where it would land. I buried my face into the steering wheel of my car with both of my arms wrapped tightly around my head. I sobbed uncontrollably, unable to make sense of the twisted truth I had just discovered. I felt a warm, heavy hand begin to rub my back in a circular motion as I drowned in my tears.

"It's going to be okay. I promise," Lynie's voice was stern and sincere.

"But he said I wouldn't have to do this alone." I was heartbroken.

"And you won't! I'm right here, Symone. I'll be here every step of the way."

I shrugged. "I don't know. I don't know if I have the strength to go on," I said to Lynie in between my depressive whimpers. "I can't do this."

"You *can* and you *will*. You have come so far Symone, you can't give up now. There's a young soul looking up to you — learning from you," she nodded towards Courtney, who was still snoozing in the backseat. "And guess what? She's gonna witness how *powerful* you are. You are stronger than you think!"

Her words fueled me. I lifted my head up from the wheel to wipe and dry my face with the sleeve of my hoodie. I looked at Lynie and she looked back at me with compassion and determination. "Thank you," I uttered to her.

"That's what friends are for," she smiled slightly.

"So cliché," a few giggles managed to escape my lips.

Lynie laughed, mostly surprised at my abrupt humor during the crisis. I looked out of my window and at the people that began to crowd the cafe. I watched as they parked their cars, walked towards the restaurant, and carried on with their ordinary lives. I envied their sense of normalcy.

"Symone?" Lynie gently interrupted my wandering thoughts. "We have to go." I still couldn't fathom the fact that I was leaving without Angelo, but I knew she was right. I nodded towards Lynie in agreement. I reached my hand around and slid the key into the ignition to start the car. My foot rested on the gas pedal; I pushed down slowly as I steered out of the parking space and onto the road.

I drove forward. Quiet and focused on my destination, I drove forward. With great purpose and without looking back, I drove forward. I pressed harder on the gas; I could see my future in front of me. I drove forward, leaving behind pain and regret. I drove forward towards healing, peace, health, and happiness. I drove forward.

CHAPTER 11

TEARS OF AN UNKNOWN FREEDOM

"I slowly exhaled out all of my old fears...Woosah."

8 Weeks Later

"Hopeful." There I was, again. Back on the huge red couch. Sitting under the tall glass windows and across from the beautiful brown sugar skinned woman who knew just how to challenge my emotions and support my thoughts with a healthy balance. She exhibited the perfect dose of compassion and strength. Her long, shiny legs extended from her red pencil skirt and crossed over each other as she leaned in forward, fully engaged in my response to her daily "How are you feeling?" question. She smiled, seeming to be both proud and surprised that I decided to return and complete yet another session with her. She understood how difficult it was for me to walk into her office each day, to answer hard questions, to relive trauma, to dig into old wounds, and to express how they were affecting the new life that I started to build for myself and my daughter. "Today I feel hopeful. Yes, I still feel devastated, hurt, sad. Some days I feel numb and empty. But today feels different. I woke up for the first time feeling hopeful more than anything else."

"*Hopeful*, wow!" Ms. Rita Fray beamed with enthusiasm. For the past two months, our therapy appointments had been mostly dark and gloomy...but that day, there was a hint of sunshine that mirrored the sunlight that blasted through the office windows and glazed our melanated skin. We were shining. The beautiful light was bold enough to wake up my spirit and it felt *good*. "This sounds like progress." She seemed to be hopeful as well.

Ms. Rita Fray pulled out her large notepad from her lap, licked the tip of her finger, and began to flip through the pages of notes from past sessions. *Here we go.* I knew that once she opened the notepad, it was time to get down to the nitty gritty of our appointment. That was when the hard work started. Though that part was highly uncomfortable for me, I knew it was a necessary part of my healing journey. I braced myself as I watched her long, white polished fingernails flicker through the pages, eventually landing on a blank, fresh sheet for new notes.

"Okay, so since you are feeling *hopeful* today, I want to do things a little different. Rather than asking specific questions, I am going to simply give you a topic, a word, and I want you to express whatever comes to mind when you hear it. You can sort of just explain what you're feeling, any progress in that particular area, concerns, updates, fears—anything that comes to your heart in relation to the topic. I want to allow you to steer our conversations for today, and I am going to assess your mood while you're doing it. How does that sound?" she asked politely.

"I think I can do that," I felt ready to tackle the new exercise.

"Perfect," she slid on her reading glasses, popped the top off of her gold pen, and began rapidly jotting and scribbling on the paper in front of her. I stretched my neck a bit, hoping to catch a peek of what she was writing down.

"Family," she looked up at me. "Tell me, what comes to you when you hear the word *family*?"

I took a moment to access my immediate reaction to her question before responding. "Well, when I think about family…I feel a sense of loss. Family as I knew it, no longer exists and it will *never* be the same."

"Uh-huh," the woman listened actively as she scrambled my thoughts onto her notepad.

"But that's not necessarily a bad thing because, family as I knew it was painful…and broken. I try to focus on the positive and remember that in order to heal, there must be adjustments and changes."

"Good, good," she rooted for me behind a slight smile.

"Adjustments and changes can bring peace and happiness if you allow it to." After leaving our home, Lynie lent us her guest room until I was able to save up enough money to pay the security deposit and first month's rent for an apartment in a nearby neighborhood. I was grateful that my supervisors at the law firm were understanding and cared for me more than I ever knew. I was given two weeks paid leave, just enough time to settle and heal my physical wounds. Once I returned to the office, I was greeted with balloons, streamers, and a huge banner draped across the front of my desk that read: HAPPY PROMOTION! I was surprised to find both Mr. Bricks and Mr. Butler standing there wearing silly party hats as they blew aggressively into the loud horns to celebrate my new milestone. I felt fulfilled. It felt like true authentic love from family. "With the extra money from my raise, I was able to secure a small cozy, three-bedroom apartment just south of Cambridge," I thought out loud.

"Three bedrooms? Why three?"

"Michael," I gleamed as I thought about how far my brother and I had come in repairing our bond. "He decided to move up to the city to begin college courses at BSU and to be closer to Court and I. In order to save money on room and board, he's going to stay with me instead of living on campus."

"*Wow*, that's awesome."

"Yea, it's like I was given a second chance to rebuild my family. Only this time, I'm stronger, wiser, and know exactly what I need to foster a healthy support system," I smiled to myself as I thought about the opportunity of a clean slate.

"Sometimes it takes a village," Ms. Rita Fray cocked her head and pointed her frail finger at me. "And it sounds like your village is coming together slowly but surely. I am happy to hear that." She looked down at her notepad. "Okay, the next word is *friendship*."

"Lynie," I took a deep breath. "She is the *true* definition of friendship. I know that I come with such heavy baggage and still, she did not let that deter her from remaining in my life. She has been with me every single step of the way," I paused for a moment to stop the volcano of raw emotions from erupting from my eyes. "She never, *ever* gave up on me and I will always love her for that. She has always been stern, genuine, and consistent. Without her..." my voice cracked as the volcano of emotions began to explode and release tears of joy. I reached over for a tissue from the coffee table before continuing. "Without her and her strength...I don't think I would have made it this far."

"Sounds like a sisterhood," Ms. Rita Fray grinned.

"She is definitely family and deserves the same type of support she has given me. I am grateful I am now in a space where I am able to show up for her...in a similar way that she has for me."

"Powerful. I am rooting for this bond and its continued growth," she flashed her pearly whites at me right before putting her undivided attention back on her writing pad. "Okay, I love what you have given me so far. But now, I want to dig a little deeper. These next two words may be challenging, but I want you to try your best. Your best is all that I need."

I nodded my head in agreement.

"Perfect. Let me know when you are ready."

I slowly exhaled out all of my old fears. *Woosah.* "Ready."

"*Jonathan,*" she stated his name boldly.

His name pierced through my ears. "I, um. I...uh," I stumbled to gather and verbalize my thoughts.

"It's okay. Take your time."

It had been two months since I'd heard from Jay. The last time I saw him, he had death in his eyes with his hands around my throat, crushing my chances for survival. It was a miracle I was able to fight my way out of that *horrific* situation. Shortly after arriving at the Boston Police Department to report my abuse, Jay was arrested in our home. I was granted a temporary protection order for me and my daughter. Knowing that he was in custody made me feel...

"Free," I professed my feelings out loud to my therapist. "When I think of Jay, I am grateful that I am alive and free from his shackles of pain and suffering."

"*Hmmm,*" she groaned out as she empathized with me.

"Yes, it gets difficult at times, no doubt. Courtney asks about him at least once a day. The painful discussion of why she can't see or talk to her dad *never* gets easy. However, it is my hope that one day she will understand why we had to leave our old life behind. I cringe when I think about how this may affect her now, and in her adult life, just as my mother's mistakes affected me." I looked down to hide my pitiful eyes.

"But there seems to be a significant difference. You left the abuse to protect yourself and Courtney. You broke the cycle and generational curse, wouldn't you say?" Ms. Rita Fray interjected.

I thought about her words for a moment before slowly lifting my eyes back up to meet hers—reminding myself to keep my head held high. "Yes," I said boldly.

"I love it," she replied proudly. "I want you to remember to not be *too* hard on yourself. Try not to forget to acknowledge your victories, even the ones you deem as small. All victories matter and can inspire you to push forward and reach the other goals that you have lined up for yourself. Make sense?"

"It does." I nodded.

"That's good. Okay, are you ready for your next word?"

"I am."

"Angelo."

My heart ached. The truth of the matter was, I wasn't ready...*at all*. It was a topic I wanted to avoid at all costs. I managed to speak about Angelo with Ms. Rita Fray just a few times in earlier sessions but could never finish a sentence without bursting into tears. Angelo—or the imaginary person I constructed in my head—was still an extremely sensitive topic for me. However, I knew I would have to face it fully one day in order to heal and move on.

"Angelo," I murmured. "Still very painful and confusing. I still can't wrap my head around the fact that he is not real. It's difficult because I know the emotions...the conversations...they all felt so *real*. How could I just fabricate his entire existence? I mean, is that even possible?"

"Well, the mind is beautiful and complex. Fully capable of creating beautiful and complex, *imaginary* scenarios. My theory is this: based on the details of the events over the course of your life that you have shared with me, there was a lot of trauma. *A lot* of trauma. This pain and discomfort made you desperate for a way out— a way to escape and alleviate the suffering that you experienced. Which is, by the way, a perfectly normal human response. It's sort of like the fight or flight method that we talk about in psychology and the medical field. I believe your flight came in the form of cutting of the wrist, which later transferred into unfortunate suicidal thoughts. When those things were unable to free you from your pain and suffering, your brain took a genius turn. Your mind was able to design a friendship with a man that you cherished. And from that, you were able to generate the bravery, guidance, and strength to leave an *extremely* abusive marriage. This could be a way we look at the brighter side of this situation. Does this all make sense to you?"

"It does…but," I stopped for a moment.

"Tell me. What's on your mind?"

"But he saved my life."

"NO. *You* saved your life." I bit my lip to fight back the tears as she continued. "Angelo has always been a part of you. You created this beautiful being because he lives within you. He *is* you."

Streams flowed from my eyes. *That's it*. It was the first time that I realized why I felt so connected to Angelo. It was simply because he was me all along. I had fallen in love with myself all over again. I inspired myself to be greater. *Wow.* "Thank you," I wept out loud.

"No, thank *you*… for trusting me with this most vulnerable part of yourself. It is truly my honor."

I managed to smile at her as I leaned over to grab my second Kleenex and quickly allowed the tissue to soak up the tears on my face.

"Okay, so we have time to zoom through a few more words. Is that okay?"

"Yes."

"Love."

"I'm learning to love again by first loving myself and the people close to me. I believe love heals and love wins."

"Perfect. Next word: *career*."

"I am excited about my future at the law firm. However, I have hopes of someday starting my own non-profit organization."

"Really?" Ms. Rita Fray slightly tipped down her glasses to reveal the impressed gaze in her eyes. "That sounds amazing! We'll have to talk more about this new business adventure next time. I'm excited for you."

"Thank you, I can't wait to share with you." I beamed and blushed simultaneously.

"Last word: *life*."

"Life," I repeated out loud as I thought about my answer. "Life has been difficult, for sure. But I have decided to not dwell on my past and life's shortcomings. Instead, I am determined to focus on all of the pleasant parts of life and work to sustain my peace. I used to toy with my life because it didn't mean much to me. I felt trapped in a rut and wanted to end my life for good. But now, life is meaningful. Life is significant. Life is trial and error. Life is full of surprises. Life has ups and downs. Life is not easy, but **life is good**…and I'm going to live it like it's golden," we both chuckled at my added Jill Scott lyrics.

"I support you, one hundred percent," Ms. Rita Fray leaned forward to initiate a high five.

"I appreciate *you*," I leaned over to slap the hand that she held in the air.

"Well my dear, that is our time for the day." We both stood from our seats. "Same time tomorrow?"

"Same time," I flashed a smile as I softly shoved my sunglasses back onto my face and walked towards the door. I left the office with a light spirit, ready to take on the next chapter in my life.

◆

I paralleled parked in the narrow space right in front of the small, two-story apartment building that I now called *home*. The building was made of a beautiful brick pattern and surrounded by a well-groomed, green yard with a small garden in the front. Each of the four apartment units in the front end of the complex had a personal balcony that protruded from the building. Our porch was on the bottom left-hand side, occupied by two lawn chairs, a mini table, and a few of Courtney's outside toys. There was a gorgeous, tall, leafy tree that stood close to our balcony, providing the perfect amount of protection from the hot sun on blazing summer days and from the rain on dark and gloomy days. Birds of all shades and colors danced and sang from the branches daily, from sunrise to sundown. As I made my way to the entrance, I looked up to appreciate a glimpse of nature. In mid-air, a stunning blue hummingbird began to tweet softly right above me. The bird wandered from the tree just enough so I noticed its flawless feathers and high-pitched voice. The beautiful earthling proceeded to follow me to the door with an angelic tune ranging from its tiny lungs.

"Hi there," I grinned up at the tiny bird as I let myself into my home.

"Mommy!" Court rushed me at the door. Her natural curls bounced from side to side as she sprinted in my direction.

"Good morning, baby doll!" I kneeled down to her height with my arms stretched wide open, ready to receive her warm embrace.

"Guess what, Mommy?"

"What, baby?" I snuggled my arms around my daughter's tiny frame as I listened to her latest updates.

"So, today we ate pancakes and strawberries for breakfast. And...we also cut up bananas and made a smiley face with them. Yummy in my tummy!" Courtney took a step back and looked me in my eyes as she continued. Her eyes were filled with excitement and her gestures were expressive. "Next, we played the makeup game."

"Oh, yeah?" I matched her energy with my enthusiasm.

"Yes. And I think that I did a great job. I used eyeshadow, blush, *and* lipstick! So, first I dipped the small brush in the blue and rubbed it on the eyelids. Then I used the brightest red for the lips! And...! And...!" she stuttered out of pure exhilaration.

Just then, her sentence was finished by the tall figure emerging from behind her. "And she even put a wig on me," I burst into laughter as I watched Michael walk into the living room with smudged lipstick on his face and a crooked, curly black wig on his head.

"Oh, you think it's funny, huh?" he snatched the wig off and threw it towards me as uncontrollable, belly-wrenching giggles escaped my body.

"I think you look *beautiful*," I said sarcastically after catching my breath from laughing so hard. "Good job, baby!" I slapped Courtney a high five.

"Why don't you like it, Uncle Mike?" Court looked up at my brother with innocent, concerning eyes.

"Oh no, sweetheart," Michael's demeanor quickly softened after witnessing Court's disappointment. He squatted down and looked into her eyes. "You did an amazing job. It's just that I'm more of a naturalist." He winked at her.

"Okay, but you're missing out," she shrugged and playfully skipped down the hall towards her room.

Michael and I giggled at the brief exchange for several moments. He grabbed a towel from the hall cabinet and walked into the small kitchen to soak the cloth in warm water. I sat at the black and chic desk in the living room. The narrow desk sat in between the maroon sofa and pale grey painted wall that was outlined in a bold and flawless white. Blue, dense curtains draped around the glass windows, which revealed a portion of the grand tree that sat in front of our apartment. I opened up my laptop and began typing away. *Click! Clack! Tap! Click, click! Tap, Tap! Clack! Click, click! Clack! Tap!*

"What are you working on?" Michael asked as he cleaned the red and blue contents from his face.

"My business plan."

"**YOUR** business plan?"

"Yes, **MY** business plan," I stated as a matter of fact. "I am developing a non-profit organization for individuals effected by sexual abuse and domestic violence."

"Word? Hey, that's going to be powerful," Michael rooted for me out loud.

"Yeah, thanks bro. I just want to give back and help others that may feel stuck and trapped in abusive situations like I once was."

"That's dope. I'm sure you're going to help a lot of people with that passion of yours, Symone."

My heart beamed with joy. "I hope so!"

"So, you got a name for your business, yet?"

Up until that point, I had not thought of an official title for my non-profit. But, when Michael asked me, my response came almost involuntarily and automatically. It left my throat effortlessly. "FADA."

"FADA?"

"Yes. Fighting Against Domestic Abuse."

"Yo! I like that. How did you come up with that?"

"I got the inspiration from an old friend," I smiled to myself. "I still have a lot to decide on for the planning phase. I know you're taking that business management course this semester, right? Do you want to help me?"

"Speaking of class," Michael began to back away slowly. "I have an exam coming up next week and have a lot of studying to do. So, I think I'm going to pass on that offer…but you enjoy!" Michael quickly disappeared from the living room and down the long hall, escaping my invitation altogether.

"Silly," I shook my head and chuckled at my brother's humor.

DING!

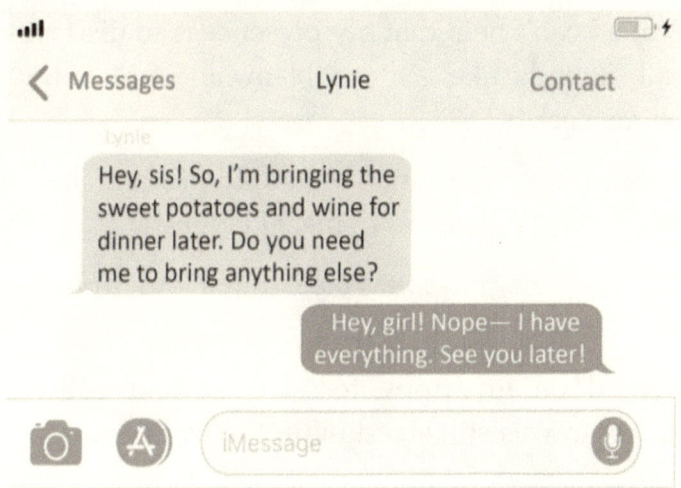

I tucked my phone away and continued to work on my project while I still had a moment of peace and quiet to myself. *Tap, Tap! Click! Clack! Tap! Clack, click! Click! Tap! Tap! Click, clack! Click! Tap!*

◆

"We are here, and we are hungry as hell! Monie, I hope the food is done. I skipped lunch purposely just to make enough room for your shrimp, broccoli, and homemade biscuits! Lawd! I can taste it already," Lynie barged into the door with her grand personality and a pan covered in aluminum foil, steaming, and reaping of fresh brown sugar and warm sweet potatoes.

"Oh, Lynie, must you always cause an abrupt disturbance when you enter a room?" I teased as I peeked from the doorway of the kitchen.

"Well, I can't help that my presence is so distracting to you all. Sounds like *your* problem, and not mine," she sassed me back.

I rolled my eyes and waved Lynie and her witty responses off. "Whatever, Lynie," I laughed.

"Hi, Symone," a soft voice called out from behind Lynie.

I stood on my tippy toes to see and address the woman who was still standing in the front door opening. "Oh, hey, Amanda!"

Amanda was Lynie's partner—a tall, slim lighter skinned woman with big brown eyes and thick, curly hair that bounced right above her shoulders. She worked as an adjunct professor at Boston State University and was kind enough to write a recommendation letter on Michael's behalf for his college application. Amanda was the complete opposite of Lynie: reserved, introverted, and book smart. She was very nurturing and a single mom of an energized seven-year-old little girl, which was perfect for Lynie because she always wanted children but did not want to go through the physical birthing process.

"Hi, Ms. Baker," a squeaky voice yelled up to me.

I looked down and spotted Amanda's daughter with two oversized puffballs on her perfectly round head and bright eyes that matched her mother's.

"Hi there, Lue-Lue," I bent down to meet the little girl. "I love this sparkly shirt! Court is going to go crazy when she sees your gorgeous outfit. She's such a fashionista these days." I winked at Lue-Lue.

"I hope she likes it! Where is she?"

"She is around here somewhere." I stood up straight and glanced around the perimeter for my daughter right before calling out to her. "Courtney! We have guests!" I waited a few seconds for Courtney to respond but heard nothing.

"I'm sure she'll be out in a minute. She's probably still getting ready for dinner.

"Okie, dokie," Lue-Lue skipped to the dining room table to take her seat.

"That's right Lue-Lue, bon appétit, Lynie followed her stepdaughter to the table and took a seat beside her.

"Aht, aht ladies! Hand sanitizer, first," Amanda rushed behind Lynie and Lue-Lue with a large bottle of Purell in her hand.

"Oh, yeah! I smelled the grub all the way from my room. Is the food ready, yet?" Michael walked in and sat at the table across from Lynie and her family. He reached his hand out and accepted the squirt of hand sanitizer that Amanda deposited into his big, dry hands. "Thank you, Ms. White," he gleamed.

"Yes, the food is ready," I carried a large pot of my perfectly seasoned shrimp and broccoli to the table where the hungry guests were waiting. "Oh! And we can't forget the biscuits." I jogged to the kitchen and picked up a large basket filled with my fresh buttermilk biscuits. I delivered the steaming hot bread to the table and placed it right next to the pitcher of red wine, courtesy of Amanda and Lynie.

"How are classes going, Michael?" Amanda asked as she began preparing a small plate for Lue-Lue.

"They're going well, so far. I feel pretty good about this semester's schedule," Michael responded right before gobbling down a hot biscuit.

"Have you met any girls?" Lynie whispered loudly across the table.

"Well, you know. I have a few contestants, but I haven't decided on a winner, yet."

Laughter erupted from the dinner table. I looked around and smiled as I watched my newly constructed family engage and enjoy each other over a shared meal. I felt safe. I felt secure.

"Aye, Symone. Where's Courtney?" Michael was curious.

"Yes! Courtney!" I suddenly remembered my daughter's absence. "I'll go get her. I believe she's still playing in her room."

I walked down the long path of bright hardwood floors that led to Courtney's pink, princess decorated door. *Tap! Tap! Tap!* I landed three knocks on the door. Nothing. "Court?" I called out to her through the closed door. Nothing. I instantly twisted the doorknob and let myself into the room.

"Courtney? It's time for dinne—" Court swiftly sat up in bed and shoved a mysterious item under the plush pillow that laid right at her pearl white headboard.

"Yes, Mommy?" the five-year-old looked at me with a startled look on her face.

"Umm…oh, nothing. I was just saying that it's time for dinner." I walked in closer to the bed but fought to keep my hand from flipping over the pillow in front of Courtney. It was obvious to me that she believed that she was fast enough and hid the object before I opened her bedroom door. She was wrong. However, I wanted to keep the peace and decided that I would investigate the scene once she left the room. "And guess what?" I retained a normal attitude in an attempt to not blow my cover.

"What, Mommy?" Courtney jumped off of her twin-sized bed and walked over towards me.

"Lue-Lue is here."

"Really?" She was excited.

"Yes. She's at dinner waiting for you."

"Yay!" Courtney began making her way out of the room.

"Hey, baby! Don't forget to wash your hands," I yelled out.

"Okay, Mommy," I heard her tiny voice travel as she was already halfway down the hall.

Once the coast was clear, I slipped my hand under the pillow and captured a thick, smooth rectangular shaped piece of paper. *What the hell is this?* My mind wondered before my eyes could even see what I was holding. I slowly slid the document from under the pillow, revealing the item that Courtney had kept hidden from me. *Oh, my baby.* My heart wept for my daughter as I looked down at the wallet sized family picture of Courtney, Jonathan, and I when we were all together. When we were a family. I flipped the portrait over and made out the sentence that was printed in Courtney's handwriting on the back: "Daddy, I miss you."

A single warm tear landed on the words and intertwined with the black ink until it was completely smeared and undetectable. Until it was no more.

NeeNee Marie

About the Author

*A*uthor NeeNee Marie is a mommy, writer, poet, educator, professional and lover of life. She enjoys learning, creating and spending quality time with her loved ones- especially her son, Carter.

NeeNee Marie is a Cleveland Native who grew up in the inner-city alongside her two younger brothers and hardworking single mother. NeeNee is a first-generation college student and attended Kent State University, where she received her Bachelor and Master's degree. She has since then, devoted her time to serving in the field of education to assure academic success for the youth. She continues to be an advocate for higher education opportunities in the inner city and Black communities.

For as long as she can remember, NeeNee has possessed a natural passion and appreciation for the arts. She has always expressed herself in a creative fashion, mostly through words. Poetry and storytelling have always been an important key in her life. When she was a young girl in elementary school- she would write poems in her journals and be one of the first to raise her hand and share her latest creation. In high school, she memorized and performed long monologues for large audiences. She also studied and practiced contemporary and historic

African dance. NeeNee used the arts as an outlet and as a fun and safe way to express herself.

After overcoming a very difficult obstacle in her life, NeeNee developed a new interest in writing novels. She began with mapping out short stories and experimenting with different plots and settings. A short while later, **Tears of a Hummingbird** *was born. NeeNee Marie has since then fallen in love with novel writing and plans to embrace her community and the rest of the world with her poetic writing style and life changing stories.*

Acknowledgements

I am thankful that God, Mommy Nature and the Universe has continued to shower me with patience, forgiveness, guidance and love during this journey. I am forever grateful that the three energies have guided me and kept me as I traveled through the different phases of this very emotional, challenging and lengthy novel writing process.

I am thankful that my mother birthed me and raised me the best way she knew how. I am appreciative of her genuine love from up close and afar. Thank you for being strong and for never giving up. I love you, mommy.

My son, Carter, has been with me every step of the way. His unconditional love fueled me during my weakest moments. His warm hugs and kisses encouraged me to keep going. Thank you, Carter- mommy loves you.

Jameel D. Davis, thank you for being so essential in my writing and publication journey- from your creative input to your constructive criticism. You believed in my story ever since 2019 when you read part of the first chapter. I am beyond grateful for your willingness to mentor, coach and teach me as I continue to learn the ins-and-outs of this industry. I am thankful for your eagerness to donate your time and energy, while fully investing into this project. What a blessing you have been through each season- the highs and the lows. Thank you, Jameel.

www.ingramcontent.com/pod-product-compliance
Lightning Source LLC
Chambersburg PA
CBHW021954010726
47494CB00003B/733